she is also an auth~~or~~ ~~2015.~~ Her debut novel, *The Stylist*, is in development as a major motion picture.

Rosie has worked in the magazine industry for over 20 years and previously held senior positions at glossy women's titles including *Grazia*, *Glamour* and *Red*. Rosie was named Editor of the Year (entertainment and celebrity) by the British Society of Magazine Editors in 2017.

JUST BETWEEN FRIENDS

Rosie Nixon

ONE PLACE. MANY STORIES

HQ
An imprint of HarperCollins*Publishers* Ltd
1 London Bridge Street
London SE1 9GF

This edition 2020

1
First published in Great Britain by
HQ, an imprint of HarperCollins*Publishers* Ltd 2020

Copyright © Rosie Nixon 2020

Rosie Nixon asserts the moral right to be
identified as the author of this work.
A catalogue record for this book is
available from the British Library.

ISBN: 978-0-00827-341-5

MIX
Paper from
responsible sources
FSC™ C007454

This book is produced from independently certified FSC™ paper
to ensure responsible forest management.

For more information visit: www.harpercollins.co.uk/green

This book is set in 11/16 pt. Sabon

Printed and bound in Great Britain by
CPI Group (UK) Ltd, Croydon, CR0 4YY

For Mum and Dad

She thought she had known love before, and she did.
But it was just a whisper of what love had to say.
Just a tea cup out of the ocean.
And so this time she sat down and closed
her eyes and listened, really listened,
to what love had to say.

JMSTORM

CHAPTER ONE

Aisha

Saturday 24th April

'Oh no,' I sighed, holding the paper between my fingers. It had been on the fridge door for a month. Four weeks in which I should have read it to the end.

Still in my slippers, baggy pyjama bottoms and a slightly tatty T-shirt – low on style, but one of the few outfits that was still relatively comfortable at this stage of my pregnancy – I padded from the kitchen to the bedroom and stood in the doorway.

I looked at him with faint hope. 'I don't suppose you read this, did you?'

Jason grunted in response; he was half asleep.

'Jason?' I said, more loudly than was strictly necessary. 'It says I need to bring a sharing dish to contribute to the lunch.' I paused, searching his features for a clue, before adding a loud, cursory, 'Great. You didn't. So I don't have a sharing dish. Aargh!'

It wasn't Jason's fault. Joining The Baby Group had been my idea and *I* should have read the paperwork. 'So now I'll have to leave the house in the next five minutes so I can stop by the deli and pick up something overpriced.'

As I flung open the wardrobe doors and pulled out my maternity jeans and a stretchy mauve maternity top, my mind was already ticking over, wondering whether I should take a nice plate on which to put the shop-bought sandwiches, with some foil to cover them, and whether perhaps there were some cherry tomatoes in the bottom of the fridge, which I could add as a garnish so no one would know they were bought. I grabbed a silver pendant and slung it around my neck in an attempt to jazz myself up a bit.

Jason had propped himself up onto his elbows. 'Is it really that bad?' he said, fixing his green eyes on me, concern mixed with a mild amusement etched across his face. That gorgeous face. He even looked gorgeous first thing in the morning, damn him.

'Yes it is. I've messed up. You're meant to take food to share with the group at lunchtime. We have nothing in the fridge. The universe is clearly trying to tell me this Baby Group is a bad idea.' I paused and looked at him. 'Maybe I won't go.'

'Baby, come on. You've *got* to go. You've been thinking about this day for weeks,' he said. He was correct, I had.

'Hmm, weeks and weeks in which I could have been better prepared. I can't face it now.'

He looked at me quizzically for a moment, probably trying to remember if we'd had a conversation about the letter; whether he was partially to blame here.

'It's not your fault, I'm just annoyed at myself,' I said, more softly, swallowing my frustration. 'Plus none of my clothes fit and I feel like a frump. I'm not up for it any more.'

'For what it's worth, I like you in that top,' he offered, as I pulled it down a bit more, watching it stretch across my impressive chest and large, round bump.

I ignored his compliment. 'You know that food preparation isn't exactly my forte. What hope do I have with no ingredients and less than five minutes to make something?'

I was brought up by a 'feeder' mother who took great pride in cooking delicious dinners from scratch and was very particular about how they looked. Her signature dish, a version of Coronation Chicken, made with a blend of spices inherited from dad's Indian mother and smothered in yogurt, was legendary in certain Leamington Spa circles. I'd inherited my love of spicy food from dad's side of the family, but none of the domestic skills. Though I was artistic enough to make a plate *look* good, the taste of its contents was another matter. Hence Jason was the main chef in this household. But he wasn't quite as good at ensuring the fridge was adequately stocked. Oh, why didn't I check the bloody letter? I managed to stop myself from swearing out loud.

'I'm sorry I'm not going with you today, Aish,' Jason said, 'I really am. But I promise you, if you pick up a few sandwiches and pastries from the deli the other ladies will be really happy. Not many pregnant women turn down deli goods, from what I've learnt.' He winked – an obvious reference to my obsession with the almond croissants from our local deli. 'Anyway, I doubt anyone else has had time to rustle up

3

a MasterChef-quality homemade dish. And if they have,' he qualified, 'well, they need to get a life, if you ask me. You must go, you'll regret it if you don't – and you never know, you might meet some like-minded people. You said yourself you're keen to make some "mum friends".'

I smiled. He knew what to say to make me feel better. It would have been nice to have Jason by my side in this first session, but I understood. We'd had this conversation a million times – he needed to put in the overtime while he could, before the baby came. Being an IT manager often meant him working unsociable hours. I didn't like it, but I was used to it.

'Thank you, Jase.' I smiled and gave him a peck on the lips. 'I suppose you're right.'

Fully dressed, I waddled back to the kitchen to look for a suitable plate for the sandwiches. To be honest, lunch wasn't the only thing I was worrying about this morning. Walking into a room full of strangers with the intention of making friends was a weird and nerve-wracking prospect. All that judgement. It made me feel anxious. And if that wasn't enough, the day was also likely to involve some awkward chat about the perineum and confronting childbirth head on. I hadn't given much thought to the actual birth bit because it made me feel nauseous whenever I did. I was convinced I was going to need a caesarean, like Mum, and the thought of being butchered in a stark operating room had cost me a few sleepless nights already.

I diverted my attention to our barely used kitchen cupboards, stooping down to poke around, looking for a dish

I wasn't even sure we still had. We'd had to shed a lot of stuff when we moved back from Hong Kong two years ago.

'Crockery doesn't travel well,' Jason had reminded me at every opportunity. He didn't have the same sentimentality for belongings as me. That was another thing I had inherited from Mum, a self-confessed 'hoarder'.

Jason came up behind me, spreading his hands over my bump from behind. He laced his fingers with mine, and I reciprocated, despite the fact I'd rarely felt less sexy than I did right now – all swollen breasts, water retention in my legs, rounder-than-usual face. At thirty-five weeks and three days, I was rapidly getting too big for even my biggest maternity clothes. I didn't understand those women in *Cosmopolitan* who claimed they felt sexier up the duff.

'You look sexy today,' he whispered into my neck, between peppering it with little kisses. 'I wish I didn't have to work.'

'You were late home again last night,' I muttered.

'You were still awake though.'

'I wasn't,' I replied, remembering how he had pushed himself into my back, in an attempt to gauge whether I could be warmed up for sex. Of course I was having none of it. We both knew that I had pretended to be asleep or had blamed my bump when rebuffing his sexual advances countless times in the last few months. Much as I fancied my husband, I just couldn't face sex at the moment. I wasn't sure how much more rejection he could take.

'You were just pretending to be asleep!' he protested.

As any woman who has ever been eight months pregnant

knows, it's practically impossible to be sound asleep anyway. Especially when your husband comes to bed late, having slammed the front door, which is just beneath your bedroom, and then starts trying to unbutton your maternity pyjamas, pestering you for sex.

I shook my head.

'Right, sure. Well the little snorts you were making weren't very authentic.' He was humouring me. Sometimes Jason didn't seem to grasp that my feelings about my body were not the same as they once were. Just because I had porn-star worthy boobs right now, didn't mean they made me feel sexy. In fact, the opposite was true: I missed my B cups.

I poked around in the cupboard for a few seconds longer before realizing this crouching position was ill-advised for a woman in my condition and I wasn't quite sure how I was going to get back up again.

'Need a hand?' He slid his hands under my armpits. 'Aren't you supposed to stop doing things like this now?'

'I can do it, thanks.' I shook him off and rose to my feet in a graceless fashion, steadying myself on the kitchen table and feeling like an overweight elephant in women's clothing. It was hard to imagine there was a time when we'd had sex on this very table.

'Listen,' he continued brightly. 'Provided I'm done before seven, which I really hope I will be, how about I take you for a burger this evening, to make up for today?'

He was pushing the right button there – along with almond croissants and custard creams, the quarter pounder with cheese and bacon from Honest Burger was another pregnancy craving. And don't get me started on the salty, skinny fries.

'Now you're talking,' I said, softening. 'I'll head home after the class, so text me what time to meet.'

'Will do. And make sure you take notes – you'll need to tell me what I've missed, so I can prepare for the arrival of whoever is in there.' Then he bent down and spoke to my belly. 'Yes, we are talking about you, little bean. Your mummy is going to be brilliant today and I love her very much.'

'We love you too.'

This wasn't the first time Jason had told me he loved me via my belly recently. He hadn't actually said it to my face – or rather the round moon that used to be my face, complete with cheekbones – very often since I got pregnant. He used to tell me all the time, back in the days when we were dating, and when we were newly married. He would kiss me like his life depended on it and constantly tell me he loved me to bits. He'd leave loving Post-it notes on the fridge and text me sweet compliments while I was at work, which had the ability to make me smile all day, and feel like I was the only woman in the world. But he didn't tell me so often these days, I'd noticed, and to be honest, I needed to hear it now more than ever.

Twisting to check the time on the cooker clock, I realized I'd have to waddle as fast as I could to the deli. I picked up my bag and kissed Jason goodbye.

After begrudgingly putting almost thirty pounds onto my card for eight ciabattas hastily stuffed with tomato, mozzarella and basil – the quickest thing they could do – and awkwardly asking the guy not to wrap the sandwiches, but put them straight onto my plate and cover the whole thing in cling film, I made my way towards the door. There was a sinking feeling in my stomach and my chest became tight. For a brief moment I thought again about not going to the class. Although I'd always known Jason would have to miss this first session, going alone suddenly seemed impossible. Plus my nagging worry that the class might involve something hideously embarrassing like acting out labour or talking about discharge with a bunch of strangers would still not go away. Imagine if we were expected to get our boobs out to practise breastfeeding or something? Could that be a possibility? Please God, no.

But I knew I had to make myself go. Jason was right, I did need to meet like-minded people – I needed some friends with babies. My closest friend Tara had two toddler boys, but she was so busy running them to and from nursery while holding down her city job that we didn't see each other as much as we used to. And I was yet to open any of the 'baby manuals' she had thoughtfully passed on to me, so I needed to learn; I had to do this for the bean.

I took a deep breath and strode towards the venue. 'We'll do this together, okay?' I whispered to my bump. 'Just you and me.'

CHAPTER TWO

Aisha

The meeting was being held in the back room of our local church. When I finally found the door, I pushed it open and saw a room full of strangers sat in a circle staring at me.

'Hi,' I said, cringing inwardly as I realized I was interrupting the introduction. 'Sorry I'm late. I'm Aisha. Aisha Moore.'

There was an intense silence as I made my way into the room. Luckily the jolly woman who had been talking didn't seem fazed.

'Hello Aisha!' she said warmly. 'Welcome. I'm Maggie, I'm a doula and your group leader! Take a seat here.' She indicated a chair opposite hers. 'I was just about to ask the mummies to tell us how far along they are and where they're having their lovely babies. You can kick things off if you like? Feel free to tell us the sex, if you know – only if you want to. No one has to discuss anything they are uncomfortable with. This is a supportive space. No judgement here.' Maggie was a short, podgy lady, probably in her late fifties, with frizzy brown hair, a wide smile and small, kind eyes. She was leaning so far forwards, smiling encouragingly with her whole body, that it looked like she might topple off her chair.

I hung my coat on the back of my seat and sat down, carefully pushing my bags underneath. I'd have to deal with the plate of sandwiches later.

'Well,' I began once I'd caught my breath, 'I'm just over thirty-five weeks pregnant and I don't know what I – *we're* – having.' I rubbed my bump and Maggie nodded eagerly.

'Where are you planning to give birth?' she asked.

'Hopefully not on the Tube!' I giggled nervously and noticed no one else seemed to find this funny. 'Hospital obviously – College Square Hospital.'

I saw Maggie's eyes flicker. 'Not *obviously*, necessarily,' she muttered. 'It's a very personal choice.'

I felt a bit stupid. It's just that a home birth had never really been a consideration for me; I wanted to be in the safest possible environment – especially if I might end up delivering the world's largest baby. Jason had recently mentioned both he and his sister were 'huge' newborns and, judging by the fact I'd put on over two stone in weight so far, there was a high likelihood that I was carrying a mega-baby too. *That* was my reality – and that, in my book, meant hospital. But I decided not to go into it, because I noticed Maggie's gaze move to the empty bucket seat on my left. 'My husband, Jason, he's working today, but hopefully he'll be at the next meeting,' I explained. 'Sorry again for being late.'

A woman with blonde highlights a few seats to my right in the circle caught my eye and gave me a friendly smile, which made me feel a little better.

'Super! We look forward to meeting Jason next week,' Maggie beamed, her eyes lingering on mine a little too long – possibly trying to scope out how I *really* felt about my absent baby daddy. Thankfully most of the group were now eagerly looking at the couple sat to my left. It was two women: a small brunette and an equally small woman with black hair. The pair looked almost identical aside from the fact that one was Asian and the other white.

'I'm Lin, and this is Susie – both spelt with an i,' the black-haired woman said, before announcing, 'She's the one having the baby – I'm just having a food baby!' The room rippled with awkward laughter. She patted her midriff, which, it had to be said, wasn't too far off the size of her partner's bump.

'We used my brother's sperm to make the baby with Susie,' she continued, turning to smile affectionately at her partner. 'It's a boy. And we're going to call him Charlie. We're planning a home birth as natural as Mother Nature will allow.'

Damn. She really stuck the knife in there with the natural home birth. Plus Charlie was on our list of possible names, if the bean turned out to be a boy. Although my instincts were currently leaning towards it being a girl, I wondered if there was any etiquette involved in choosing the same baby name as someone in the group. Should you stake your claim, so they wouldn't think you copied their chosen name? I thought about interjecting: 'How funny! We're thinking Charlie too! Loved that name from the moment I got pregnant. Bagsy Charlie!' But would that seem too intense? Weird? Passive aggressive even? Really everything about being here felt strange because I wasn't sure where the boundaries lay.

I stayed quiet and tried to focus on how maybe Charlie wasn't such a great baby name anyway, given we once had a family cat called Charlie when I was very little, and he got run over. Surely a bad omen. That settled it – Charlie was off the list. I made a mental note to tell Jason later.

'And how are you feeling about the birth, in general, Susie?' Maggie asked, drawing the other woman into the conversation.

'Well I'm not a fan of Western drugs,' Susie said, her voice quieter than Lin's – I had to strain to hear her. 'I'm opting for a drug-free, home water-birth involving hypnosis. And we've been researching a Balinese ritual involving burying the placenta in a special cemetery as soon as possible following the birth.'

'Or we'll have it made into tablets,' Lin chipped in, looking a little cross. 'We haven't made a final decision yet. And we're both planning to breastfeed. I'm about to start a ground-breaking course of hormones to make that possible.' She squeezed Susie's hand.

They seemed so resolute in their wishes, it made me feel even more insecure about my fears and lack of concrete plans. I made a mental note to google placenta tablets.

Maggie nodded and clapped her hands together with glee; hearing a more unusual birth plan seemed akin to Christmas to her. 'How wonderful!' she exclaimed. 'That's fantastic. You've clearly spent a great deal of time thinking about this. We'd all love to hear more, I'm sure.' I wasn't sure I did, but Maggie looked desperate for further elaboration.

Susie launched into a detailed monologue on how

'placenta parties' were a big trend in areas of San Francisco, where they simply popped the 'delicacy' into a blender along with whatever fruit, veg, even alcohol, they fancied and whizzed it up into a nutritional 'placenta smoothie' to be shared with family and friends. It sounded quite bizarre.

Relieved the heat was off me while she spoke, my attention wandered and I took the opportunity to look around the room properly.

It was then that I spotted an array of pretty plates and ceramic dishes brimming with salads and cakes laid out on the table behind us. I thought again of the shop-bought ciabattas under my chair. If Jason had been here, I could have nudged him to take them up, but as it was I felt too self-conscious to stand up and make another fuss after my late arrival. Under my chair they would have to remain.

As Susie's lengthy explanation of the nutritional merits of eating human placenta came to a close, we all turned to look at the couple to Maggie's right, a pretty blonde woman with elfin features and her equally blond, small husband. They were holding hands and looked very young, probably mid-twenties. I could imagine the petite, blonde, blue-eyed little baby they were cooking up in that perfectly neat bump. They introduced themselves as Helen and Ian Edwards.

Ian spoke first; he had a timid voice and piercing blue eyes. He reminded me of a gerbil. 'Hi everyone, we're having our first baby. Well I guess that's pretty obvious, this is a group for first-time parents!' he said, before laughing nervously. 'We are thirty-five weeks. Don't know the sex and College

Square Hospital for us, too.' He turned to Helen: 'Anything you want to add, babe?'

'No, that's it,' Helen replied self-consciously, before shrugging and smiling at no one in particular and then fixing her eyes on the floor. I smiled back at her; she seemed sweet and strait-laced. But maybe I was being too quick to judge. She might have a naughty streak.

'That's fine, dears,' Maggie said, trying to mask her disappointment that there wasn't another juicy set-up or alternative birth plan to discuss. 'Welcome to The Baby Group.'

Next was the woman who had given me a friendly smile earlier. She looked well put-together, with red lipstick, a neat flick to her eyeliner, fresh highlights in her tousled shoulder-length hair and a black Gucci handbag. She gave the impression of someone who had a successful career and a decent amount of savings in the bank. Of everyone, she was probably the closest in age to me (around her mid to late thirties), which made me instinctively gravitate towards her.

'Hi all, I'm Lucy Raven, baby boy, due May 31st. Looking forward to starting maternity leave in a few weeks. Still got a ton of nursery prep to do at home though. My partner, Oscar, is also working today. He'll join one of the other classes. That's me, I guess.' She folded her arms and sat back in her seat, signalling she'd said her bit and wasn't opening the floor for questions. She seemed to have her shit together – it was a little intimidating.

Maggie nodded; she seemed impressed too. I noted Lucy wasn't wearing any rings on her wedding finger.

Seeing Lucy here on her own made me feel better about

Jason's absence, but I wondered how she really felt about it. She certainly came across as perfectly happy and confident, so I decided to take a leaf from her book and sat up a little taller.

The last couple to be introduced were sat on my right: a tall black guy with a chiselled face called Will, who could easily have been a model, and his partner, a white woman called Carol, who was not unattractive but not nearly as head-turningly gorgeous. Were Will single, I'd have been tempted to trade Jason in for him; he had 'swipe right' written all over him. There seemed something mismatched about them. Will did most of the talking and while he spoke, Carol delved into a little blue bag hanging from her chair and retrieved her phone, which she cradled in her palm as if she might need to 'phone a friend' at any moment.

'The baby is due on the 22nd of May and it will be a hospital birth for us, too,' Will informed us in a matter-of-fact way. He had a deep, thespian voice.

'My husband, Christian, will join one of the other sessions,' he continued. He paused for a moment, gauging correctly that we had all naturally assumed Carol was his other half. Carol gave us a small shy smile, while Will seemed to enjoy the attention from his captive audience. His timing was brilliant; I wondered if he was an actor, as well as a model. 'Carol is our surrogate,' he continued. 'She's had a baby before, but fancied a refresh, so we enrolled in this class. You'll get to meet Christian soon.' He turned to her and they exchanged a warm look. 'Christian and I are both planning to be there for the birth, and then we will be the legal parents – the two dads. Carol will be moving back to the Ukraine.' He looked at Maggie with a neutral face, as if waiting for her to ask a question.

Maggie simply smiled and said, 'How wonderful!'

Will had delivered his lines beautifully and he had made me stop and think. I had been so consumed by my own pregnancy journey, I hadn't really appreciated how difficult it might have been for other couples to conceive. You kind of assume that for everyone else it's easy. Having some more unusual family set-ups in the group was going to make it more interesting.

'Right then,' Maggie announced, when the introductions were complete. 'What a great group! You're all wonderful humans, in my eyes.' She really was an eccentric character. 'First up, we're going to discuss birth choices. But, before we go on, I have to tell you that nothing is off limits here. In fact, let's just get something out of the way before we get in too deep, shall we?' She paused and I unscrewed the lid of my water bottle, feeling self-conscious about what 'getting in too deep' might entail. Then she flung up her arms as if she were a cabaret singer ready to make an encore and cried out: 'VAGINA!' at the top of her lungs.

This was an inopportune moment for me. At the exact same time that Maggie made this dramatic announcement, I took a swig of water from my bottle. Instead of swallowing, the whole mouthful came flying projectile out of my mouth. A tsunami of warm filtered water sprayed not only down my top but also all down my jeans and on to the area of floor directly in front of me. I wouldn't be surprised if Lin caught a light mist too.

'Oh my God. Sorry!' I yelped, trying hard to stifle hysterical giggles – my default reaction when in shock or when something embarrassing has happened to me.

Maggie looked at me in horror. 'Are you okay, Aisha?' she asked.

A brief silence was followed by a nervous titter, this time from Will. I wanted the ground to open up and suck me under. This was excruciating. Plus I was really quite wet.

Once I'd composed myself a bit, I nodded. 'Yes, I'm fine, sorry about that.' I dabbed at my face and top with one of the deli napkins from under my seat. At least the close proximity of the bag had come in handy.

'Good dear, try to keep calm, we don't want any early labours do we? There we go – I've said it,' Maggie continued, 'the V word. You'd better get used to it, ladies and gents. Now, after three, let's shout it together loud and proud! One, two, three—' She paused to looked around the room, especially at me, her eyes wide with excitement, as we simultaneously tried to avoid her gaze and stifle our sniggers. 'VAGINA!'

There was nothing loud or proud about our pathetic, quiet chorus. I prayed to God there wasn't a service going on in the chapel next door, then quickly realized the irony of that thought. I looked around the room to see whether anyone else was finding this hilarious. Will caught my eye and put his hand over his face, his shoulders shaking. 'This is bizarre,' he mumbled, between guffaws. Carol seemed a bit annoyed or perhaps confused.

Helen and Ian were looking at each other with pink cheeks. Lin and Susie seemed nonplussed, and Lucy seemed to be trying not to laugh too. I thought how hilarious Tara would find this. Shouting 'vagina' with a group of strangers was nothing short of ridiculous and I wished I had someone to cringe about it with.

Maggie ignored Will's comment. I managed to pull myself together.

'There we go – well done. That woke us all up. And didn't it feel great?' No one replied. 'One thing you should know about me is that I *love* vaginas,' she continued, clearly revelling in our puce faces. 'I love talking about them and I absolutely love marvelling at the magical and wondrous things they can do. No fannying around here. And I love nipples too. Basically, I'm vagina and nipple mad.'

Will suddenly exploded with laughter again. 'Sorry!' he murmured. 'But this is... unexpected.' Carol gave him a quizzical sideways look, and I couldn't quite determine whether she agreed with him or if his announcements were embarrassing her.

Maggie glared, unimpressed. 'Well, William, dear, with babies you need to expect the unexpected. You'll see.'

That told him. Will rolled his eyes. I liked Will; he was showing more spark now.

Right now my vagina wasn't feeling particularly magical or wondrous. I was also painfully aware of what my poor unsuspecting vag was going to go through in not-very-many weeks' time: scrutiny by various members of hospital staff, some painful war-wounds delivering my gigantic baby... It all felt pretty terrifying.

'Lovely,' Maggie continued, undeterred and looking happy

again. 'Now that we've broken the ice, let's get to the nitty-gritty. Hands up who's made a birth plan already?'

Helen, Lucy and Susie raised their hands. I instantly felt insecure again, for not having done mine.

'I have it here,' Helen said, putting the rest of us to shame. She had taken a folded-up piece of paper from a pocket at the back of her pristine notepad and was waving it excitedly, as though it held the meaning of the Da Vinci code.

'That's great, ladies. You don't have to tell us what's in it – I'm always happy to have a natter one-on-one if you'd like to, it's a very personal choice. But I would say that writing a simple and informed birth plan – or a "vaginal instruction plan", a V.I.P. as I call it – is a useful exercise to help ensure your wishes are known by your partner and birth team, and, of course, your beloved vagina.' She paused for dramatic effect, and presumably to check our cheeks had remained a shade not far off beetroot. I was starting to think Maggie wasn't the kind of person I would want in close proximity if I was actually in labour. I imagined her doing something embarrassing like shouting about my 'magical vagina' instead of finding someone to give me an epidural in my moment of need.

'So, for those who have not yet created their V.I.P., let's look at the options,' she continued, before adding to the three who had raised their hands: 'You might want to change your plans at the last minute – so you should find this relevant and useful too.'

I reached into my bag again, this time for my notepad and pen. Like most of my notepads, it was filled with half-finished sketches and doodles. I turned to a blank page and scribbled down 'Write Birth Plan', underlining it twice. Then I doodled 'V.I.P.' next to it, noticing my hand was shaking slightly. I felt thoroughly out of my depth.

CHAPTER THREE

Lucy

I hoped I hadn't made too much of an effort with my appearance, wearing a new black maternity dress bought especially for this occasion, new 40-denier tights and my trusty Golden Goose trainers. I'd applied more make-up than I'd worn in previous weeks, including a neat cat-eye flick to my eyeliner and a slick of a new scarlet Urban Decay lipstick. There was nothing like red lippy to put a spring in my step, even if those steps were more of a waddle, and my stomach was full of fluttering butterflies, as well as a baby. I'd given myself an eight out of ten, and hoped that my smart appearance would help me to give a good impression. The day had come to go forth and see if I could make a friend, or two.

Once the introductions and discussions about birth plans were done, we broke for lunch.

I watched with pleasure and relief as everyone made appreciative noises as they tucked in to my salad. It was the only dish that was completely polished off and I couldn't help feeling a little smug. I played down the fact it had taken me nearly all of yesterday to create and actually felt a bit silly for having put in so much effort, when clearly most of them had bought their offerings from a shop that morning. When Helen and Susie asked me about the ingredients, I told them it was a family recipe. Helen and Ian had brought a pasta salad with tuna, cherry tomatoes and sweetcorn. The tuna had started to turn brown, since it had been left out all morning. I felt sorry for them as it was barely touched, but there was no way I was going to risk eating it.

Aisha wasn't much of a cook either, judging by the shop-bought ciabattas. She seemed to be a little embarrassed because she set them down on a pretty plate, blurted out that she hadn't read the part of the letter about bringing a sharing dish until this morning, and then made an excuse to get some fresh air. She needn't have worried though, because they were delicious and all gone within a matter of minutes. Will and Carol had supplied deli-counter offerings from the big Sainsbury's, so my biggest rivals for 'dish of the day' were Susie and Lin, whose decision to bring dessert would have been a good one, only their box of 'vegan superfood brownies' tasted more like bird food than the glorious stodgy 'proper' brownies from Gail's bakery down the road. What a wasted opportunity – with a room full of pregnant ladies, chocolate brownies would have been a much better idea.

I checked my phone while everyone else continued chatting and saw that Oscar had WhatsApped.

O: How did the salad go down?

Me: Really well, thank goodness. 😋

O: Excellent. How is it then?

Me: Fine. Although the teacher is obsessed with vaginas.

O: A woman after my own heart.

Me: Haha.

O: Well I suppose it's a legit thing for a midwife to be obsessed with.

Me: True

O: I'm thinking about your vagina now.

Me: 😳 Are you on the plane? Are you drunk already?

O: Yes and slightly. I wish you could join the mile-high club with me, I miss you.

Me: You've only just gone! But you'll be back soon enough. Class is about to start again – me and my vagina had better go.

O: Call you when I land.

Me: OK, safe flight.

O: Still thinking about your vagina.

Oscar had left for New York early that morning.

'I'll miss you, but I'll cope,' I'd said as he stopped for a moment and asked whether I was really feeling okay about him going off and not coming to The Baby Group, especially when my due date was getting so close. He had reassured me that his phone would stay on all night and he'd drop everything and come home immediately, if anything started to happen.

As he'd walked away from me down the hallway to retrieve his shoes, I'd watched his slightly gangly walk, and marvelled at how I'd ended up with a man so kind and considerate, albeit lanky.

Then he came back into the kitchen, shoes on, and gave me a peck. 'See you in a few days – I'll go straight to the office probably, I'm on the red eye. Proper kiss?' He lifted my head to his lips. He was a good kisser. But I couldn't press my body into his like I used to do when kissing him. I ran my fingers over the front of his trousers and he ran his over my bump.

'I *really* wish I didn't have to rush off this morning,' he whispered.

And then we kissed again. When our lips pulled away, he was still holding my head in his hands. He fixed me with a look; a look of lust mixed with wonderment.

'You're having a baby!' he cooed.

I smiled and shrugged. It was wonderful to see him genuinely engage with this pregnancy – a scenario I once feared would never happen. I pulled my chin from his fingers, conscious that time was ticking and I needed to get ready.

He hesitated. 'Good luck today. WhatsApp me when you get out, tell me how it goes, and if there's anyone you're considering being friends with. I'll be able to reply from the plane.'

After the break, Maggie tried to make us believe that the delivery of a baby through a surgical incision in the abdomen and uterus was a barbaric torture involving a long recovery process and thus should be avoided at all costs. I closed my ears and kept quiet for most of it, having already decided on an elective C-section. It was surprising how judgemental people could be about childbirth, when surely the aim was just to have a healthy baby, however it might be born. Half of me wished Oscar was here now; he would have struggled to keep silent and would likely have challenged Maggie on that. I wondered if there were any other secret caesarean sisters in the room. Carol's expression had failed to give anything away all day, although my guess would be her as the most likely candidate.

During the afternoon break, I nipped to the bathroom, took the red lippy out of my prized handbag and topped up my lips with three strokes in the mirror. Perhaps Gucci had been a bit too fancy for today.

'You're so glamorous,' said a quiet voice at the sink next

to me. Lost in thought, I had barely noticed Aisha come out of the cubicle. She turned on the tap beneath her and we smiled awkwardly at each other in the mirror.

'Well I suppose I won't be wearing it much once the baby arrives,' I replied. 'May as well make the most of it.'

'Yes, the red lippy will have to go – your baby won't appreciate it when you're smothering him in kisses, believe me!' came Maggie's booming voice from behind a locked cubicle door. 'Unless you both want to look like clowns, that is.'

Aisha and I looked at each other and smiled broadly. 'Does she literally hear everything?' I whispered, as Aisha silently giggled.

'Noted, Maggie!' I yelled back. 'No more rouge for me.' I slung the lipstick back into my bag for dramatic effect.

Aisha had put her hand over her mouth to stop her laughter.

Maybe I might make some friends here, after all.

CHAPTER FOUR

Aisha

As I was leaving the group, Dad texted to tell me he had transferred £500 into my account to buy us a cot. I had panic-texted him during the meeting, when almost everyone else mentioned they had prepared cribs for their babies, just in case they arrived early. Obviously, Jason and I didn't yet own one. I was just trying to work out how to tell Jason about the payment, because I knew Dad's hand-outs were a source of tension for him, when he phoned.

'I feel like such an amateur,' I told him as we chatted while I walked home. 'The others seem so organized, whereas *my* only plan so far has been to survive the birth. As it turns out, not-dying isn't a birth plan.' I sighed loudly, for dramatic effect. 'It's made me realize that I – *we* – still have a lot to work out.'

'Oh honey, we'll get there,' Jason replied. 'People have babies every minute of every day and I bet loads of them are a hell of a lot less prepared than us. You attended a Baby

Group for starters. Surely that counts for something? Isn't the whole point of going to a Baby Group, to learn and plan?'

'That and make some new friends. I'm not sure I'm going to succeed in that either,' I said.

'I can't believe they were *all* psychos or boring, were they? Tell me about them.'

I took a deep breath. 'Well, there was "Perfect" Helen and "Earth Mother" Susie who both had their birth plans all laid out. One of them is going to have her placenta made into tablets. I'm not even entirely sure where to find my placenta,' I stroked my bump, 'let alone how to make its funeral arrangements. I mean, is that bad?'

He chuckled in response. 'Sounds quite mad to me.'

'Then there was this "Deliciously Ella" one, who had prepared a salad that looked like it had walked off the set of its own cookery show. *And* she was wearing red lipstick. Jason, I don't think I've worn any lipstick for the last three months, let alone a red one. I've never felt less cool. She turned up with a Gucci handbag too. She looked like an Instagram post.'

'Aisha, it's a Baby Group, not an influencers' convention. I don't think anyone cares what anyone else is wearing,' he said. 'I couldn't give a toss. Excuse the salad pun.'

'But *I* care,' I sighed. 'Anyway, how was your day?'

'Philip offered to pay me double overtime when I mentioned I'd missed the meeting. I'll get at least two hundred quid,' he declared, sounding genuinely chuffed. 'I'll tell you more over dinner later.'

'Every cloud.' I sighed again. I didn't dare tell him about

the money from Dad, which we were going to badly need because Jason's £200 wouldn't cover kitting out the nursery, not judging by the baby list Maggie had said she was going to email us all this evening. 'I'm just popping home for a quick change of clothes and a rest. I'll see you in an hour.'

When I reached Honest Burger, Jason was standing outside holding a bunch of yellow tulips. He looked so sweetly apprehensive.

'Tulips for my love,' he said, bowing down dramatically. 'I'm so sorry I wasn't there with you today; it doesn't sound like you had the easiest time.'

'I suppose I can forgive you,' I said, taking the flowers from him and lifting my head to give him a kiss.

He knew yellow tulips were my favourite. They had been hard to come by in Hong Kong (whereas red roses had been ten a penny) and they had reminded me of home. Now I bought a bunch almost anywhere I found them. I loved them so much that when illustrating my last children's book – yet another incarnation of a story about learning how to share – I put yellow tulips in almost every scene. When my new editor questioned it, I had my answer at the ready (I hadn't been in this game for eight years and learnt nothing): 'It adds another dimension. Once the adult reading the book becomes aware of them, the child can begin to search for them on every spread. I've done so many bunnies, cats and bears. Yellow tulips symbolise cheerfulness and sunshine to me. Please?'

I got to keep the tulips.

When we sat down, Jason slid an arm around me,

enveloping me into a tight hug. 'You're going to be an amazing mum, you know,' he said earnestly, turning my face so my gaze met his.

My eyes filled with tears. 'I hope so.' I took a deep breath. 'I was thinking, with my overtime money, we could shop for a cot.' He fixed me with a look of pure love. 'Perhaps we could go and find one tomorrow, a really great one.'

I smiled. There was a time when a bonus would have meant going straight to the pub, and blowing it all on margaritas and later a Thai meal at our favourite local restaurant, and now here he was getting excited about buying a cot. Even though I would give almost anything for a margarita right now, it felt good, after his initial wobble when I got pregnant, to see Jason enthusiastic about the baby. It meant he was finally getting his head around becoming a daddy and it made my heart swell with happiness. This was quite a moment, because it was the first time it had been *his* suggestion to go shopping for nursery items. The last time I mentioned getting a cot, he had suggested we use the time to go on a date instead. He had looked exasperated when I had explained that the baby was likely to be in a cot for up to two years so it was important to do the research. But really, it wasn't even about the cot – it was about us coming together to plan. Jason seemed to think having a baby was a fleeting moment in time.

'A cot – can I just check I heard you correctly?' I asked sardonically.

'You did,' he said proudly, moving a stray piece of hair that had flopped across my face. 'I know it probably sounds ridiculous, but it's like I'm finally really excited about all this.

I was genuinely gutted not to be able to come with you today. I felt like I'd let you down.' He paused. 'But more than that, I felt as though I'd let our baby down. It felt horrible – and I don't want either of you to feel like that again. I promise I'm going to be a good dad, Aish, I'm going to give our baby everything he or she needs – nothing will be too much.' He looked down at my swollen belly and whispered behind his hand. 'You hear that, little bean and your little placenta, wherever it may be?' He glanced at me comically. I beamed. Jason had always been able to make me laugh. 'I'm going to give you everything you need. Including a gold-plated cot, if that's what you want. Well, maybe not gold-plated, but a super-cosy one. I love your mummy very much, you know.'

Although still not addressed directly to me, they were, at least, the words I had been longing to hear, but there was still a nagging worry: that Jason was managing to give the conversation a financial slant. He was still not over the fact his salary since moving back to London was quite a way beneath what he once earned in Hong Kong. Jason had been obsessed with earning money when we lived abroad; I had hoped things might change when we moved back to London, but when he failed to find a role with a large basic salary he put in for all the overtime available. I tried not to dwell on it, telling myself that all our baby really needed was love and his presence. And we were planning now, at least.

The conversation moved on to kitting out the nursery, and I downloaded the overwhelming list from Maggie entitled, 'What to buy for baby and you'. It contained buggies, bottle sterilisers, changing mats, something called a 'jungle gym' and a number of strange gadgets – I mean, do you *really* need a machine to get wax out of the baby's ear? I tried to push to one side the strong doubt that £200 would come anywhere near covering the cost of all this. I decided not to tell Jason about the money from Dad – plus the fact I might need to ask him for more – because I didn't want to spoil Jason's happy mood.

CHAPTER FIVE

Lucy

I had missed Oscar loads this week and it wasn't just because of a mild concern that I might go into early labour and would end up having to ask our creepy neighbour to take me to hospital if I couldn't make it into an Uber on my own. I missed having him around the place. I missed him wrapping an arm around what used to be my waist and planting kisses on my forehead. I missed his conversation.

There were some plus sides to him being away though – having as many pillows as I liked in bed was one. Also especially satisfying was the fact that it took me all of five minutes, with a hammer and some tacks, to put up the pictures I had chosen for the nursery walls, rather than a convoluted whole afternoon involving a painful discussion about why it was best to do this properly – i.e. the time-consuming way, involving a spirit level, drill and proper picture hooks. DIY techniques were a constant battleground for us.

'What's cooking?' he asked, nose in the air like a sniffer

dog the moment he had set his suitcase down. I took his hand and led him towards the kitchen, where he guessed correctly that I'd been busy cooking my speciality boeuf bourguignon this afternoon.

I puckered my lips. 'Supper, for my man.'

Oscar smiled and put his arms around me. Despite the fact he was six foot three with long arms, I'm pretty certain they didn't meet at the back. 'It smells beautiful – but not as beautiful as you look, darling Lucy.' He paused to look at me. I enjoyed accepting his compliments and stopped for a moment to bask in his besotted gaze, before shuffling out of his hands and turning to retrieve the oven gloves from the side. I gave the pot a stir, releasing some more juices, to labour the point that I really was a bloody good cook.

'Something tells me some nesting has been going on,' he declared, with an air of sarcasm.

There was no point denying I had become a pregnancy cliché. 'Wait until you see the nursery.'

He followed me upstairs.

I reached behind the nursery door and turned the light off for some added drama as we both stood on the landing outside the smaller of two spare rooms, which had been turned into the nursery. He planted a kiss on my lips. As I edged open the nursery door with my foot, he whispered, 'Maybe we should leave the lights off...' Then he pushed himself into my back and ran his fingers over my breasts and over the bump. It occurred to me that my body was not too dissimilar to a camel's, with two humps, right now. 'I just find you so sexy.' As he pressed himself into me, I felt he was hard.

'Sexy now – but will I be sexy to you when my breasts are lactating and I've not slept for weeks?' I muttered.

He gently turned my face towards his. 'What do you mean?' he said. 'Of course I'll find you sexy. You've never looked more womanly – I love it.'

'You'll still want me, when I'm a mum?'

'Even more so,' he whispered, hungry for me. 'You'll be sexier than ever to me when you're a mum. You are blooming, Lucy.'

I turned to face him and we kissed slowly and passionately.

'The Baby Group woman was saying that sex can bring on labour at this stage,' I whispered, my bump between us, stopping us from pressing into each other as closely as we wanted to.

'I don't care, I need you,' he panted, before gently biting my lip with a passion I had felt many times before.

'Even with boeuf bourguignon in the oven?' I smiled into his lips as we went in for another long kiss, soft and warm. Swapping sex for food was the only thing guaranteed to work with Oscar.

'You've got a point there, Miss Raven, but your curves make me feel horny,' he said. 'I'm going to be even crazier for you when this little one arrives, but I know I'll have to fight for your attention, because I'll have competition. I need to make the most of having you to myself.'

I pulled back to take in his face. His eyes were sparkling in the landing light. He looked handsome. I was aware that the dinner really was going to be spoiled if we carried on right now. I peppered his lips with shorter kisses until our mouths separated again. When I opened my eyes once more, Oscar was beaming at me.

'Why are you laughing?' I asked, thinking something about my appearance must be humouring him.

'I'm so happy,' he said. 'I didn't think it was possible.' I knew it was his way of acknowledging not just the passion we shared, but our deepening bond. 'Our future is so bright.'

I smiled into his lips once more. 'I love you, Mr Bright.'

CHAPTER SIX

Aisha

Saturday 1st May

A week later, Jason and I were on our way to the second Baby Group meeting when his phone rang. I knew instinctively it was bad news.

'Seriously?' he said loudly, stopping in the middle of the pavement. I watched him put his hand to his forehead and took an educated guess that it was his boss, Peter, on the other end. Then Jason said: 'I'll be there in thirty,' and hung up. My heart rate quickened.

'The system's gone down again,' he said. 'It's a nightmare, Aish, I thought we'd fixed the problems yesterday, but apparently not. Peter is going nuts because no one's getting any emails.' He blew air out of his mouth harshly. I wanted to feel sorry for him because he genuinely was having a work nightmare, but right now, I was more sorry for myself – *and* our baby.

I sometimes wished Jason worked for the ambulance service. At least then the unsociable hours and emergency calls would have the payoff that he was saving lives in the process. Instead, I have an IT manager who gets all the stress and upheaval, but with none of the genuine heroism.

'At least you're not actually in labour, hey?' he said lightly, as if this was a sweetener.

'Yeah, because if I was in labour, I'm assuming you wouldn't be going in!' I snapped.

'If you were, I'm sure I could remote in, and keep working,' he retorted.

I failed to see the joke and looked around self-consciously, hoping that no one else from The Baby Group was witnessing this. I was royally pissed off. Jason was going to miss another meeting. Not to mention he knew how anxious I was about going into labour.

'Oh baby – Aisha – chill out, okay? Of course I wouldn't leave you if you were actually in labour.' He said it as though this was slightly funny. He reached for my hand.

My eyes burnt and my bottom lip trembled. I wondered if this was the kind of stress that could bring on contractions. 'I just feel like you constantly put work ahead of me,' I said, trying to stop my voice from wobbling.

'Ahead of you and our baby, never,' he said, sincerely enough to make me straighten a little. 'Ahead of this group today, I'm afraid, yes. I'm as pissed off about it as you are, I promise, but this is my job – I'm doing this *for you*. We both knew what I was taking on and Peter wouldn't be asking if he didn't really need me.' I said nothing. 'Baby, we talked about this and how if I put the hours in now, I can be around for you in a few weeks' time, when you're *really* going to need me. You *and* our baby will need me. We discussed that, remember?' He looked at me with those big green eyes. 'Isn't that what we agreed – I work my arse off now, so I can be around for as long as possible when it's here?'

'We still need you today,' I replied, trying really hard not to cry. 'I need you.' I knew I was labouring the point, but I couldn't help it, and stroked my bump for added effect. The thought of walking into the meeting alone again filled me with dread. It was just going to be so embarrassing having to explain why he wasn't there for the second time.

'I'm *really* sorry,' he said, dropping my limp hand, because it clearly wasn't going to show him any love right now, however hard he clasped it. 'I'll be back as soon as I can – with any luck, it will be quick to sort out and I'll get an Uber and come and join you for the afternoon. I'll be thinking of you, you're amazing, you don't need me, you can do this.' He lowered his face to my belly. 'I love you and this little bean so much. I do, you know.' Then he kissed me on the forehead and dashed off in the opposite direction to the one we were meant to be going in.

Fortunately I was one of the first to arrive at the group – only Helen and Ian had taken their seats – so I had a quiet word with Maggie.

'Jason got called away for work suddenly. He's a manager for the IT department of a bank – in the city,' I said. 'There was an emergency situation with their systems going down, something to do with a software update.' I was babbling.

'He's the manager.' I immediately felt silly for going into so much detail and feeling the need to repeat the manager part, in case she hadn't heard, as if this somehow validated his absence. Who was I trying to kid? I just hoped he would be there next time.

'It sounds terribly techy, I don't have a clue about all of that,' Maggie said, her chirpy voice a comfort to me now. 'We'll miss him, but I suppose it can't be helped.' She paused to look me in the eye. 'Are you okay, dear?'

'Absolutely fine,' I lied. 'He'll be here next week.' And I took my seat.

When we had all settled into the same places as last time, Maggie began: 'In today's session, we're going to act out a vaginal birth and also a caesarean section and then we'll be talking about body awareness, breathing and massage.'

I watched Helen sip from an extra-large Caffè Nero cup and wished I'd thought of picking something up myself. How I missed my daily caffeine fix. If you gave me a pound for the number of times I'd hoped a barista would accidentally make it a proper coffee rather than decaf, I'd be handing over a piggy bank heavy enough to pay for a new deluxe iCandy stroller by now. Though I'd bet Helen was sipping something herbal.

'Would anyone like to share if they are planning to go the caesarean route?' Maggie asked. Her dark, piggyish eyes darted around the room expectantly.

I averted my eyes from hers and immediately thought of Mum. Lately I'd been thinking about her more than ever. As I saw my bump grow, resembling the colourful, inflatable beach ball I'd played with on childhood holidays in France, sometimes my whole body ached for her. There were so many questions I wanted to ask her, but would never get the chance.

Did she suffer the same debilitating morning sickness I had endured for the first sixteen weeks? Had she opted for the caesarean section birth, or was it an emergency? I remembered her showing me her faint scar, but I couldn't recall the whole story and it bothered me that I hadn't paid more attention. Perhaps the combination of the sickness and the C-section was why my mum had stopped at one child. After the sickness I had experienced, I didn't blame her. Perhaps I would feel complete with one child too. Mum always led me to believe she couldn't imagine loving any other child as much as she loved me, but I never knew if there was really another reason. All I knew was that I could be headed for a C-section too, but that at the end of the day did it really matter, because this baby inside me was so very wanted and so deeply loved.

Lucy was the only person who raised her hand. I clocked the empty seat next to her and it offered me a little comfort to see that she was also flying solo again today. 'I'm electing for a caesarean,' she said confidently. 'It might seem controversial, but I have my reasons and I'm sure this is the right route for me.' She folded her arms and sat back in her seat. I admired her ability to shut down a conversation.

'Wonderful,' Maggie said awkwardly. 'Feel free to discuss your decision with me at any time, if you'd like to. I'll be asking you to pair up to practise a few of the breathing and massage techniques first,' she continued. 'We'll save the

C-section until after lunch.' Presumably so it didn't put any of us off our food. I felt a little sorry for Lucy and the way Maggie had made it sound like something she frowned upon. Lucy clearly had her reasons – and it wasn't as if I hadn't considered one too, because of Mum. Pregnancy could make people so judgemental.

The idea of practical demonstrations made me shift uncomfortably. Don't split up the couples. Please don't split the couples. I didn't want someone else's husband's hands on me. Although perhaps I could make an exception for Will…

'Aisha and Lucy, you can work together please,' Maggie said.

I successfully caught Lucy's eye and we exchanged a shy smile in acknowledgement. Seeing as we were both partnerless, it made sense for us to work together, even though the idea of giving and receiving massages from another pregnant woman – and especially someone as well put-together as Lucy – wasn't exactly making me feel relaxed.

'Sorry, you seem to have drawn the short straw,' Lucy said as Maggie indicated I should move to the chair next to Lucy.

'Not at all, I'm just relieved she's not using me to demonstrate,' I replied.

Maggie turned to us: 'Okay ladies, ready to give it a go?'

'There's still time,' Lucy muttered, smiling sweetly, and I cringed in response.

A minute later, following a description of what we were to do from Maggie, all of the couples moved into position and Lucy slowly manoeuvred herself into a kneeling position behind me.

'Well, this is embarrassing,' she whispered. I could tell from her voice that she was trying not to giggle and the fact she was letting her guard down made me warm to her. 'I've never felt less mobile.'

Meanwhile, I was on my knees, leaning over a chair, so I couldn't see how mortifying it was for her because I was wrapped up in my own ridiculousness.

On the other side of the circle, I could hear Lin and Susie getting into the exercise. Susie was making loud, appreciative noises as Lin clearly hit the right spots.

'Fabulous ladies! Great work over there,' Maggie encouraged them. 'Don't hold back – remember that, everyone; it's really important that you let out those moans and groans. And when you reach transition stage – that's the bit right before the birth – if you want to moo like a big beautiful pregnant cow, just do it. Let it out! That's right, Susie, "Moooo!"'

'I don't hear any mooing coming from you, Aisha,' Lucy said sarcastically, as I felt her tentatively knead my shoulders. It was embarrassing doing this with a woman I barely knew. If it wasn't so funny, I'd be livid with Maggie for putting us through it.

'I don't think I'm at the mooing stage yet,' I replied, 'I'm more in the "get me out of here" stage right now.'

'I'm with you,' Lucy giggled. 'If it wasn't so hard to move out of this position, I'd leg it out of here with you.' We both snorted with laughter.

'Whoa, Lucy dear! That position isn't necessary for you!' Maggie suddenly exclaimed, rushing over to us, her too-wide-for-her-body-shape navy trousers flapping and revealing the top of a white towelling sports sock. 'That's what the birth partner would do, yes, but it isn't safe for you to do. I'll come and assist the pair of you. I don't want to be responsible for any injuries – let alone early labours!' She held up her hands and gave me a worried look, like I was about to shoot a baby out of my vagina unannounced. 'You okay down there, Aisha?'

'I think so. Do I stay here?' I asked, feeling vulnerable.

'Yes please, just for a moment Aisha. I'll demonstrate another gentle relaxation technique on you, if you don't mind, and then it will be Lucy's turn.'

I rolled my eyes at Lucy and mouthed: 'Told you.'

She winced, and mouthed back, 'Sorry!'

At least it felt as though I had a comrade here, because all of the others seemed to be taking this extremely seriously.

Maggie turned to the group. 'Now, don't be embarrassed if any of you ladies fart during this exercise – either from the rectum or vagina – it's perfectly normal to be gassy.'

At that, Lucy let out a guffaw like a schoolgirl, shooting one hand up to cover her mouth as her shoulders shook and she struggled to contain herself. It took all my strength not to collapse into giggles too – or to fart.

Maybe she was okay after all.

CHAPTER SEVEN

Lucy

Fortunately, when the relaxation demos were over and Aisha and I had composed ourselves, Maggie granted us a comfort break. We joined the others in the tea-making area and I almost wanted to hug Aisha when she pulled a packet of custard creams out of her bag.

'I've been craving these,' she smiled, offering me the packet.

I had been trying to avoid refined sugar, as a general rule, but they were exactly what I needed right now. 'Oh yes please!' I said. 'I thought I was going to lose it for a moment then. It was the most bizarre thing—'

Just then Helen joined us: 'That was so interesting, I had no idea about the mooing,' she commented. 'Aren't our bodies incredible?' She looked deadly serious. I really did not understand how a person could not find the idea of mooing remotely amusing.

'Well I'm going to moo that hospital down!' Susie interjected, lightening things up. I liked her, she seemed a cheery personality.

'You'll definitely know when Susie's arrived,' Lin added fondly.

'I just hope it doesn't happen too soon,' I said. 'I've got a lot to pack into the coming weeks. I'm not ready to turn into a full-blown sow just yet.'

'When are you finishing work?' Aisha asked, offering the biscuits around again. I gladly accepted another.

'I've still got a fortnight left at work. We're down to the final two in a huge client pitch, plus I've got a campaign that's about to go live, and my deputy is showing no signs of picking up the reins right now. I've got to supervise everything she does. It's hard to focus on buying nursery equipment until I can get all of that tied up and delegated. Although I'm *trying* to multi-task… the nesting instinct is real and I'm desperate to get stuck into it. What about you?'

Aisha hesitated. I suddenly felt maybe I had said too much; been a little full-on about work. When you're in the fast-paced world of consumer PR it's easy to be swept up in the urgency of everything.

'I'm still at it, but I don't have to go into an office at least; I'm freelance,' she answered quietly.

'What do you do?' Susie asked, joining the conversation.

'Illustrator, of children's books,' Aisha said.

'That's so cool! Would we know any of your books?' Susie continued.

'Probably not. Well, I don't know, maybe, I've done six over here,' she smiled, her cheeks flushed as though she was embarrassed to have the attention on her. Aisha seemed to lack confidence, which was a shame because she was clearly talented, not to mention beautiful, modest, funny – she was easily the most interesting in this group, in my eyes.

'What about you?' Aisha asked.

'Primary school teacher,' Susie replied. 'There's barely a children's book I don't know, perhaps I'll know some of yours. I'm just hoping this little one can hang on until half term and then I'm all good.' She patted her swollen belly. 'I can't wait to stop now – you wouldn't believe the probing questions I get on a daily basis from a class of six-year-olds. They seem even more obsessed with my placenta than Lin is!' We all chuckled.

I had noticed a missed call from Katie during the session, so I took the opportunity to grab a brownie from the table – another Susie and Lin special, my sugar craving was strong this morning – and popped out into the street to phone her back. Katie had been my closest confidante since we bonded on day two of university and was the kind of friend who always saw the funny side of situations. I knew she'd love the massage demonstration story.

'I need to show you something,' she had said on that day we first met twenty years ago. Her expression was somber, as though she'd been telling me my cat had been run over. Then she'd ushered me down the corridor of our halls and into her bedroom, where her face had lit up into a wide smile and, giggling, she had pointed to a magnum of Cava. 'From my parents. Want to help me find some hot guys to share it with?'

Katie had perfectly managed the delicate balancing act we faced at university – of attempting to be functional adults while having a strong desire to get drunk at every opportunity. I had loved her from the moment I met her and simultaneously discovered my love of bubbles. And, of course, we had managed to land ourselves the hot guys, for the short while we were together at uni anyway. Katie had always been there for me, even after our student days together had been cut short.

'So?' she asked. I could sense a mix of excitement and trepidation in her voice.

'Nothing to report,' I replied. 'Not yet, anyway.'

'I've been thinking about you all day,' she sighed, disappointed.

'But I am learning that doulas are vagina-mad, that I have a fear of farting from my front bottom, and that having a baby is totally insane. I can't believe so many people do it. Tell me the details of your birth story again? It will make more sense to me now.'

She sighed. 'Two words – car crash. Don't you remember Daisy and I were in hospital for four days afterwards because I lost so much blood? I'm not sure it's a good idea to remind you.'

'Oh yes, of course, I'm sorry. Maybe don't tell me then. Actually, I need to know. Knowledge is power.' I felt bad that I couldn't remember the details of Katie's birth story, but the truth was that before falling pregnant myself, I had found it difficult to engage with other people's pregnancies and births. I had kind of blotted out the fact that a number of my friends were getting pregnant and having babies around me and I had purposely distanced myself from them, because I was finding it so hard myself. I did it with Katie too, and

I'm sure it must have hurt her. For a while it had stung too much – she seemed to have it all, and I felt resentful, even though I had hated myself for it.

I think my body had been waiting, waiting for The One – for the same feeling of true love I had been lucky enough to experience once before, a long time ago.

I had spent years basically on a treadmill of long periods of being single, trying out various dating apps, going on dates and having relationships lasting a few months at most; many of them enjoyable and some involving plenty of good sex, but none that I felt could go the distance.

Like Lennox, the builder who had come to do some work in my bathroom and ended up drinking a bottle of wine with me one Friday evening. We went on a few dates and he was good at foreplay, but the fact that he had never read a book and still holidayed with his parents, aged 39, had soon put a stop to things.

And Rich, the wealthy banker who, if I'd drunk a number of cocktails, we were sitting in the right light, and I squinted, looked passable for Ryan Gosling. He had taken me to some of London's most expensive bars and restaurants – even a couple of swanky hotels in the New Forest – during our six-month courtship, but he had absolutely no sense of humour. He didn't even find it amusing when I introduced him to the new Snapchat filters and sent him a video of myself singing 'Do Ya Think I'm Sexy' half naked while looking like a fluffy white bunny. It was never going to work. There'd also been Tom from Norway, and a couple of other one-night stands whose names I couldn't remember.

I had taken a few risks along the way too, having unprotected sex in the middle of my cycle, then watching and waiting for the slightest sign of a pregnancy or a period symptom, wondering whether, if I was expecting a baby, I could give it a go with the father; if maybe there was a chance for us. But no pregnancy had come.

Curious to know about my fertility, I undertook tests which revealed, at the age of 35, that I had a low egg count. When I'd asked my gynaecologist how he thought it would affect me, he'd said brightly: 'The best way of finding out is to get on with it!' Noticing the silent tears appear in my eyes, he'd then asked: 'Have you ever been pregnant?' He had touched a very raw nerve.

'Once,' I'd replied quietly. 'I had an abortion, a long time ago.'

'Well that's good news,' he'd said optimistically. 'I suggest you keep trying, and it will happen.'

I had never seen my abortion as 'good news'.

I felt a despair and loneliness that the years since the abortion had failed to completely shift. When friends all around me had seemed to be gleefully falling in love, getting pregnant or talking about starting a family, I had withdrawn from socializing with them. Friends were easy to lose, it seemed. As time had passed, I had begun to think more and more about the person who got me pregnant when I was 19. I had viewed him through rose-tinted glasses and still wondered how different life might have been if I'd told him the truth, instead of ending our relationship. Would we have kept the baby? Would we still be together now, as a family?

But today, finally pregnant again, at last I felt able to make up for lost time with Katie. I listened with renewed interest – plus a mix of trepidation and awe – as she recounted her birth story, wondering what my experience would turn out to be.

'Anyway, I'd better go back into the group, we'll be starting again in a minute.'

'Keep me posted,' she commanded.

'I will.'

This time I didn't return to my usual seat, I deliberately sat next to Aisha.

CHAPTER EIGHT

Aisha

Sunday 2ⁿᵈ May

I had a dream last night that Jason missed the birth.

It was just before the baby arrived. I had gone into labour, but I couldn't find him anywhere. I searched frantically around the house, panting as my contractions got more severe. Barely able to stand on my feet, I called him endless times, but he didn't pick up. I called our mutual friends and family, and some of his colleagues, begging them to help me track him down, but no one could find him. I panicked that maybe something had happened to him. Finally I called an ambulance and I could hear its siren whirring down the street coming closer and closer to our house to take me to hospital. I was all alone…

Then I woke up.

The dream left me feeling unsettled; a feeling that, if I was honest, I hadn't been able to shake since the day I found out I was pregnant.

I had delayed taking the test until I was sure my period was three days late – and even then I promised myself I would wait until the following morning to take it because you're meant to get a more accurate result first thing. Jason had pulled an all-nighter at work the night before, and at 10 a.m. sent a text to say that they still weren't finished and he would probably be home very late again. 'At least I'm clocking up the overtime. I can probably afford that trip to Paris I've been promising you,' he quipped, in an effort to placate me. It was hard to tell over text whether he was being sarcastic or not, and it was typical that he happened to be on an all-nighter at the exact same time that I was going to discover if we were pregnant. I knew he'd be so excited too and I wanted to share the moment with him. But the suspense was killing me. It was a moment I'd waited for, for some time. Jason might describe us as 'casually' trying, but it was anything but casual for me.

Jason and I had been open about our desire to have children since we'd started dating six years ago, so once we had got married three years later in Hong Kong I imagined we would start trying straight away, but Jason had been adamant about laying stronger foundations for our financial security before we did. When he'd been transferred to the London branch of the city trading firm he worked for in Hong Kong, 'Project: Baby' had been nearly ready to begin, and when he'd racked up a reasonable amount of overtime after a few months, it had finally been green-lit. But then another whole year had passed, without a hint of a pregnancy. Admittedly, neither of us had been fastidious about keeping track of the all-important dates in my cycle for the first six months, but I then began paying close attention. With Jason's increasingly erratic work schedule, it had sometimes been challenging to pencil in any night of hot sex, let alone on the days I'd been most fertile. And whenever we *had* found ourselves able to spend a cosy evening at home together, one of us – mostly Jason – hadn't felt up for it. Scheduled sex had never felt less sexy. When he rebuffed an advance, I had sometimes got the impression that perhaps Jason wasn't ready to be a father yet, but I had pushed these thoughts out of my mind and carried on. As the weeks had passed, my wish to fall pregnant had grown stronger and stronger; I recalled myself as a young girl pushing my dolly around in the miniature pram Dad had bought me. She was called Brenda. I had loved that doll so much. A strong maternal instinct had been in me from such a young age so when it didn't happen as quickly as I always imagined it would, I began to get superstitious about it.

If I'd happened to spot a solitary magpie on my jog around the common, I'd saluted it and muttered under my breath: 'Hello Mr Magpie, how's your wife and children?' while urgently scanning the area for his mate and feeling deflated when I couldn't find them. Each time I'd neared the end of my cycle, finally two weeks post-ovulation, I had obsessed over whether I was going to get my period or not. Each trip to the toilet had become a heightened experience as I hoped there wouldn't be blood on the loo roll; each day I had been overly aware of my body, wondering if a slight sensation in my abdomen was a premenstrual ache or a tiny, fertilized egg implanting itself in my womb. And then when my period had come, there had been a brief dalliance with denial, wondering whether the first drops of blood were spotting related to implantation. I had googled pregnancy symptoms so exhaustively I knew every possible scenario. But this hope had always been followed by the crushing disappointment and acceptance that I was not pregnant again that month.

At 35, I wondered if I'd left it too late. A year of trying wasn't long in the scheme of things, but when you were suddenly desperate for something, it felt like an eternity.

But that morning, my period slightly late, I felt different.

I woke up feeling really positive. After receiving the text from Jason, I decided to walk up to Clapham Common to keep myself occupied. Just a short stroll from our flat, I approached the common on the south side, taking my usual short cut through the back streets to reach the open space for a light morning run. I saw two magpies and then three, fluttering playfully between two big oak trees, almost bare of leaves, as crisp and clear as anything. It was a bright day, the air felt fresh and smelled of moist bark, and the dew hadn't yet dried on the grass.

I stopped to watch the magpies as they hovered around the low braces of the tree, coming together for a moment and then scattering, their movements so rhythmic and graceful, they had to be a little family.

'One for sorrow, two for joy, three for a girl...' There were definitely three. 'A girl,' I whispered under my breath. 'It's happening – I'm having a girl.' I felt it in my gut and there was nothing I could do to stop a huge smile spreading across my face.

After a shorter than usual circuit of the common, buoyed by Mr Magpie, his wife and child, I called Jason. He didn't answer, so I sent him a message:

Hey baby – call me asap!

I tried to get on with some work. But although I read the email from my editor at least five times, as she detailed the list of amends to my latest illustrations, nothing was sinking in.

I tried ringing him again – no response. Even when the little white ticks on WhatsApp had turned blue, so I knew he had read my message, he still didn't reply.

An hour passed, then two, and still no word. I just couldn't wait any longer. I decided to take the pregnancy test on my own.

After drenching the stick and my hand in pee, I sat nervously on the closed toilet seat, my knickers still around my ankles, waiting for the result. I started trembling as one minute passed and the control line appeared. Then, slowly but surely, I watched in delight and disbelief as two clear blue lines came into view inside the 'pregnant' window.

'Oh. My. God,' I said slowly, out loud. 'Oh my God. I'm pregnant!' And I looked to the ceiling and personally thanked each of the three magpies that had brought me luck that Friday morning.

Finding out you are pregnant is one of the most defining moments in a woman's life. The moment you realize that nothing will ever be the same again. And sharing that news has to be handled in the correct way. It was times like this that working from home as a freelancer was particularly hard because although I was glad not to have to contend with the claustrophobic, hot London Tube during rush hour each day, I was all on my own. The cosmos had shifted significantly, I was cradling an enormous secret in my abdomen, but I had no one to tell.

For a moment I was transported back to the times when Jason and I would meet after work when we lived in Hong Kong.

We'd had a small, but really cute one-bedroom apartment in Kowloon, high up on the twentieth floor and with a tiny balcony. The slightly batty porter, who had often been found talking to himself as he manned the security desk downstairs, had had a soft spot for me.

'*Mèilì*, Lady Aisha!' he would say –'beautiful' – when I walked past him most mornings, my arm interlocked with Jason's as we'd head into the city, to our workplaces together.

'Hey, she's mine!' Jason would joke in return, squeezing me tightly.

The thrill of seeing him waiting to surprise me at lunchtime outside my publishers' building amongst the high rises of Central Hong Kong, looking handsome in his smart suit and attracting a few admiring glances from my colleagues – both male and female – had always lifted my spirits. After work we would meet for cocktails and dinner, or simply get on a tram, travel up to the Peak or explore a new area of the city, always holding hands. It had felt amazing to be on an adventure together...

I checked my phone again to see that Jason had still not

responded, so I googled: 'What should you do when you first find out you're pregnant?' and was confronted by a host of instructional lists telling me to work out the due date (20th May), find a midwife and figure out my finances, all the while avoiding a host of food and drinks, including caffeine, soft cheese, raw fish and alcohol: four of my greatest pleasures in life. I suddenly hankered for a double espresso and a cream cheese and smoked salmon bagel.

I looked at the clock. It was midday. I was going to struggle to survive a whole seven hours in possession of this huge secret until Jason came through the door late tonight. Besides, the little blue lines might have faded by then and I wanted him to see them too. I touched my stomach, trying to work out if I felt pregnant; it was all very surreal.

I took a shower and stared at my naked body in the bathroom mirror as I searched for non-existent signs that I looked different this morning. I tried calling Jason one last time but still no reply. Nothing for it – I'd take a leaf out of his book from when we lived in Hong Kong and go and surprise him at work for lunch. I had to tell him the happy news in person.

When I reached Jason's office building near Moorgate, he still hadn't responded to any of my messages so I asked the man on reception to let him know I was there.

The City building couldn't have been more different to my cosy workspace at our kitchen table. I looked at my reflection in the tall, mirrored wall next to the elaborate reception desk. It was still me all right, but if I wasn't mistaken, I looked a little paler than usual, perhaps a bit fuller around the face. Could pregnancy hormones be kicking in already?

When the receptionist had located Jason, he finally appeared through the lift doors. 'Hey, what are you doing here?' he said, looking more concerned than overly happy to see me. I became conscious of my jeans and trainers, a contrast to the smart pencil skirts with matching jackets of the women walking with purpose around me.

I took in his appearance – unkempt hair, bloodshot eyes, and the same shirt he was wearing yesterday, only now it looked like it had been thrown around a dressing room by a team of rugby players.

'You look awful,' were my first words. They were allowed because I was his wife and it was true.

'Thanks, I feel it too,' he murmured, not looking me in the eye.

'I'm serious, you look shit.' I bit my lip; stress wasn't good for the baby. He was spoiling my special news.

'It's been a long night, babe, don't make me feel any worse. Please,' he said, firmly and slightly too loud, because a woman nearby glanced over at us.

Self-consciously I rubbed my wedding band. 'Did you get any sleep at all?' I probed.

'A little, in one of the pods,' he replied defensively. 'I feel like I'm coming down with something too.'

'And you had a few beers?' I continued. I knew the smell of last night's alcohol and he reeked of it. It reminded me of our early dating days, when he'd sometimes rolled into bed at my flat at 3 a.m. stinking of beer, but desperate to see me, blabbering soppily. A heightened sense of smell was another pregnancy symptom I'd read about.

'A couple – we popped out at God knows what time to try to unwind for a bit before going back,' he admitted. I wondered who the 'we' was, knowing that late-night shifts were often a solitary job. But I didn't interrogate him further; he was clearly shattered.

I pressed my fingertips into my belly. Somehow I had expected him to know instinctively why I was here, meeting him for lunch like this, out of the blue. I'd only ever done it once before, and that was on his birthday.

'Shall we get a sandwich or did you come here just to tell me I look like shit?' he asked, heading towards the revolving door. He hadn't even kissed me or reached for my hand. It wasn't like Jason. I wondered if this was a bad idea after all. Maybe I should have just waited for him to come home in his own time. He seemed awkward about me being here.

We walked in silence into the warm day outside. From nowhere I felt tears fighting their way up to the corners of my eyes. But I wouldn't let them break free, not here, amongst the pencil skirts and wafts of Elnett.

I forced a smile. 'Where shall we go then? I'm starving.'

Jason suggested Pret so we got takeaways and, as it was such a nice day, headed to Finsbury Circus Garden. The pregnancy test was burning a hole in my bag. I wanted to steal a look at it, to check it still had a positive reading. That I hadn't imagined it.

'So, I didn't come here to tell you off,' I said, taking a deep breath and feeling a little stronger for it as we sat down on the grass together. 'I came because I have some news. Some good news.'

I delved into my bag and encased the little stick in my palm. I moved fractionally closer to him, so as not to show it off to the entire garden, which was busy with office workers eating their own Pret sandwiches.

I revealed the tip of the stick and unclasped my fingers from around its body, so the two blue lines in the 'Pregnant' box were clear to see.

I watched his face for a reaction. He was staring at the stick, unmoving.

'I'm pregnant,' I whispered, in case he needed it spelling out. He can't have thought I'd come here to show him a negative result.

His eyes were wide with shock, yet he still said nothing. I looked up at him, my eyes just as big. 'You're going to be a daddy, Jason!'

'Wow. Oh wow, Aisha,' he said at last, sitting upright, inhaling deeply and blowing the air out loudly. He took the stick from my hand and held it, not caring who might see. 'Oh wow.' He was almost laughing. 'This is for real, right?'

'Yes, baby – of course it is!' I said, my eyes darting between the stick and Jason. 'I really wanted to do the test with you this morning, but you weren't home and I couldn't wait any longer. I'm sorry.'

I paused. Willing him to say something – anything – to suggest he was happy.

Another couple of seconds passed.

'Isn't it *brilliant*?'

'It's amazing!' he smiled at last. 'It's fantastic!' and almost immediately it was Jason who was dabbing tears from his eyes.

'We're going to be parents,' I beamed, finally able to let a feeling of pure joy wash over me. 'We're going to have a little baby.'

'It's – it's mind-blowing,' he said, and put a hand on my stomach. 'To think our child is growing in there.' And with those words, tears welled up in my eyes too. No amount of blinking could make them stay put.

'I promise I'll be a good dad,' he whispered, tears rolling down his cheeks. 'I swear, I'll try my best.'

I pulled him into a big hug and he buried his face into my neck, breathing me in as he cried.

'I know,' I murmured. 'You'll be the best daddy ever.'

Five minutes later, I was still trying to console Jason, who was properly sobbing, on the grass, in the middle of Finsbury Circus. Was this normal? Surely this scenario should really be the other way around given I was the one with the raging hormones?

'I don't know if I'm worthy of this,' he said, before adding, 'but I'm so pleased you got your wish.'

He was right, I *had* got my wish – but wasn't it his wish too?

In that moment, being pregnant was all that mattered. However, looking back, I couldn't help but wonder exactly what he meant by not feeling 'worthy'.

CHAPTER NINE

Lucy

Wednesday 5ᵗʰ May

The third meeting of The Baby Group was at Aisha's house that evening and, as she only lived around the corner from me, it meant I didn't have to carry my heavier-than-it-looked best ceramic dish very far. I had made an organic spinach salad with shaved carrot, toasted pine nuts and mango pieces, topped with a lime dressing – not my best effort compared to the first salad, but still impressive, considering I'd pulled it together after a full Wednesday at work. I needed to start taking things slower. After having a few Braxton Hicks contractions in the night I was fearful the baby was going to arrive ahead of the date of my planned caesarean on 24ᵗʰ May. I still had a week and a half left at work as I was keen to maximize my maternity leave, so this little baby needed to stay put. I turned down Oscar's offer to carry the salad dish for me, but was heeding his advice to give up going anywhere on the Tube. From now on, he insisted I took an Uber to and from the office, because the last thing I wanted was for my waters to break somewhere between Clapham Common and Leicester Square. So this Baby Group was already proving its worth, allowing me to retain the semblance of a social life, right on my doorstep.

'You're basically paying for new mates,' Oscar had joked when I first told him about joining the group.

'No, I'm learning how to have a baby!' I had protested.

Despite owning a sizeable number of pregnancy and childbirth books, most of them had remained unopened. And I *had* joined the group to grow a network here on my doorstep. I hadn't found it particularly easy to build strong connections with the women at work and many of my old friends, including Katie, had moved out of London in recent years. I was still making up my mind about some of the others in the group, but Aisha had surprised me and was so far the lead contender for a new buddy.

It was a beautiful evening that felt properly warm, and as I strolled to her house in my flats and a long, clingy black dress – the only dress that still fitted me – I marvelled at how pretty this part of South London was. Most of the homes on the streets around here were well looked after, with pruned roses and the odd palm tree in the front gardens, white slatted blinds at windows and shiny gloss finishes and brass trimmings on front doors. You had to earn a substantial amount to afford one of them.

Oscar and I had only moved to the area two months ago. But our fling had begun two years ago. At first it had been exhilarating. I had never quite been sure if there were other women too and, initially, I hadn't cared. It had all been part of the fun – stolen evenings in hotels during 'business trips' or booty calls after nights out. The sex had been intoxicating. But as time had gone on, my heart had started to yearn for his full attention, just as much as my body longed for his touch. I was falling in love with Oscar. He crept into my thoughts more often, although I questioned whether he was as into me as I was into him.

Then, one evening in January last year, Oscar had called to ask if he could come and stay with me that night. When he came over, there had been something different in his voice. He'd seemed willing to discuss the 'us' that had so far been off limits. 'I'm ready to focus on the future now,' he had said, before kissing me passionately all the way to the bedroom. The thought that he might want to be with me officially had been electrifying.

We had decided he would still live half the week in his Marylebone bolt hole, and the rest of the week he would spend at my Brixton flat. But my dreams of him and I going the distance, which, in my mind, involved having a family together, had soon become unfounded when he continued to make it crystal clear that he had already done the marriage and babies thing, and he didn't want to do it again. Not getting married I could live with, but I had been devastated he didn't want children with me.

So that was when I had had to take matters into my own hands. I had to think about *my* body; *my* biological clock. I was fed up of people making assumptions about me. I had to make a decision.

My getting pregnant changed everything. And now here we were – happy – I was so glad he had finally embraced it.

The only thing left to sort out had been where to live – we couldn't keep the Marylebone/Brixton arrangement with a baby.

'Clapham seems nice,' I had suggested, imagining long walks on the common with my baby. Having a newborn in summer had to be the best timing, and I had envisaged a sun-drenched maternity leave of sitting outside pubs sipping a cheeky glass of prosecco over lunch with my new yummy mummy pals, while our babies dozed soundly in their prams next to us.

It wasn't hard to find the perfect house to rent just south of Clapham Common near the chi-chi and sought-after Abbeville Road, with its handy array of independent delis and boutiques, including an overpriced butchers, a *fromagerie*, a Gail's bakery and a gastro pub that buzzed with locals at every time of day or evening. For me it had to be that area – and through a turn of fate, an acquaintance of Oscar's ran an estate agents in that patch, and found us the perfect place which we snapped up before it even went on the market. It all fell into place so easily. It was a good idea, wasn't it?

CHAPTER TEN

Aisha

'It's ridiculous!' Jason had shouted when I mentioned the new washing machine arriving this morning had been paid for by Dad. 'I should be supporting us fully now. I don't want your dad's money.'

He had a real issue with it, although I was sure that Dad was only doing it to appease his guilt at barely ever seeing me. Dad had just happened to call last week as I was battling with the machine's temperamental dial. Barely a few hours later, his PA had swiftly emailed me details of the new one she had arranged to have installed for us today. To me, it was simply a kind gesture from a dad with more money than time. But Jason saw it differently.

There was some history with me and money. I had been brought up by parents who were never short of cash. My father, a self-made, high-flying businessman – thanks to a successful property-investment company in Leamington – had kept my mum and me in well-made clothes and luxury holidays from as early as I could remember. We had a gîte in France to escape to over the summer, and there were weekends skiing in Gstaad in the winter. But I couldn't remember a single time my father had been home early enough to read me a bedtime story. I was pretty much brought up by a single mum, until she passed away.

When I had not long been out of university, my dad had bought me this flat in Clapham. At first I had lived in it with a house-mate, then with a former boyfriend. Then over the years it had been rented out several times, until Jason and I had moved in when we returned from Hong Kong. It had seemed the most practical thing to do; the tenant happened to be moving out and we knew how lucky we were to be mortgage-free in London. But the fact I owned the flat had always seemed to bother Jason. Although Jason was easily the major earner in our relationship, he had struggled with not being the wealthiest. As such, although he had never explicitly said it, he had always given me the impression that babies should wait until he'd earned enough money to support us both 'properly'. Whatever 'properly' meant.

I genuinely wasn't bothered about whether Jason was wealthy or not – I'd fallen in love with the man who had left adorable sticky notes for me on the fridge and pinned me against the wall of our Hong Kong apartment as he kissed me so passionately I never wanted him to stop. I didn't care how much cash was in his wallet. But since I had fallen pregnant, Jason had thrown himself into work even more heavily, putting in for overtime whenever it was available, prioritizing his earning potential ahead of spending time with me. I'd spent a lot of today thinking about this, while doing what felt like an Everest-sized mountain of washing using the new machine – at least I wasn't going to be forced to find a launderette – and then I had spent most of the afternoon reorganizing my knicker drawer and tinkering with some illustrations.

That meant that despite having spent the entire day at home, I left it to the last minute to get things ready for the breastfeeding class and then had a wardrobe crisis about what to wear ten minutes before they were all due to arrive. This late stage of pregnancy had made me more indecisive and anxious than usual. To say I was regretting offering to host the meeting was an understatement.

At the end of the first meeting, when Lucy had put herself forward to be the group admin by connecting us all on WhatsApp and email, and Susie and Lin had offered to make their already legendary brownies again, I had felt as though I should volunteer something too and before I knew it, my hand had been in the air and I was agreeing to host this class. Still, it was a breastfeeding session, with no men allowed, so at least it was a smaller group to accommodate, and it would be over in two hours.

'What was I thinking?' I complained to Jason when he got home from work. 'It's the last thing I feel like today.'

'I wish they weren't coming too,' he offered, looking pensive. 'I shouldn't have gone to work on an argument this morning.'

'It's okay,' I replied softly. This was the closest I'd seen him come to an apology about a comment made over money. But right now I had a more pressing situation on my hands.

I was stood in front of the mirror in our bedroom watching the buttons strain on a shirt I had bought in Zara only two weeks ago. How gravely I had underestimated my size. I really wasn't comfortable with this bigness. I peeled off my pregnancy jeans (they were beginning to chafe anyway) and pulled on a figure-hugging dark-green cotton dress – a hand-me-down from Tara, who had been infinitely better dressed during pregnancy than me.

'This, with a scarf?' I turned to Jason, holding up a silk scarf with a leopard print on it.

'Yeah, nice.' He was now sat on our bed, hunched over his laptop.

'No, it's not,' I replied irritably, before wriggling out of the dress and throwing it and the scarf down on top of the shirt. 'It's too garish. Plus Tara was half the size I am now, the dress is too tight.'

'Why don't you just wear something comfortable?' Jason offered.

'*Comfortable*,' I repeated, with real bitterness. 'Have I become a woman who should only wear *comfortable* clothes? It's not fair Jason – you can still wear a slim-fitting grey T-shirt and jeans and look fit. And *comfortable* too. Nothing has changed for you.'

'That's not what I meant,' he said.

'Imagine having a space hopper permanently strapped to your middle while fighting chronic fatigue, on top of hot and cold flushes. With a side order of swollen ankles and bad skin!' I snapped.

'I know babe, I can see it's not easy. I'm sorry.' He turned away, but he sounded cynical to me.

'It's not just about clothes,' I said. 'I don't think you have any idea how my life has been turned upside down.' Tears appeared at my eyes. 'I miss Mum so much at the moment.'

He touched my shoulder, in an effort to try and soothe me. 'I can only try to imagine,' he said tenderly. 'I'm sorry about this morning. I'm here for you Aisha, I promise.'

I took a deep breath and forced myself to be calm; there wasn't time to be upset.

'But, for the record, you *always* look good, whatever you wear. And even if you decide to wear pyjamas, I don't think anyone will care.'

'But *I* care,' I whispered; his compliment didn't sound very convincing. 'Anyway, you need to go out,' I ordered. I would be glad to see the back of him.

'Text me when the coast is clear!' he called, as he disappeared out of the flat.

Once again, everyone had been instructed to bring a plate of something to share, so I didn't really need to offer anything other than drinks, but I decided to make some bruschetta.

Half an hour later, while Lin and Helen chatted in the living room, I tended to the cloud of smoke and smell of burning toast that I had left under the grill for too long.

I heard the doorbell and panicked, but luckily Lin popped her head round the door and said, 'I'll get it!'

'Come in Lucy, Aisha's upstairs, handling a little emergency in the kitchen,' I heard her saying, making me cringe. 'Luckily we've put out the fire.'

'I've put the kettle on,' added Susie from the top of the stairs. 'We still have drinks! Are you tea, coffee or herbal?'

'Oh, *always* coffee for me,' Lucy said.

'What about you, Aisha, can I get you something to rehydrate you following the bruschetta drama?' Susie asked, turning towards me. I felt my eyes prickle as another joke was made at my expense, though I knew it was because I was already feeling overly sensitive this evening.

'I think I need a coffee too,' I replied to Susie, trying to sound more cheery than I felt.

Probably unlike most people here, I hadn't managed to kick the single-shot lattes completely this pregnancy. I usually saved them for a weekend treat when Jason would also indulge me in my craving for almond croissants. But this evening I decided to make an exception.

'Decaf, of course!' Lucy added to her order.

'Me too,' Lin smiled. 'I may not be the one expecting, but caffeine – yuck!' She pulled a disgusted face.

'Decaf for you too?' asked Susie. It felt as though they were all looking in my direction.

I paused for a moment.

'I'll have a weak, normal one,' I replied, feeling rebellious.

To my relief no one actually fainted.

Lucy came into the kitchen and set a dish down on the side.

'Oh wow – look at that work of art!' Lin exclaimed, peering over the salad. 'I want to put my face in it, it looks so good.'

'I happened to have ingredients in the fridge to use up,' Lucy smiled proudly. 'I just threw it together really. Do you need a hand, Aisha? Let's face it, most people have probably burnt bruschetta at least once in their life.'

I was struggling pathetically with the skylight, trying to let out some of the smoke from the smouldering bread. I felt a twinge of jealousy listening to the admiring comments about her salad from the others. I had failed all over again. 'No, it's okay, it's all fine. Please, go through to the lounge, I won't be a minute,' I said, flustered.

I found I was actually grateful for Susie and Lin's bossiness because at least they had made sure everyone had a hot drink in their hand.

When I eventually rejoined the group in the living room, everyone had arrived, including Camilla, our breastfeeding instructor. She had dyed red hair and elfin features. She stood up from the leather pouffe on which she was sat, and reached out to shake my hand. 'Hello Aisha! Do call me Mila. Ready to start?' I noticed a plastic doll, a knitted breast, a plastic contraption that looked like a foghorn and a lever-arch file full of printed sheets next to her. Who knew breastfeeding was so complicated?

'Sorry about the bruschetta,' I bit my lip. 'But luckily we've got Lucy's amazing salad, some spring rolls, a pack of chocolate fingers, Susie and Lin's legendary brownies and an emergency tub of Pringles. A slightly random menu, but we won't starve, will we?' They all made reassuring noises about how they preferred salad, spring rolls, chocolate fingers and Pringles to bruschetta anyway, and then the room fell into silence.

Initially I felt a little self-conscious about our flat; with all the photos on display, it felt very exposing this early into our friendships. A couple of times I caught people looking at the photos. Sometimes it was strikingly obvious that we had only been friends for a few weeks and barely knew anything about each other's lives before being pregnant. But I supposed that the current collection of framed milestones in mine and Jason's life would soon be replaced by baby images, so I might as well show off my pre-baby life while I could.

'Your wedding will seem *so* insignificant once you've given birth,' Tara had told me, only half-joking, on the phone the other evening. 'You thought marriage was a commitment? Honey, you will barely remember that day. Having a baby together supersedes *everything*. Having a baby is tough. It's lucky you're *married* to Jason because it makes it harder for either of you to leave. Planning a wedding is merely training for how organized you need to be when getting out of the house with a newborn. And don't even get me started on leaving the house when you're weaning. You don't know what's about to hit you. Mark. My. Words.'

In my living room, Helen had opted to sit on the floor with her legs crossed in a pretzel position. Presumably to demonstrate her suppleness – what your body was capable of if you got knocked up at 20, or whatever young age she was.

At 36, I was classified as a 'geriatric' mother. I hated this fact. It had influenced a midwife to ask me whether I was planning to opt for a caesarean birth, because she assumed I might be fearful of complications during a natural birth, due to my age. I certainly didn't feel geriatric. But when it came to breastfeeding, I was definitely keen to give it a go, so I needed to pay attention.

Lin sat next to Susie who was in the middle of the sofa, with Lucy at the other end and I took the armchair. I was relieved that 'Call me Mila' was running the class, so thankfully we didn't have Maggie and her vagina obsession to contend with again this evening. She seemed a much more reassuring teacher.

Mila talked us through the drill like a breastfeeding sergeant to our rookie battalion: 'Tummy to mummy, nipple to nose, angle the dangle and – latch!' The baby started kicking a lot during this part, and if I wasn't mistaken, my nipples started to tingle as she repeated it over and over again, like a children's nursery rhyme. I looked around the room, wondering whether anyone else was experiencing the same sensation, but they were all fastidiously making notes, writing down the song's words. I wondered if Mila was frustrated at finding herself a breastfeeding tutor rather than a professional singer, as she had quite a good voice. She told us she had two children of her own and was full of anecdotes about how 'breast is best'. Despite my initial fears, and a limited discussion around painful cracked nipples and mastitis, keeping a newborn alive via the boob sounded relatively straightforward. I had attended enough midwife appointments by now to know that breastfeeding might not come easily to us all, but that I was to try at all costs, or else. Or else what? The breastfeeding bobbies might come and arrest me?

Mila then talked us through the 'rugby hold', using the old doll that looked as though it had indeed been chucked around a rugby pitch. When Lin was handed the doll to hold in the correct 'rugby hold' fashion, she decided instead to cheekily throw it in my direction. I reacted swiftly, catching the doll with a skill to make any professional scrum half proud. Mila tutted loudly, disapproving of Lin's joke, and Susie put a hand to her head in despair and mild embarrassment.

'I'm so sorry, Mila. Lin sometimes gets over-excited about the wonders of the human body and all the different options available to us,' she said, on behalf of her partner.

'So this is when I tackle her to the ground, is it Susie?' I added, making everyone – including Mila – chuckle. It was swiftly becoming apparent that Lin was the non-conformist amongst us.

Later on, Mila enlightened us that the 'foghorn' was actually a breast pump contraption and we should all get one. Thankfully no displays of actual nudity were necessary during the class, which did something to ease my anxiety. That was what the fairly ancient-looking knitted boob was for. I couldn't help but notice the crocheted nipple was particularly well-crafted. I pondered for a moment, about whether there was a circle of grannies, perhaps living in a nursing home in a remote Scottish village, who spent their days knitting boobs for breastfeeding classes like ours. Someone had obviously lovingly made this one. The thought tickled me, and I noticed that I was smiling. The class had lifted my spirits after the argument with Jason, and despite the disastrous start to the evening with bruschetta-gate, I now wasn't in any hurry for it to end. I was really enjoying myself. Hosting wasn't as bad as I first thought and they were certainly an entertaining and supportive group of people.

When she had brought the class to a close, with a sage reminder to stock up on savoy cabbage, Mila hurriedly packed up her bits. 'Got to get back for my sitter,' she announced, clapping the lever-arch file shut and shoving in a few rogue bits of paper. 'Well done all of you. Feel free to email me at any time, should you have any questions.' She dropped a small pile of business cards onto the coffee table, before leaning towards me a fraction. 'And special thanks to our hostess, you did great this evening.'

Lin put her hands together and led everyone into a small applause. 'To boobs and milk production!' she said, cherishing the role of class joker.

Mila picked up her empty mug from the coffee table and glanced in my direction. 'I'll leave this in the kitchen, shall I?'

'You just head off,' I told her, 'there's hardly anything to put away.'

Soon after her, Lin and Susie left too, then Helen. When it was just Lucy and me left in the flat, she offered to stay and help me clear up. We gathered up the Pringle crumbs and left-over chocolate fingers in silence for a few moments, until something seemed to catch her attention on one of our book shelves.

She was staring fixedly at a photograph – a framed one of Jason posing with the Bristol University football team.

I hadn't looked at it in any great detail for some time myself, and now I realized its silver frame looked in dire need of a polish, almost turning black at the corners. I felt embarrassed about that.

When she sensed I was looking at her, Lucy quickly averted her eyes. 'Your photo frames,' she remarked. She seemed startled I'd noticed her looking. 'They're so pretty. I love all the different styles.'

I smiled awkwardly. 'Thanks. Although I'm sure they'll all be full of baby photos before long.'

'I expect so – mine too. You make a gorgeous couple,' she added, studying our wedding photo, which stood pride of place in the centre of the shelf above the football one.

'Are *you* married?' I asked, keen to move the attention off myself.

For a moment she seemed surprised by such a forthright question.

'No,' she said. 'Not out of choice, but Oscar was married before. He's in no hurry to…' Her voice trailed off.

'Sorry, I didn't mean to pry,' I added. With my right hand I picked up two mugs from the table by their handles and they clanked together loudly. 'Photos don't ever tell the whole story though, do they?' I muttered, trying to make her feel better. 'Deep down I'm terrified about how Jason is going to cope with a baby.' I stopped myself, fearing this was too deep for what had been such a fun evening.

She looked concerned. 'I'm sorry – are you going through a rough patch?'

'A bit – I mean, no, not really. It's nothing.'

'Because, it's okay if you are— Do you want to talk?'

'We're fine, I meant how *we* will cope. You know, on a practical level. I had no idea what "weaning" actually meant before tonight – I thought it was something to do with mopping up wee!' I cut her off, keen to lighten the conversation.

Lucy giggled, and I felt pleased to have won her around again. 'Don't,' she said, 'I once googled "weaning" only to wish I hadn't. Who knew that grapes were a potential death trap? And that there can be terrifying allergic reactions to strawberries?'

'Not to mention that, according to Mila, it can take just a few seconds for your baby to choke to death on a raisin,' I added. 'Let's hope that "how to perform the Heimlich manoeuvre" is on the agenda for the next meeting, shall we?' We both chuckled.

'Knowing Maggie, she'll have us paired up and practising it in no time,' Lucy laughed.

'I wouldn't put it past her,' I said. 'But perhaps we should all add "do a Baby First-Aid Course", to our already extensive to-do lists. If I'd have known it was all this complicated, I might have put it off for a bit longer!'

Lucy smiled, as that last flippant comment hung in the air between us for a moment. The length of time taken to get pregnant could be a contentious issue, I knew that, and I sensed I had hit a raw nerve when Lucy didn't offer any response.

We both busied ourselves by taking out the last bits to the kitchen. When I had stacked the dishwasher, I glanced at my phone and noticed Jason had texted:

'Looks like the time has come to allow the other half back in,' I said.

'Thanks for this evening,' Lucy smiled, and I watched with awe as she gracefully lifted her Gucci bag over her head and across her body. It fell neatly to one side of her bump. She was effortlessly stylish. 'Gorgeous home, I love all your personal touches,' she added. I felt myself stiffen. If the designer handbag and posh salads were anything to go by, Lucy was probably just being kind – her home was likely to be something straight out of *Elle Decoration*.

I smiled politely, 'Thank you – and thanks for helping me clear up. See you at the next one.'

CHAPTER ELEVEN

Lucy

As I walked home after the class, I felt edgy. I played over the moment Aisha had caught me looking at her photos. Sometimes I felt like a pressure cooker, the internal tension rising and rising inside me. But thankfully I didn't blow it. Not yet. I was holding things together okay and no one seemed to think I was weird – if they did, they didn't show it. The knitted boobs were much weirder, let's face it. To take my mind off things, I FaceTimed Oscar, who was in New York on business. I told him about the rugby ball incident and he found it amusing. I also mentioned how Aisha had burnt the bruschetta.

'Well, you can't expect everyone to be as culinarily endowed as you, my sweetheart,' he teased.

'Culinarily endowed, is that even a phrase?' I asked. 'Typical of you to turn everything back to sex.'

'Excuse me, you're the one with the dirty mind!' he retorted. 'Thinking about how well endowed I am, are you?'

'Oscar!'

'Well, you can tell me in person tomorrow. I'll be home off the red eye mid-morning. Why don't you go in late?'

'But I've got a meeting—'

'I'm the boss, so it's fine,' he cut me off. 'I can't wait to see you.'

I didn't realize until I had reached our house that I'd left the empty salad dish at Aisha's. I was too tired to go back, so decided it would be the ideal excuse to ask her out for a coffee.

Thursday 6ᵗʰ May

The following evening, sat on the sofa, Oscar flopped his arm around my belly and nestled into my body. He cocked his head to one side and looked at me; I mean *really* looked at me. 'I missed you darling,' he cooed.

'I missed you too, honey.' I planted a kiss onto his lips and took his hand in mine. I silently marvelled at how we had become a pregnant couple who referred to each other as 'darling' and 'honey'. It should have made my heart sing, but instead it made me feel uneasy.

My desperation to be a mother had been so strong, for so long. But now I was here, on the brink of my dream finally coming true, it wasn't quite the perfect situation I had hoped for. There was one big problem.

I went upstairs to look at the nursery. I had been a woman on a mission all week, working full days in the office before racing home to nest like a mother hen. The five vests from

Petit Bateau and ten sleepsuits from the Little White Company were folded neatly in a drawer of the dresser I'd ordered from John Lewis, with a few outfits for 'best' hanging in the small matching wardrobe. A 'family' of soft, brown, cuddly bunnies sat in height order down one side of the cot. It was all extremely satisfying. If this were the backdrop for a celebrity's baby photoshoot in a glossy magazine, the reader would think it all absolutely idyllic. But how misleading first impressions can be.

I flicked on the light switch, then stopped and caught a glimpse of myself in the large mirror I had somehow managed to successfully hang over the cot earlier today, using a row of ten tacks bashed into the wall. Miraculously, it was straight. I hadn't noticed until now that I had flour down my black dress from cooking earlier. My hair had nearly all fallen out of its ponytail.

I stroked my large bump. I had been lucky with the pregnancy, suffering no morning sickness. The lack of alcohol had done wonders for my complexion and I loved my new curves. I found myself dressing to accentuate them, wearing dresses far tighter than I would have dared before. Before, I'd always considered my figure 'boyish' rather than voluptuous, and I'd never had much of a waist to speak of, but now that I had curves in all the right places, I wanted to make the most of them; I really wouldn't have minded staying this shape forever. But it wasn't just about the curves, it was far deeper than that; it was *everything* – I just felt so grateful to be having a baby at last.

Once I had got over the initial shock of finally falling

pregnant, the planning had kicked in and I had embraced every moment of it. I was barely two months gone when I began obsessively checking out cots from Mamas and Papas and covertly shopping on the Petit Bateau website when I should have been preparing pitches at work. As the weeks passed, I relished any opportunity to discuss my growing foetus around the coffee machine when someone politely enquired how I was feeling at work. Sometimes I would catch myself sounding like the baby bore I once swore I would never become. Could this be the same Lucy Raven – the ambitious PR professional on a trajectory to Managing Director? I barely recognized myself some days, having never guessed I'd be in this situation.

I stared at my reflection.

Can you really do this? I asked myself internally.

I didn't have the answer, but I knew that I was getting closer to finding it.

CHAPTER TWELVE

Aisha

The day after the breastfeeding class, my phone buzzed with a message:

WhatsApp:
Lucy Raven has added you to: 'The Baby Group'.

The symbol was a baby bottle full of milk. There were a few more notifications as numbers were added, before another message:

Lucy: Hey everyone, finally got round to connecting us all on here. Looking forward to seeing you for the next class on Saturday. I don't seem to have Carol's number, can you give it to me please, Will, so I can add her to the group? And let me know if I should add Jason and Ian? Lx

Helen: Thanks Lucy! Hope everyone (and bumps!!) are

doing well. No need to add Ian (he's a grump on WhatsApp!).
Helen xx

Susie: Great to be connected, see you all on Sat. S&L x

Me: Thanks Lucy, don't worry about adding Jason either.
See you all soon. Ax

Will: No need to add Carol. I'll just pass on any relevant
info. Thanks Lucy. Will x

Then I received a private WhatsApp message from Lucy:

Lucy: I'm off work tomorrow, so thought I could pick up the
dish I left at yours in the morning, if that's ok? We could
also go for a coffee, if you're free?

It didn't take much to distract me from work at the moment
and I had enjoyed chatting with Lucy yesterday, so I replied
quickly:

Me: Love to! Does 9ish at Gail's work?

Lucy: Perfect. See you then. Lx

Me: Great, don't worry about picking up the dish. I'll bring
it. Ax

'Would you like tea or coffee?' Lucy asked. She was already in the queue when I arrived at Gail's at ten past nine.

'Tea would be great, thanks. Builder's,' I replied. 'I'll get us a table.'

'Drinks will be here shortly,' Lucy said when she joined me.

'Thanks. I haven't managed to kick the caffeine completely – unlike some.'

'Ha! Lin and Susie are such earth mothers,' she smiled. 'Good for them, but that weird burial plan for the placenta. Really?'

I smiled back. 'I'd forgotten about that. Ooh but what about Will and Carol? I wonder how many babies she's carried for other people? It's fascinating.'

'I bet she's making a fortune,' Lucy said. 'I mean, it can't be something you'd do unless the reward was huge. But I wonder if she ever finds it hard to give the baby up? It can't be the easiest thing to do.'

'I know. I just couldn't imagine it. And especially with a baby daddy as handsome as Will. I mean, who wouldn't find that hard?' We both giggled in unison and looked up at each other, registering the connection.

I got my purse out of my bag to offer Lucy some money for the drink.

'No way – it's on me. You did more than enough hosting the other night.'

'Thanks so much, I'll get them next time then,' I replied. 'So, are you feeling ready for the baby?'

'As ready as you can ever be, I guess. I mean, there's always more to do, but I've almost got the nursery sorted,' she replied.

I was beginning to realize my initial assumption of Lucy as the power-dressed, organized CEO-in-waiting, wasn't quite on the mark. She was actually a lot softer than that.

'What about you – is the cot up?' Lucy asked me.

'We don't have one yet – we're going to choose it this weekend. John Lewis probably. My dad's getting it for us.'

'Aw, that's nice, you're close to your parents then?'

I paused. A tight feeling took a hold of my chest. 'My mum passed away fifteen years ago.'

'I'm sorry,' Lucy said, looking into her coffee cup.

'It's okay. Dad's still around, but he lives in Dubai with his girlfriend. He wanted to move closer to his parents in India. I don't see any of them very often. He likes to send me lavish gifts to make up for that fact.'

'That must have been a tough time, losing your mum in your twenties,' Lucy said.

'It was,' I sighed. 'When I was 21, life changed forever. All Dad's money couldn't prevent Mum from being diagnosed with Stage Four breast cancer at the age of 50. I would have done anything to keep her in our lives for longer.'

'I'm sure she'd be so proud of you,' Lucy smiled kindly. 'A husband, baby on the way, successful career...'

'Mum would have loved Jason – she probably would have seen the same spark and drive in him as my father had when she met him. But if Dad had been less concerned with earning money when I was a child, I often wonder whether we'd have had a closer relationship now. I've only seen him once in the last two years, and whenever I do see him it's always stilted and formal. He keeps promising a father-daughter trip to India to meet long-lost relatives, but the invite never actually comes. Anyway – family! Enough about mine, what about you?'

Lucy exhaled sharply. 'Families, indeed. We're not close either. I mean, my parents are around, and in my life, but we're different. So different. You know?'

'I can relate to that. Funny how it can all go wrong. Up until my early twenties, there wasn't a time I ever worried that my parents wouldn't be around. I always got everything on my Christmas list and had birthday parties that were the talk of the playground for months afterwards. But I never imagined I'd lose my mum so quickly. It broke me and Dad.' I felt a heavy sadness descend again.

'I'm really sorry,' she said, and she leant across the table and placed a hand on my forearm. 'That must have been so hard. And especially now – being pregnant. It can bring so many feelings to the surface.'

I took a deep breath and looked into her eyes. 'You can say that again.'

Lucy moved her hand and smiled graciously as a waiter interrupted this conversation by depositing our drinks, plus two almond croissants on the table. 'I've had a serious craving for these recently,' she said.

'Snap!' I exclaimed, sounding a little more enthusiastic than was necessary, I was so glad of the distraction. 'Maybe it's a pregnancy thing. This is sweet of you, thanks. Anyway – how are you feeling about getting close to your due date?'

She stroked her bump. 'Yes, I'm really excited about meeting this little man. I'm sure he's dropped in the last few days. Do you feel like that?'

'I wish.' I shifted on the chair. 'My bump still feels so high, I can feel it pressing against my ribcage a lot of the time. I can't wait for it to drop. Sleeping is becoming really uncomfortable. Jason keeps complaining I wriggle too much. And you should see the number of pillows in our bed.'

'Your bump is perfect,' she said, her eyes fastened on me. 'I bet Jason thinks you look amazing – because you do. You're glowing.' Embarrassed by receiving such a big compliment, I looked away. 'I just hope my other half, Oscar, is as ready as he says he is, when the baby actually arrives. You know, is he prepared for the sleepless nights and changes to our lifestyle?' She stopped and gazed out of the window.

'I'm not sure any of us have got our heads around it yet,' I tried to reassure her.

'Oscar already has two children, you see, from a previous relationship. It's a lot to ask of him, to do it again. I just hope we'll cope okay.'

'I know what you mean,' I admitted. 'Jason's been working late so much recently. I guess he's only trying to clock up the overtime payments, but I do worry sometimes too. He didn't react brilliantly when I got pregnant.' I stopped myself. Perhaps this was also too heavy for our first coffee date. 'Have you lived in Clapham for long?' I asked quickly, keen to change the subject.

'Not long, actually,' she revealed. 'The house is still quite sparse. I'm kind of loving being free of clutter, but it doesn't feel like home yet either. The walls need more pictures, we need a rug – I've got my eye on one from Graham and Green. I've been nesting like mad – with Oscar away so much for work there's been plenty of time for online shopping.'

'Where were you living before?' I asked.

'Only down the road in Brixton. We needed more space—'

'So you bought a house,' I finished her sentence.

'We're renting actually,' she continued, making me feel slightly better about our modest flat around the corner. She paused. 'It's a trial, I guess.'

'A try before you buy?' I asked, wondering if they were in the market for a plush townhouse in the neighbourhood.

'That too, but Oscar's already got a property in central London. I meant it's a trial for him and me – it's a fairly new relationship,' she revealed, catching my gaze once more. 'We met at work. He's divorced, you see. Well, he is now.'

'Oh, right.' I could see she was weighing up whether or not to tell me something. I kept quiet, hoping she would elaborate.

She took a breath and nibbled a piece of croissant before continuing: 'Oscar's actually my boss, and he was married when we first started seeing each other. I've worked at Bright PR as an account manager for two years and then one of my accounts – a popular tissue brand of all things – really took off and I got promoted. I managed to get the *Daily Mail* to vote them "Number One Snot Saviour" when the flu virus was big news and boxes flew off the shelves. I was fast-tracked to Director of Consumer PR.'

I chuckled. 'Yay you!'

'That's when Oscar and I became close. We were on a work trip to New York, to visit a potential new client – a hotel group, handily – and he kissed me in the lift after a boozy dinner. It was the best kiss I'd had in a long time. And that's when it all started really – the snooping around, the secret snogs in hotel rooms, the hundreds of naughty WhatsApp messages during important meetings, sometimes involving what he wanted to do with me over the boardroom table.' Her cheeks flushed and there was a wistful look in her eye as she no doubt enjoyed a hot flashback.

'It must have been exciting,' I encouraged her, my eyes shining. This had turned into a juicy conversation.

'It was hard not to be excited: he was a successful, wealthy guy – not my usual type, being really tall with barely any hair, but he was good-looking and charismatic – and the sex was amazing!'

'Was he married then?' I asked quietly, aware that we could be overheard.

'His divorce was almost finalized, and I had been single for the best part of two decades,' she continued. 'I hadn't been in love since my first relationship at university. I mean I dated men, on and off, but always found a reason to end it. Most of my friends were busily getting married and having babies; but for me it wasn't so straightforward. I knew a love so perfect while at uni, I wanted to find that again. I didn't want to settle for second best when it came to starting a family.'

I nodded, relating to what she was saying.

'Oscar and I had an instant chemistry and I thought that

I'd finally found a proper "grown up" relationship. But Oscar already had two kids and was adamant he didn't want any more. And then I found out I had a really low egg count.'

'Oh no, I'm sorry,' I offered. 'But it clearly worked out in the end.'

'I decided to freeze the few eggs I had, and I started looking into the IVF route. I didn't tell Oscar about this at first because I didn't want him to suddenly agree to have children just for me. Although it looked, at that moment, like he might never be ready.'

'But he was, in the end?'

'We split up for a bit, but ironically, nine months later when his divorce finalized, we got back together and decided to make a serious go of it. I had IVF and it worked.'

'That's brilliant news. And so lucky. How did you tell everyone at work?'

'Oscar thought the best way would be to gather staff together one Monday morning and tell them the news in a short company meeting, to nip any office gossip in the bud.'

'Had anyone suspected?' I asked, thinking this sounded like the storyline from a Netflix drama.

'Probably! It had to be one of the worst-kept secrets in the company, because no one seemed particularly shocked. It changed my relationship with most of my colleagues, though – I got invited out to lunch less, and I certainly wasn't as popular on company socials as I once was. They probably thought I might tell Oscar who got pissed on their lunch break and who was the worst at bending their expenses! That's why I joined this Baby Group: to make some new friends.'

She paused and looked at me. I saw a new vulnerability in Lucy. She seemed in need of validation. After a few seconds, she carried on: 'But knowing I was having a healthy baby made up for everything. It felt like my greatest wish had been granted. Besides, I'll be off on maternity leave soon and after that? Who knows.'

'Do you think you'll go back to Bright PR?' I asked.

'I'm not sure. Maybe I'll become a stay-at-home mummy, and pursue my dream of writing a cookery book or starting a small business, or perhaps I could become a yoga instructor. I try to practise yoga as often as I can. I feel like the world has finally opened up for me. What about you? Will you keep working?'

'Well, as a freelancer, it's hard to stop completely. You worry that "out of sight is out of mind" and the commissions won't come,' I said, acutely aware that my life story wasn't nearly as compelling as hers. 'But I really love illustrating, so I'll probably continue, if I can fit it around childcare. So, yes.'

We had both finished our croissants. Lucy dabbed at her plate, picking up the last crumbs with her index finger and putting them into her mouth as we moved onto the topic of baby-friendly days out in London, and the things we wouldn't miss about work when on maternity leave.

Then Jason texted. He offered to take an extra-long lunch break to take me shopping – a token gesture, but since the breastfeeding class I had become obsessed with buying a bottle steriliser and a breast pump, so I took him up on it.

'Where are you?' he asked.

'Gail's, with Lucy,' I replied. He suggested I walk home and he would meet me there shortly.

As I left the café, strolling out into the bright, fresh daylight, I felt buoyed by my chat with Lucy. It felt like we had both really opened up and I was happy to be making a genuine new friend in her. I hoped she and I would get to hang out together again. The fact that she had told me about her illicit relationship with her boss stayed with me. It sounded so thrilling and passionate. I wondered whether I would be capable of such a thing, but doubted it. She was certainly full of surprises.

CHAPTER THIRTEEN

Lucy

When Aisha left, I wandered up the road to Sainsbury's to pick up a few bits, including some ingredients to make another dish for tomorrow's meeting. Confiding in Aisha had felt strange, but good, and I was feeling slightly giddy and free. She was so easy to talk to. That foreboding feeling cast a shadow over it all, reminding me that things weren't quite right, I tried to push it away, but it became a little dry spot at the back of my throat. Ever present.

As I hunted down some pine nuts for the salad, I spotted Will by the sushi counter.

'Rubbing it in are you – you can still have sushi, but we can't?' I joked.

'Lucy! Hi. I'm sorry, it's not fair is it?' His face lit up to see me. An equally gorgeous guy appeared beside him. 'Lucy, this is Christian, my husband.'

Christian stretched out his hand. 'Hi. I was saving my big reveal for the group tomorrow, but you've got in first.'

'I'm truly honoured,' I replied. 'I would curtsey, if I was capable of it.'

'Will tells me that Maggie is quite the character,' he said. He was as good-looking as Will, except a blond, white version. Together, they looked like an Abercrombie & Fitch poster.

'She's a strong personality all right. Get her onto vaginas and you'll be fine.'

He ran a hand over his face and gave a puzzled laugh. 'Not exactly my specialist subject.'

'Of course! Sorry.'

'Don't worry, I'll make sure he's fully prepped,' Will said, holding a tray of fresh sushi in his hand. I looked at it enviously.

'I'll let you get on. Enjoy the sushi – lucky things!'

CHAPTER FOURTEEN

Aisha

I was determined to take a leaf out of Lucy's book and get organized for tomorrow's Baby Group meeting. Fortunately I was ahead of schedule with the draft illustrations for the new book I was working on. It was entitled *Santa's Busiest Christmas Ever*. Christmas in May sounds ridiculous, but this was actually a short turnaround in the world of book publishing and my deadline was looming. I had been knee-deep in decisions about shades of red, types of sleigh and how big a pot belly to give my Santa for weeks now. I had gone for round and cuddly, with the snowiest of long, curly beards – verified as spot on during a FaceTime call with Tara's boys. The next challenge was to ensure he didn't look like he was headed for a stint in rehab by Boxing Day. Goodness knows 25th December is busy enough for Mr Claus. The thought of his 'busiest one ever' made me want to have a nervous breakdown on his behalf. That, and a strong G&T. Oh how I missed gin. If there was one thing I craved the most and couldn't have during pregnancy, it was gin.

Before I was pregnant, Dad used to send me cases of wine and gin on almost a monthly basis, but they had been replaced by random deliveries of kitchen appliances and John Lewis vouchers. I had to tell Jason that the masticating juicer that appeared in the kitchen a few weeks ago was second hand. I felt guilty about it, but at the same time couldn't face another discussion with him about why Dad's 'treats' needed to stop.

Stressed-out Santa sorted, I gave myself the rest of Friday off to try to write a birth plan and work out how to bring a better contribution for lunch than the previous times. I knew better than to try to compete with Lucy, so I decided to make something simple. We had a couple of overripe bananas to use up, so banana bread it was. How hard could it be? Easier than bruschetta, I hoped.

It had started out well, and for a brief while I had visions of myself whipping up cakes and cookies regularly, the baby snoozing contentedly in a rocker beside me, a cute dusting of flour on both of our noses. It all started to go wrong after I took a call from my editor while I was halfway through measuring the flour, and then couldn't remember whether I'd already added baking powder, so decided to assume I had, rather than risk too much. Then the consistency of the batter seemed too thick, so I added a healthy glug of milk. Mum was never a stickler for following recipes to the letter either, I told myself.

The resulting cake was more of a dense banana-flavoured scone. That wouldn't have happened to my mum. But in the absence of any desire to bake the bloody thing again (besides, there were no bananas or eggs left), I decided some creamy icing would improve things, and it wasn't as if badly made banana bread had ever had an adverse effect on an unborn baby. To the best of my knowledge, anyway. Probably best not to google it though.

My excitement must have been contagious as Jason was seemingly enthusiastic about coming to this Baby Group at last. Because of the last disaster, he'd sought permission from Peter to have the whole weekend off – whatever IT malfunction occurred. I think having me telling him that that if he didn't come to this one, it was grounds for divorce, the message had finally sunk in. At this stage in my pregnancy, with hormones raging, I had only been half-joking.

Saturday 8ᵗʰ May

Jason and I were the first couple to arrive at the church hall the following morning. After placing the cake on the lunch table, displayed on the fanciest plate I could find, and confident that the icing actually made it look quite tempting, we took our seats opposite Maggie. She greeted us warmly, seeming as relieved as I was that Jason had actually come today.

Helen and Ian arrived and took their seats in the same spot as always, directly next to Maggie, like the teacher's pets. They greeted me warmly and even Ian showed enthusiasm at meeting the 'infamous' Jason.

Next came Susie and Lin, who entered hand in hand. There was something about them that reminded me of Russian dolls, with their bobs and classic pear-shape bodies. Even though she wasn't carrying the baby, Lin seemed to waddle sympathetically and be a completely proportionate version of Susie. They also greeted us like old friends. It felt nice to feel such familiarity amongst us already. They all made an effort with Jason, which I appreciated.

Will arrived after them, this time with a guy. I'd bet there were gym-honed bodies under their Ralph Lauren sweatshirts.

He stopped in the middle of the circle. 'This, as you probably guessed, is Christian,' he declared. Christian turned around to the group, making eye contact with us all individually. Holding hands, they made their way to another pair of free chairs. I caught Will's eye and smiled. He nodded warmly back.

Lucy rushed in last, on her own again. 'Sorry I'm late, couldn't find my house keys,' she muttered as she took her seat. She looked up and gave a small, strained smile in my direction. I smiled back warmly. Will and Christian raised their hands to Lucy and it seemed as though she had met Christian before, as she mouthed, 'Hi,' to him. 'Oscar's working again this morning, but he'll join the session after lunch,' she revealed once she had regained her breath. I was excited to meet the man I'd heard so much about.

'Lovely! *Almost* a full house.' Maggie clapped her hands together. 'Let's get going!'

Thankfully there were no more chants of 'Vagina!' today, although I was a bit disappointed Jason and Christian didn't have to go through that particular rite of passage. The conversation quickly took a turn for the comedic, though, when

Maggie began to explain how to identify the different shades of poo in your baby's nappy. We obediently handed around images of the sticky, dark-green meconium that our newborns would be ejecting from their perfectly formed peachy bums on days one and two, followed by photos depicting a 'mustard yellow'. And then Maggie revealed her *pièce de rèsistance*: a nappy with some yellow papier mâché gunk attached to it. When this slightly disturbing visual stimulus reached Ian, he became the most animated I'd ever seen him. He held the nappy up to his mouth and pretended to be sick in it. Ian found this a lot more amusing than Helen, who shrieked, 'Ian, that's disgusting!' before handing the full nappy back to Maggie.

It hit home that having a baby was not glamorous, however hard you tried to dress it up. It was unfortunate that this topic was covered just before lunch, because it reminded me of my stodgy banana cake lying beneath its thick layer of icing just a few feet away from us.

Jason's earlier enthusiasm seemed to have disappeared quite quickly. I wasn't too surprised when he popped out for some 'air' after the nappy segment. But when he went for a toilet break twice, then outside again to check his phone, it started to irritate me. If he couldn't sit through one meeting, how was he was going to cope with a newborn baby? His behaviour seemed uncharacteristically fidgety. We hadn't even broken for lunch when Jason failed to return from a third trip to the toilet. I checked my phone and found a message:

Feeling dodgy. Have popped out for air, and to go home to change into a less hot jumper. Jx

What kind of excuse was that? It meant I was left on my own for the part about what your partner can do for you during labour, like identifying tension points in your muscles and practising relaxation techniques. I was livid, and far too cross to text Jason back.

At lunchtime, Oscar joined Lucy and she introduced him to everyone in the group. He was as tall and bald as Lucy had described him, but he was attractive and he looked trendy, dressed in turned-up dark jeans and a black, what looked like cashmere jumper. A pair of cherry red socks were visible under the turn-ups and he wore box-fresh white trainers, giving him a creative edge which I appreciated. He definitely had charisma; his confidence was obvious and I could see why Lucy had fallen for him. When it came to my turn to be introduced, he shook my hand firmly and smiled, 'Aisha, lovely to meet you. Lucy has told me so much about you.' We all helped ourselves to the food, Oscar making loud, appreciative noises about how good it all was. He even took a slice of my not-quite-banana-cake.

Oscar was good at socializing. He greeted everyone with firm handshakes and eye contact as he repeated each person's name and found something interesting about them. He made everyone feel special. It was quite an art form to witness and made me feel even more frustrated that Jason wasn't here making an effort too.

'I'm Oscar, pleased to meet you.'

'Oscar – hi, and you are?'

'Hello there, Susie, I'm Oscar, and this is…?'

'Lin. It's great to meet you too, Lin. Susie and Lin, how fortuitous to fall in love with someone so beautiful.'

'Will, it's great to meet you, sir. What a fantastic group of people.'

And so on, back slaps and handshakes, air kisses and compliments, as he made a point of greeting each individual in turn.

'How's the salad going down? She's a pretty amazing chef, this one,' he had added, nudging Lucy proudly.

I kept myself busy by serving up my almost inedible banana bread to the others, watching self-consciously as Susie graciously nibbled it. It was typical that Lin was the only one who wasn't shy about telling me it didn't fit in with her vegan, sugar-free and gluten-free diet – hence the free-from-everything cacao brownies she had made again. Helen might have thought I didn't notice her fold her piece of banana stodge into a napkin and deposit it into the bin untouched, but I did. I smiled affably as she caught my eye.

I had been intrigued to see Oscar and, from what I could see, he was certainly allaying any worries Lucy previously had to do with whether he was ready to be a dad again. He seemed to ooze enthusiasm and Lucy looked justifiably proud.

A dark, nagging concern about Jason's readiness for fatherhood and his unpredictability descended on me again. I pulled my phone out of my jeans pocket and checked it. No more messages from him. No indication of whether or not he was coming back, never mind an apology for leaving me here alone yet again.

As the class came to an end, Maggie reminded us that there was only one group session left. I couldn't quite believe we were soon going to be left to fend for ourselves. Lucy had suggested earlier in the week that we should decamp to the local pub after today's meeting. Part of me wanted to go home, but I was still so furious with Jason that another part of me wanted to punish him. Perhaps the pub was a good idea. Leave him wondering where I had got to, for once. Although the idea of a heavily pregnant woman going on a bender was ridiculous.

'Coming for the drinks?' Lucy asked hopefully. I noticed a frown across her forehead. The fact that she was clearly holding out for me to go helped make up my mind.

'Sure,' I replied, as breezily as possible, pulling my cardigan off the back of my chair and gathering up my things.

I stuck it out for a whole hour before excusing myself to go to the bathroom, where I sat on the loo going over the events of today. Jason still hadn't even bothered to send me another text. I was gripped by anxiety again and couldn't help thinking about the day I told him I was pregnant. Was this weird behaviour another sign he wasn't up to the challenge of fatherhood? I tried to distract myself by scrolling blankly through my Facebook feed and randomly liking things, until I decided it was now a respectable time to claim I felt tired and face Jason. One advantage of pregnancy was always having an excuse to leave a rubbish party.

When I got home, Jason was already in bed, AirPods in his ears, watching something on his phone. It was unusual for him to be so subdued. Perhaps sensing he was in the dog house, he didn't say anything, but watched me for a while as I moved around the room, taking off my jewellery and changing out of my clothes. It irritated me that he had got into bed without even closing the curtains, so I pulled them together loudly, making the point.

Finally, he took a bud out of one ear. 'Everything okay?' he asked. I noticed he looked pale.

'Shouldn't I be asking you that question?' I said, feeling the familiar tightening in my chest. Jason had pushed things too far today, with his unreliability. It made me seriously question his readiness for all this.

'I didn't feel well,' he said morosely.

I knew there had to be more to it, but I was tired and not in the mood to start a big conversation right now. I went into the kitchen and ate some dinner on my own. We went to sleep in silence.

CHAPTER FIFTEEN

Aisha

Sunday 9th May

I woke up the next morning to a WhatsApp message from Lucy. She had sent it late the evening before.

> Lucy: Hey, just checking how you and Jason are? Hope all ok.

I spent a while considering how to respond. I was so angry that Jason had put me in this position, where I had no option but to lie to my new friend in order to cover up my embarrassment and shame that I had had no idea he was not coming back to The Baby Group yesterday. I eventually responded:

> Me: Yes, all good. Jase had a funny turn, think he's coming down with the man flu!

Lucy: Oh dear, sorry to hear that. Nothing's as bad as man flu. Fancy another coffee and croissant this week? Maybe in town this time, while we can?

Me: I'm actually meeting a friend at Selfridges tomorrow, for tea and a look round the baby department. You're welcome to join us?

Lucy: Sounds great, love to! I've got to pop into the office first thing, but I've got some holiday to use up, so I'll take off the afternoon. Just let me know what time. Lx

Monday 10th May

With less than two weeks until my due date, I was feeling nervous about travelling too far from home on my own. The possibility of my waters breaking, a 'show', or the onset of contractions in a public place, when I wasn't in easy reach of our house or with Jason, scared me. But with Jason's unreliability reaching new heights in the last few days, I was starting to think that Lucy cared more about me anyway. She was certainly looking out for me more than he was right now. I hadn't seen Tara for a few weeks, so when she had suggested taking a day off work for a shopping trip to the Selfridges baby department, followed by tea and macaroons in the Foodhall, I decided there was safety in travelling as a pair. Plus I really needed to speak to someone about Jason. I told Lucy to meet us slightly later, in The White Company concession, so Tara and I could talk before she arrived.

Tara kindly offered to get an Uber from Crystal Palace to Clapham Common station so we could get the Tube into town together. She greeted me with a hug so warm and familiar it made my eyes water on the spot. I felt a lump in my throat that no amount of deep breaths and light-hearted chat about what her kids had been up to could make go away. As we sat next to each other in the Tube carriage, travelling towards Stockwell, her eyes landed upon my face and settled there. She read me like an open book.

'You're not your usual bubbly self Aish, what's up? Is it Jason?'

I nodded in response.

'Is he working too much again?'

'He's still doing all the extra hours available, but there's more to it than that, Tara,' I said. My eyes filled with tears. She took my hand in hers. I noticed a woman sat opposite register that I was on the brink of crying and felt a pang of shame. She smiled sympathetically at me. It wasn't a healthy look for a heavily pregnant woman to be in tears, unless she's in labour. It was just a pity that my husband had barely noticed how close to the edge of despair I was.

'You can tell me,' Tara continued, reaching into her bag for a pack of tissues and placing them in my lap.

'I just don't think he's ready. For fatherhood. And I'm scared,' I uttered hesitantly. They were such big words to say aloud.

The train stopped at Stockwell and we stood up to cross the platform onto the Victoria Line. I swallowed hard and wiped a rogue tear from my eye with one of the tissues.

'Maybe I could speak to him?' Tara offered. I knew it pained her to see me like this.

'I don't think he'll listen,' I replied.

'Or perhaps I could ask Hugo to take him out for a beer? Maybe he'll open up to him?'

I shrugged; it was sweet of her to make suggestions, but Jason and Hugo weren't close. Besides, deep down, I knew this was mine and Jason's situation to work out.

We were making cooing noises around The White Company baby clothes, when I spotted Lucy walking towards us.

'Fancy bumping into you! Literally,' she joked, as we embraced each other and our bumps touched. My middle felt especially massive now, so black had become my staple colour. Lucy looked great in a leopard print coat and her trademark red lipstick. She was holding a cashmere onesie in each hand, one grey, one navy.

'Aren't they cute?' She cocked her head, to take a closer look at one of them. 'Found them in the Ralph Lauren sale area. I still can't get my head around the fact that they're going to be filled with an actual baby soon.'

'They're gorgeous, you should get them both,' I replied, before turning to Tara. 'This is Lucy, from The Baby Group.'

'Really? I'd never have guessed!' Tara rolled her eyes sarcastically.

'Guilty,' Lucy smiled, looking down at her bump, which was poking out of the coat. 'This thing is a bit of a giveaway.'

'This is Tara,' I continued, 'one of my oldest friends. We met at primary school.'

Tara smiled warmly and held out a hand, which Lucy shook enthusiastically.

'Lovely to meet you. I could go wild in here,' Lucy said, replacing one of the cashmeres on a nearby rail. 'I need restraining.'

'Me too,' I replied, thinking Lucy really could go wild in here if her Gucci handbag and the fact Oscar ran his own company was anything to go by.

I suggested we go to the Foodhall to take the weight off our swollen ankles.

Over mint tea and macaroons, Lucy explained how Oscar would be working flat out this week and going on his last work trip before the baby, so she'd be home alone most of the time. I told her she could call me if she needed anything and Jason and I would try to help. I got the impression she didn't have family nearby. She had never mentioned them.

'How's Jason coping with the man flu?' she asked. My instinct told me she had sensed things hadn't been quite right between Jason and I that day.

'Still pretty bad. But he's dragged himself into work today, so he'll live, I expect,' I replied. 'We're both asleep by nine o'clock most nights at the moment, so I'm sure he'll manage to sleep it off.'

'Sounds familiar,' Lucy said. 'Oscar and I had a "date night" last night. It involved a Chinese takeaway that gave me chronic heartburn, so I had Gaviscon for dessert and then I fell asleep half an hour into a film. Rock and roll.'

'Ladies, I hate to burst the beautiful baby bubble, but a takeaway and a film *will* be a hot date night for the next, ooh, eighteen years. Welcome to your new life!' Tara giggled. 'Anyway, I've got to dash, I need to get back in time to pick the boys up from nursery. You take care of each other okay, no dashing around or buying up the whole macaroon display. I know what your sweet tooth is like, Aisha.' She looked at me affectionately. 'And you two preggos will travel back to Clapham together, right?' Lucy and I nodded obediently. 'Good. Lovely meeting you, Lucy. Look after each other!' And she rushed off.

We finished our macaroons and ordered seconds. I figured I already weighed the same as a Smart car, so a few more macaroons wouldn't hurt. I got the impression Lucy wasn't in any hurry to get home either. A couple of times she looked like she was weighing up whether or not to tell me something.

'It was weird the other day, in the meeting,' she offered at last. I bristled, thinking for a moment that she was referring to Jason's behaviour; that she was going to pry. 'Having Oscar there. I found it weird.'

I visibly sighed with relief that she wasn't going to interrogate me; I didn't feel strong enough today, to continue pretending everything was okay. But the idea that perhaps there was a chink in her seemingly perfect relationship gave me a little comfort.

'Weird, in what way?' I asked.

'Because this baby was made differently—' she stopped herself abruptly mid-sentence, her eyes a little watery and her cheeks flushed all of a sudden. I leant forward, studying her, wondering what was coming next. 'He's... an IVF baby.'

A waitress came over and refilled our tea cups from the pot between us.

'You told me, and that's not unusual,' I said lightly, trying to make her feel at ease. I could tell she wanted to talk but I knew better than to push her. Lucy seemed quite fragile today. Her eyes were reddening. She sat up straight in an effort to pull her emotions into check.

'This probably isn't the right time or place. I just – well I don't really have many other people to talk to.'

'It's fine to talk. I'm all ears, if you want to.'

'What I didn't tell you the other day, in Gail's, is that Oscar and I were actually on a break when I found out I was pregnant.' I sat up straighter, intrigued. She was certainly full of secrets. 'It was a tough time, you know. The IVF was under way, but he got cold feet. He panicked, big time, and called it off.'

'Oh that's awful. What a thing for him to do. It must have been such a tough time for you,' I sympathized. 'You must have been devastated. But you obviously got back together?'

'Yes, on the first day of my second trimester. Oscar changed his mind. He told me breaking up with me was his "biggest regret". Said he was determined to be there for me and the baby, and would pay me attention like never before.'

'Was it easy to forgive him?'

She thought for a moment.

'Aisha, as you probably know, all relationships reach a point where you have to think with your head as well as your heart. I know from friends that bringing up a child isn't easy and I already knew that Oscar was a great dad; he has a fantastic, close and loving relationship with his children Evie and Ollie, and although he is probably a little rusty, I figure he can probably still remember how to change a nappy, with some practice. Plus we have great sex.'

I squirmed. I'd always been prudish about talking about either my own, or other people's sex lives, especially in public.

Lucy didn't seem to mind though. 'We're definitely compatible in the bedroom. I mean, it wasn't easy at first, but he really did mean it this time, I could tell. I came to the realization that good things often come after a fight and the *best* things are worth waiting for.' She stopped in her tracks, as if afraid she might have said something shocking, or out of turn. 'Sorry, is this too much?'

'No, not at all,' I replied. 'I'm intrigued.'

'We began seeing each other properly again – there were trips to the theatre, days out visiting art galleries and a couple of weekends away at country spa hotels. The sex was unreal. Turns out I've never felt sexier than with these curves. I was five months gone when he asked if we could become a bona fide couple and move in together. Neither of us wanted to waste any more time.'

'Wow,' I said, enthralled. 'So are you happy now?'

'Yes, we are. I love him. He's close enough to the full package.' She shrugged.

I giggled. 'And "close enough" is all any of us can ask for, right?' She had, at least, made me feel a little better about Jason and me, by reminding me that all relationships go through difficult times and 'close enough' is sometimes, enough.

'Sorry if I went on a bit, I hadn't planned to come out with all that; to get heavy,' she said.

'It's not heavy,' I reassured her. 'Anyway, we're friends, aren't we?'

She smiled, and for a moment I thought she had tears in her eyes. To think, when we first met I assumed she had everything figured out. It occurred to me that perhaps she was lonely.

Tara texted me later on:

Tara: Lucy seems lovely. Really down to earth.

Me: Yes, I think we could be good friends.

Tara: But not besties, I hope. I knew you first, remember?! Xx

Me: Of course 🌚 Ax

CHAPTER SIXTEEN

Lucy

When I got home from town, I found a note from Oscar on the breakfast bar: 'Popped out to meet a potential new client. Will be home by 7. O.'

I set down the two yellow Selfridges bags. I felt so exhausted, I was glad he wasn't home. Shopping normally gave me such a buzz and today I had been fairly extravagant spending more than I planned to on 0–3 month items – some of them as pricey as adult's clothing – but instead of feeling elated, I felt wrung out. The conversation with Aisha had left me feeling conflicted. I had planned to take one of the bags upstairs, unpack its contents and put it neatly away in the nursery, before Oscar could ask too many questions, but I felt too tired.

I took off my coat and shoes and filled the kettle before glancing at the oven clock: 4.25. I had a while before he'd be back. I made myself a peppermint tea and sat on the sofa, flicking through a magazine, but failing to properly concentrate on anything.

I felt the baby kick and decided to head upstairs. When I passed the spare room, I stopped. My legs were aching; we'd been on the go for most of the day. I sat on the edge of the spare bed and looked out of the window at the backs of the houses beyond our little garden. The buildings might be tightly packed around here, but the view was still pretty. The house directly behind ours was partially covered in ivy, and from an open window I could hear the soft tinkle of piano keys.

I took a sip from the mug of tea I'd brought upstairs with me, and looked towards the desk in the corner of the room. A piece of paper was poking out of the middle drawer of the filing cabinet beneath it, stopping it from closing properly. I stood up and gently pushed it back in. A blue folder behind it prevented it from sliding in easily. Its little plastic header caught my eye; it was written by Oscar and entitled 'Divorce Docs'. I pulled out the file. Oscar had shown me his divorce certificate before, but I still found it morbidly fascinating to look at.

In the High Court of Justice Principal
Registry of the Family Division

Between PHILIPPA JANE BRIGHT Petitioner
And OSCAR LEOPALD BRIGHT Respondent
On 10 May 2019

I noticed goosebumps appear on my arm as I realized it was two years ago to the day. I recalled how the reason for the breakdown of this marriage had been squared at Oscar, basically for working too hard and being absent.

And now we had set up a home together. We shared a filing cabinet. A joint bank account. There was a baby on the way. Although I was very grateful for the life I had with Oscar, there would always be a niggling doubt about whether he really wanted any more children and what he would be like when the baby arrived.

I placed the folder back into the drawer and had almost closed it, when another large file grabbed my attention. This time the label was in my handwriting: 'IVF Docs'. I remembered writing it. I lifted the folder out, coming across a few printouts of correspondence I had had with the fertility clinic in the run up to having IVF. There were some leaflets they had given me about pre- and post-procedure care when I had begun the process; I had dutifully kept them filed away for future reference, although I'd never actually read them again. As I flicked through, my heart began to race. I stroked my bump as I remembered how badly I had wanted this pregnancy. How much time, effort, heartache and money had gone into producing this unborn child.

I noticed the date at the top of an email – almost nine months ago – confirming my appointment for the embryo transfer that week. As I tried to focus on the email, my mind wandered back to that day…

It was a warm day, and as I walked the short distance from the Tube to the IVF clinic, I almost wished I'd worn a dress. I felt clammy and sweaty in all the wrong places; a toxic mixture of nerves and hangover; a bag of jitters. But I didn't want the physician implanting my little embryo to think I had dressed up for him or her. I wanted to be bland today, just another patient, just another cervix – the whole thing was shameful enough; imagine if they knew what had happened last night? So I wore my staple blue skinny jeans and a thin grey T-shirt. Subconsciously I thought that tight trousers might somehow hug my body and encourage the embryo to stay put and stick. I'd run out of time to shave my legs anyway; it had ended up being a rush just to make myself look and feel presentable, before hurrying across London in time.

After paying for the procedure and completing all the paperwork, signing my name several times against a signature for a representative from the embryology team, the reality hit me as the nurse asked me one final question:

'Is there any chance you might already be pregnant today?'

'No,' I replied, my heart rate speeding up. She barely looked up as she noted down my response and passed me a pee-stick anyway. I went to the toilet and took the test. I noticed my hand was shaking as I tried to aim on the stick. For a moment I wondered if this whole thing was a good idea. My heart pounded in my chest. But as a second line failed to appear on the stick, confirming I was not pregnant, I took a deep breath and returned to the consultant's room. I had come too far to change my mind now.

I was then asked to remove my underwear and change into a clinical green gown. None of the romance involved with having your knickers pulled down in a moment of passion with the man of your dreams. A flashback swept across my mind.

As I lay there, half naked, my legs in stirrups, I stared at the ceiling while the doctor delved around my uterine cavity and a sonographer made encouraging chirps by my side.

At last my discomfort was broken by the sonographer announcing: 'Super. Well done, Lucy. I'm very pleased with how the transfer has gone. So all that's left for you to do now is get dressed and go home and rest. You don't need to do anything in particular, just take it easy for a few days – try to avoid any sharp jolts, speed bumps, sex – and then you can get back to normal life. Stick to the rules of course.'

She handed me a sheet of paper with a list of things that it was sensible to avoid if you might be pregnant, including caffeine, alcohol and raw fish. I put the paper straight into my bag. I knew it all already. She placed a hand on my shoulder to stop me getting up just yet. 'Wait at least twelve days before taking a pregnancy test. Here's one for you.' She produced a long, unmarked white box from a draw and handed it over. 'Do you know how to use it?'

I nodded; I'd done more than my share of pregnancy tests over the years.

'We'll call you back after fourteen days anyway for a blood test, to double-check the result. If you can't wait that long, you can come in for a test at twelve days and we'll give you the result then.'

She smiled. 'Everything looks good on screen, so now we just have to hope your body will do the rest. Do you want to go and see Amelia?'

'No, I'm good,' I shook my head resolutely, refusing the counselling session again. 'But thanks.'

'You take care and we'll be in touch.'

She handed over the papers in an unmarked envelope. And that was it. In under an hour, in a very matter-of-fact, clinical way, we had just, potentially, made a baby.

I got dressed quickly, keen to leave the clinic as soon as possible. Stepping back into the roasting sunshine gave me a little lift; I felt warm in my jeans, my cheeks still flushed both from the procedure and the alcohol still in my body. It was hard not to feel like a piece of meat in there. But I had done all I could do now; it was time for Mother Nature to pick up the reins, and although hungover, heaven knew I'd given her a reasonable head start.

I hailed a cab – the Tube was far too hectic for my head to cope with again today – and on the journey home I tried to distract myself from wondering whether I felt any different already.

I had imagined the sensation of having a tiny foetus inside me so many times in recent years, when I had willed my body to be pregnant, only to face disappointment, over and over again. And now look. The synergy of what had happened last night was so bizarre. The last time I had had a fertilized embryo inside me I was 19. And now, twenty years later, I had a fertilized egg inside me with a real possibility of a successful pregnancy. This didn't feel real. I closed my eyes and willed the taxi to get me home as quickly as possible.

Katie texted when I was in the cab:

Katie: All good? Hope you're okay. Let me know if you need anything. Chocolate? Hummus? Kx

Me: All fine, the deed has been done. Going to get an early night. Call you tomorrow x

When I got home, I considered curling up on the sofa to watch TV, but my mind was scrambled and my ability to focus lost, so instead I climbed back into bed and under the duvet, setting down a large mug of peppermint tea next to me. I had only just managed to stop myself from popping two Nurofen and making a G&T in the kitchen, forgetting for a moment that I was meant to be off regular drugs and alcohol right now. Half of me was thinking what a fat lot of use this recently purchased Nespresso machine was going to be. The other half of me thought carrying on like I might be pregnant was futile. And I was desperate for coffee.

Of course, I hadn't yet thought to stock up on decaf pods.

Back in the spare room, I took another slurp of tea, although it was barely warm now. Going through all this probably wasn't a good idea right now. I gathered the papers up into a pile and pushed them into the folder. I was about to put it back in the cabinet when my attention was drawn to another folder. The label said: 'Donor Docs'.

The sperm donor documents were filed alphabetically next to Oscar's 'Divorce Docs'. It seemed quite bizarre that two such momentous, life-changing events for us now amounted to a few pieces of paper sitting cosily alongside each other in the same cabinet. So close, yet light years apart at the same time.

I went through the pile, licking my finger and casting my

eye over each piece of paper. There had been a consultant I particularly warmed to when I'd had my embryos frozen; she had sent me a very kind and supportive email, following the awful task of having to tell me that my eggs were of such poor quality, there was only a slim chance of one being successful. It was also following a consultation where I had opened up to her that I wasn't quite sure when I would be able to use them anyway, because my 'boyfriend' didn't want any more children. 'Don't lose hope,' she had said at the end, 'I know it's hard to process right now, but there are other options. Looking for a sperm donor could be worth exploration.' I remembered the pain anew as I read it.

There were a number of leaflets and letters from the sperm donor bank. Profiles of a few possible candidates. And then a long trail relating to the one I'd chosen, plus a lengthy signed contract.

There was a gap of three months between being told my eggs were poor before I was to return to the same clinic for the IVF procedure. Also inside the folder was the pregnancy test I had used at home and which had revealed the positive result. The little screen which once showed two blue lines had almost faded completely into an off-white now. I wondered whether it was crazy to keep something like that for sentimental value. For a while I had referred to it daily, such was the disbelief that this moment had finally arrived for me again.

Falling pregnant had been a lot to get my head around. Only Katie knew what I had been going through and she'd even offered to be there when I told my parents that the IVF had been successful, although I'd chosen to do it on my own and had ended up telling Mum on the phone. My parents were conflicted in their emotions – on the one hand thrilled at the prospect of becoming grandparents at last, but on the other, tinged with the sadness of this substandard set up. I could practically hear my mother's mind ticking over as she tried to fathom how she would explain this to friends at dinner parties. It was almost amusing.

One evening, about three weeks after I had the IVF, Oscar had offered to come round. I had been feeling a little low that day and did what I often did when I was feeling vulnerable – called him. I hadn't been in the office for a few days, claiming to be 'working from home'. I almost wanted to wrap myself up in cotton wool in those critical early weeks. Oscar and I weren't together, and he didn't yet know I was pregnant, but even hearing his voice on the phone was a huge comfort…

'Everything all right?' he asked urgently, the moment I answered the front door.

'Yes,' I sighed, 'everything's fine. Come in.'

We were sat on my sofa having just ordered a Thai takeaway. My mind was ticking over as Oscar was flicking through Netflix, trying to find a series someone had been raving about, but he couldn't remember the name of. He gave up, moved to the coffee table and set about opening the bottle of red wine he had brought round. When he passed a glass to me, I knew I couldn't keep the secret any longer. I just blurted it out.

'Afraid I'm not drinking,' I said, pushing it away. 'I'm pregnant.'

He looked at me in shock. To be fair, it was a huge

bombshell – both the pregnancy and the fact I wasn't drinking wine. His eyes widened. 'Are you serious?'

'Yes, Oscar, I am. I'm just a few weeks gone, so it's still very early days.'

A moment passed. 'Wow, Lucy, this is big news.'

I smiled weakly.

'I had no idea you were so keen... *still* so keen to get pregnant.' He said it slowly, still processing my news.

'I'm 38, with no baby-daddy prospects,' I said measuredly. 'Of course I want children – a child. You know this Oscar. But I didn't think it was going to happen any time soon, so I had to go for it. I froze some of my eggs and I had IVF. It appears to have worked.'

I said it in a matter-of-fact way on purpose, wanting to make light of it. Even though there was nothing light about it at all.

'How are you feeling?' he asked.

'Okay, so far,' I said, 'A bit more tired than usual, perhaps.'

'Were you going to tell me?' Oscar asked, turning the conversation back to himself, somehow making it sound like he'd been hurt in the process.

'I'm telling you now aren't I? I didn't tell you before, because I know you've got a lot on your plate with your own family and we're not together. Remember?'

He looked crestfallen, and for a moment it riled me slightly. 'You made it quite clear to me that you don't want any more children, Oscar – you broke up with me over it – so I figured you didn't need my IVF plans cluttering up your life.'

He paused.

'Can I ask who the father is?' He sounded dejected, which took me by surprise. It hadn't even crossed my mind that he might jump to the conclusion that I'd miraculously found a man willing to make a baby with me in the last few months.

'You can, and it's no one I know – I went the anonymous sperm donor route. I chose from a list of distinguished characteristics: high IQ, a clean bill of health, tall and as close to Channing Tatum's looks as possible. It was all very scientific really.'

He breathed a sigh of relief. 'So it will be just like me then.'

I smiled. His joke had released some tension.

Oscar seemed fascinated by the anonymous sperm donor and asked if I thought I'd ever want to discover who the father was. I had thought about this a lot at the outset and decided that I wouldn't want to find out, but that if my child wanted to know, when the time came, I would support them. I hadn't ticked the box on the consent form which ruled that out entirely. I believed they should have the choice, wherever it led. And I'd be there to support them in that journey. I waivered as I recounted this to him, adding that I imagined it might get complicated one day.

I must have given something away, by the way I told Oscar all this. He gave me a funny look.

'What are you thinking?' I asked.

'I'm trying to work you out.'

'Work me out?' I paused.

He had touched a nerve and he seemed to know it. I paused for a moment and a shiver ran down my spine. But again I decided to keep quiet and not tell him any more. This big secret sometimes felt like a fish bone lodged in my throat. It constricted my breath at times, but I didn't know how to release it, or what the consequences would be if I did. It was a ticking time-bomb.

'I guess it's not exactly the way I dreamt of bringing a baby into the world – not knowing who its father is – but it's my story now,' I said at last. '*Our* story,' I indicated my stomach, which so far wasn't showing any signs of having a baby in there. 'I wanted to be normal, but it didn't happen for me.'

He sighed heavily, and I realized Oscar had taken this as a veiled dig at him.

'Oh, I didn't mean that I blame you in any way,' I said quickly.

He placed a hand on my hair and tenderly stroked it and the side of my cheek.

'You're going to be the most amazing mother,' said Oscar. 'I'm here for you both.'

He pulled me in for a hug and I lost whatever control I had and leant into him. I hid my face as tears collected in my eyes.

We were glad of the new Netflix drama taking our minds elsewhere as we ate the takeaway together.

Oscar held me for an extra-long time as we embraced in the hallway before he left.

'Do you need anything?' he asked when we pulled apart.

If only I could tell him how confused a part of me felt; if only he knew what a mess it all was.

'I'm fine, just going to take the doctor's advice and be kind to myself. I'll work from home for a bit, but they advise you carry on as normal, so I just have to hope for the best.'

'Of course. Let me know if you need supplies.' He was a generous man, Oscar. He might not be the most practical, but he was considerate and had the budget to facilitate anything I might need.

I smiled. 'That's sweet of you, but I'm fine.'

'Okay, I'm here if you need me,' he said. 'I've got Evie and Ollie this weekend, but we could easily swing by if you want some company. We're dog-sitting for Pippa too. You could join us on a walk. Otherwise, see you on Monday, Lucy,' he said sweetly. 'It's your birthday if you hadn't forgotten, so I'm taking you out for lunch, to Nobu, whether you like it or not.'

Dear Oscar. He hadn't had the easiest time himself recently. He was a good, strong person, and he had given me space for the last six months because he knew it wasn't fair when he didn't want any more babies. But there was no denying we enjoyed each other's company, and he was making a big effort to ensure we stayed friends.

'Thanks, Mr Bright,' I said, tears welling in my eyes.

I must have lost track of time and dozed off on the spare bed. I awoke to the baby kicking energetically and I propped myself up on my side. My back ached.

'Ouch, you feisty little thing,' I muttered, receiving another kick just as I rose up to sitting, one hand on my back, feeling like an elephant rousing from an afternoon nap.

I heard the key turn in the front door downstairs.

'Lucy?' Oscar called out, checking where I was. That meant it must be around seven o'clock.

'Upstairs!' I called back, trying not to sound as though

I'd just woken up. I moved towards the desk and shoved the donor paperwork back into its file. 'Been doing some tidying.'

'Not like you,' he exclaimed jokily. And then I heard him kick off his shoes and come padding up the stairs to find me.

'Well, if you must know, I also fell asleep.'

I stretched backwards, giving my body a little reprieve, and made a mental note to check whether there was a drop-in yoga class I could make tomorrow. Yoga always helped me to feel calmer.

'Nothing wrong with a little nap,' Oscar smiled. 'And I see nesting extends to filing. I like it.' His eyes wandered to the open filing cabinet.

'I was going to slim down the paperwork and ended up looking through some old bits and pieces,' I explained, motioning to a folder sticking out of the drawer, the one containing his divorce papers.

'Let's put it all away now...' Oscar pushed the file back down.

'Right,' I smiled, watching him close the drawer.

CHAPTER SEVENTEEN

Aisha

Wednesday 12ᵗʰ May

Jason had been very quiet since we'd arrived at the fifth and final Baby Group meeting, a shorter evening session back in the room at the local church. It had been a battle getting him to attend it at all. I knew he was tired from work, but he'd behaved like a petulant teenager, asking silly questions about whether everyone else was going to be there, how long it would last and so on. I was so cross.

'You can't do this to me, Jason, not after last week,' I had fumed, panic-stricken, as I practically forced him out of the front door.

'I wasn't well!' he'd exclaimed, as if I was being ridiculous.

'So what's your excuse this time? What are you afraid of Jason – are you getting cold feet?'

'It's not that,' he had snapped. 'I'm just exhausted.' He'd seemed on the edge, emotional.

I wasn't convinced.

'It's Movie Night!' Maggie declared enthusiastically, making small talk while we waited for the last two couples to arrive. 'Baby Group-style. We are going to be watching a live birth and talking about the first few weeks as new parents.'

I immediately felt anxious about being made to watch something as intimate as a birth with a room full of people. I was easily embarrassed, and seeing full-scale nudity in this environment gave me sweaty palms.

To pass the time, Maggie asked Jason an innocent question about whether he was planning to take any paternity leave, but he didn't seem to hear her – he was looking at his phone.

'Any plans to take paternity leave?' she asked again, more loudly and slightly irritated this time.

I kicked his foot.

Jason coughed into life, but his voice came out sounding hoarse. I suspected he'd been smoking this week. Although he claimed to have stopped the habit when I got pregnant, I recognized that gravelly cough and had noticed the faint smell of tobacco on his coat.

'Oh, sorry,' he said eventually, pushing his phone into his coat pocket. 'What was the question?' Six pairs of eyes looked at him.

'Paternity leave. Your fatherly right?' Maggie repeated, unamused. 'I was just wondering if you're planning to...'

'Use it? Oh right, yes, of course,' he stammered. 'I'd – *we'd* – be mad not to. Free holiday! We can't wait.' He squeezed my hand.

'Free. Holiday.' Maggie repeated the words slowly under

her breath, a wry smile dancing on her lips. 'Let's see about that. Do feel free to take your coat off, Jason, you look like you're about to go somewhere.' It was obvious she hadn't particularly warmed to him, especially after his disappearing act last week.

I glanced across at the rest of the group, clocking that Ian seemed to find Jason's response amusing. Maggie noticed this too and folded her arms; she had a strong matron game going on this evening.

'On the subject of paternity leave – I hope you've told your employers? Remember, guys, you should have told your work place if you intend to take a week or two of paternity leave – or shared maternity leave,' she added, glancing at Susie and Lin. 'I hope you've all got this in place. How many weeks along are you now?' Maggie continued, looking at Jason, who turned to me, searchingly. If this was an exam, he had failed miserably.

'Thirty-eight weeks and six days,' I answered on his behalf, feeling annoyed. 'It's okay, Jason let his work know a while ago.'

'The guys never remember the weeks, do they!' Maggie chuckled, slightly pityingly, trying to make light of something that was important – and should have been important to Jason, considering I was this close to full term.

'Well, it's hard to remember yourself half the time,' I added, defending Jason, despite this being a complete lie.

Lin coughed loudly, suggesting she had never forgotten a single day during Susie's pregnancy.

I had never lost track of my dates and I'd bet the other

pregnant women in this room hadn't either. The whole of my pregnancy had been punctuated by important dates and significant numbers: dates of doctor and hospital appointments, numbers of weeks plus days, heart rates, blood pressure, my increasing weight, the circumference of my belly and, of course, the all-important due date.

Susie and Lin smiled at me in sync. I wasn't sure if they were smiling in solidarity or with sympathy because they could see I was flustered that Jason and I weren't exactly gelling this evening.

Once Will and Christian had arrived, Maggie muttered, 'Still waiting on Lucy and Oscar,' and pulled out her phone from the Eighties-style corduroy jacket on the back of her chair.

'A-ha,' she said reading a message. 'Lucy won't be joining us unfortunately; she's not feeling up to it. Hopefully she's okay. Not a problem folks, let's get started.' She rubbed her hands together.

I felt a little disappointed. I'd miss Lucy this evening. We'd become good friends. I sent her a quick message:

Me: Hey, Maggie said you're not feeling great. Hope everything's ok?

I waited for a minute but she didn't reply.

Maggie got up and began wheeling an ancient TV set and VHS cassette player out from behind her.

'Bloody hell,' Jason whispered to me, 'they're almost as old as her! I better give her a hand.' He jumped up, suddenly seeming brighter, more engaged. Maybe Maggie's scolding had shown him he needed to up his game. 'Here, let me help,' he insisted, and manoeuvred the TV into place in front of us all.

'It might look like a museum piece,' Maggie acknowledged, wiping a little sweat from her brow. 'But I'm reliably informed it works. Modern technology isn't everything, you know.'

After a few minutes of awkward clicking and nothing happening she finally managed to turn the system on and prevent the VHS tape from being repeatedly ejected by the machine.

Suddenly we were all confronted by a close-up of a vagina, covered in a lot of very fuzzy black pubic hair. There was a great deal of moisture around it, and the top of a baby's head poking out.

When I say a lot of very fuzzy hair, I mean a *staggering* amount of curly black pubes forming a large fluffy afro atop the woman's private parts. I had never seen a vagina look so well dressed. There was a halo of light around the edges of the fuzz as bright hospital lights shone down on this most intimate of moments.

My immediate reaction was to laugh hysterically, and I let out a bellowing guffaw, which Maggie pretended not to hear.

'I'm sorry!' I squealed, covering my mouth with my hand. 'It was just a surprise!' As I sank back into my chair feeling like a naughty schoolgirl, desperately trying to contain my full-scale laughter, I wished Lucy was there, because she would certainly be doing the same.

Jason was also trying not to laugh. He nudged me with his elbow, but I didn't dare look at him, for fear I would explode.

I looked to my left to see if anyone else found this amusing. Helen's cheeks had turned red with embarrassment, and Ian was tittering slightly. To his right, Will and Christian were shifting uncomfortably in their seats. Next to them, Susie and Lin didn't seem too fazed.

I tried to stop my shoulders from shaking uncontrollably, eyes watering as I desperately stifled my giggles. The longer the image stayed paused on screen, despite Maggie pressing a series of buttons, the worse my hysterics seemed to get.

'Tsk, some naughty person forgot to rewind it to the beginning, and now it seems to be stuck,' Maggie said, stony-faced.

When Jason put a hand on my leg to try to calm me, it only made it worse and I waved him off. I couldn't wait to tell Tara about this. And Lucy.

Finally, after she had pulled out the plug from the wall and restarted both the TV and video recorder, the film finally rewound. We were all at least now prepared for the vintage birth moment featuring a lovely couple called Janet (she with the large bush) and Peter, who bore an impressive handlebar moustache and brown flares. It was all very late Seventies.

The birth was natural and fairly straightforward (if you call straightforward watching Janet look like she was about to explode from pushing) and in a relatively short space of time they were in their Cortina driving little Eric back to their pebble-dashed semi in Essex. It might have offered me some comfort, if I hadn't found it so funny.

I noticed that Susie seemed quiet, and also slightly uncomfortable this evening, holding onto her bump and wincing slightly through the video. I wondered if she was getting sympathy contractions.

'Jeez,' she muttered at one point. 'To think I was considering foregoing the pain relief. I think I've just changed my mind.'

After we had finished discussing the film, Maggie started to explain what the partners could do in the immediate days ahead of the due date. I was relieved to see Jason taking the pad and pen from my lap and making notes, following Will and Christian's lead. They were both scribbling away.

I peeked across to see what pearls of wisdom Jason had written down:

'Things for Jason to do/think about' – he had scrawled as a section head, underlining it. Underneath was a series of bullet points, many of which made me smile:

- Identify Aisha's favourite foods/dinners
- Order frozen meals, and set up online shopping. Don't forget savoy cabbage (for boobs)
- Get biscuits and coffee for visitors. Limit visitors in early days
- Remember Aisha's favourite pillows when going to hospital – important
- Buy a sling, learn how to use it

I felt relieved that Jason was finally engaging today. This was, at least, a step in the right direction. A couple of times, I caught Helen looking at him. I noticed her pass Ian a pen, but he just fiddled with it.

Maggie held up a small white plastic instrument with a digital screen and a button halfway down. 'Does anyone know what this is?' she asked enthusiastically.

Will's hand shot up. 'Is it a kazoo?' he asked.

This time it was Maggie's turn to giggle. 'Oh heavens, no dear, some of us have a lot to learn. This is a baby thermometer.'

Sometimes I got the impression Maggie despaired of this class.

CHAPTER EIGHTEEN

Lucy

I lay in bed feeling anxious and burnt-out. At one point, I had had to make a sudden dash to the toilet, thinking I might be sick. I had looked in the bathroom mirror and seen that my face was pale and sweat was beading on my forehead.

I focused on breathing slowly; I didn't want to alarm Oscar. He came into the bedroom to start packing for a trip to Paris the following morning – his final client foray before he went on baby lockdown. He pottered around the bedroom collecting things for his suitcase. I knew that case well – I had travelled halfway around the world with it on work trips when we were first seeing each other. I had even hurriedly packed it one morning when he feared his PA was on her way to our hotel room in Milan to give him some important documents and he bolted out of there as fast as possible to meet her from the cab. It wasn't professional to be shagging the new account manager. The memory offered me a momentary reprieve from more pressing thoughts.

'How are you feeling my love?' he asked, shooting me a look.

'Okay, mostly tired,' I replied. 'It was the right decision to miss The Baby Group today.'

'Yes, it was probably for the best. You need to conserve your energy now.'

I propped myself up in bed with pillows. 'What if something is wrong with the baby?' I said, filling a moment of quiet, as Oscar stood in the en suite gathering his toiletries. The subject had been on my mind, on and off, throughout the pregnancy, but until now I'd kept this distressing thought strictly inside my head, wanting to focus on the positives.

'Darling, what made you think that?' he said, dropping his wash kit into his open case. He sat down on the side of the bed.

'I was just thinking about being older,' I replied. 'It wasn't covered in the textbooks – or by Maggie.'

'How can she even begin to cover that?' he said gently. 'But you mustn't worry – all your scans have been perfectly normal, the doctors and technology are so good these days, they can tell pretty much everything. You would have been told if there was any cause for concern.'

'But if anything does go wrong – how will I cope?' I placed my hand on my stomach.

'*We*,' he took my hand and held it. '*We* will cope. You're not on your own. I'm here for you.'

'Really?'

He crouched down now, to my level, so he could look me straight in the eyes. He took my other hand in his and held them tightly. 'Lucy, I know this pregnancy journey hasn't been easy for you, but things have changed these past months. You have blossomed – no, rather *we* have blossomed, into a proper couple. I know I let you down before, but I'm committed to the baby. I love you.'

The tender moment was broken momentarily by the sound of a text appearing on my phone. I wriggled one hand out of his and reached for it on the bedside table. I read the message slowly. Although my heart was hammering in my chest, I tried to keep my face neutral. I would reply later.

'I love hearing you say that,' I said, calmly laying the phone back down, overturned on the table, and taking his hand again. Oscar seemed keen to reassure me that he wasn't going to freak out and desert me when the baby arrived. I should have welcomed this moment, but I was barely able to concentrate.

'I mean it,' he said earnestly.

I thought back to when we officially got back together.

Oscar had asked if he could come over one evening after work. It was the first day of my second trimester and I had decided to treat myself to a pizza takeaway for dinner. At least I could relax a little, now I'd passed the three month mark, although I still hadn't told anyone at work my news. I couldn't face all of the questions that would come with it.

Arriving at my door, Oscar looked jittery.

'What's wrong?' I asked.

He stared at me. His eyes twinkled. 'You.'

'Me? What have I done?' I asked, slightly amused. We had

been spending an increasing amount of time together recently but I still sometimes found Oscar hard to read.

'I've got you on the brain. Can I come in?'

I invited him into my flat. Sometimes I felt a little embarrassed when he came here. My Brixton pad in no way matched up to his swanky crash pad in Marylebone. But it was great that he finally wanted to talk about the 'us' that had so far been off the table.

'I've been struggling to fathom a life without you in it,' he said, holding my hand tightly.

'If you'll have me back, I'd really love for us to give it a go. I want to bring up this baby with you, Lucy,' he said.

We talked for hours that evening about how it would work, and Oscar convinced me he was ready – ready to be a father and a committed partner again. It was butterfly-inducing.

I melted into his arms and inhaled him several times. But as he hugged me, stray tears silently fell from my eyes onto his cashmere jumper. Happiness, it seemed, could be bittersweet.

Now officially back together, and with my three-month scan in the bag, I at last felt able to let my bump blossom. That's why, when the news finally came out at work, people naturally assumed he was the father. The situation suited us both and I convinced myself that I felt happy and settled. Yet a fear that maybe Oscar didn't really want any more children sometimes crept back into my mind, when I thought how home life would change for us once the baby arrived. No more spontaneous mid-week meals out to Michelin-starred restaurants, or sexy European minibreaks. Life would come with cots, nappies and prams for the foreseeable. I hoped that Oscar had got his head around it.

A couple of months after we had rekindled our relationship, Oscar asked if I fancied bringing up the baby in a bigger home – a joint home, rather than my small flat – and I was happy to agree; it was my suggestion that we rent a house together in Clapham – close to the 'Nappy Valley' area of London . We found the perfect house and moved in a few weeks later.

From there, with the secret still swirling inside me, I had an idea and decided to join a local Baby Group.

Thursday 13th May

The next morning, I saw Oscar off on his trip with a long, passionate kiss and promise of an X-rated FaceTime call. There was still eleven days until my C-section on 24th May, unless anything happened earlier. While I was feeling excited about meeting my little man, the feeling of anxiety followed me around like a gradually swelling dark rain cloud.

I was making my morning decaf when my phone lit up with a message on the Baby Group thread:

Lin: Fuck! Susie's got contractions. It's so fucking painful!!

This was it. I had to get my head around it.

CHAPTER NINETEEN

Aisha

Saturday 15ᵗʰ May

I was lying in the bath when the first contraction came. I gripped the sides of the tub, my knuckles turning white as the sudden tightening pain ripped through my insides. When it passed and my breathing returned to normal, I managed to cry out for Jason.

'Baby! I mean, Jason! I think the baby is coming early!'

He managed to help me out and wrapped a towel around my dripping wet body. He looked at me, his face pale with fear, mirroring my own. My mind buzzed with what we should be doing at this moment, and I tried to picture the notes I'd made in The Baby Group.

'Your phone – where is it?' I asked frantically. 'Aren't we meant to be timing this?'

Where was his phone? Why wasn't he springing into action? He was just standing there.

'I'll find it in a sec, try to stay calm, Aish,' he urged. 'It's going to be okay. Shit! It's happening early! Where did I put my phone?' He grabbed another towel to absorb the drips of water falling off my hair. 'There we go. Oh my God, Aisha, can you believe it's happening? Do you feel okay? Try to stay calm. If that's the first contraction we could be here for a while, right?'

He had verbal diarrhoea.

'*Me* stay calm? I am calm! Anyway, you're meant to be the calm one!'

I got dressed into my new pyjamas – bought from & Other Stories especially for this moment. I'm not sure why I bought something new, and now I had them on, they felt ridiculous and not nearly as comfortable as my old clothes. The buttons barely did up, and it wasn't easy to move around, so I waddled back to the wardrobe, took them off and tried to locate my cosy, very old, oversized grey pair. They weren't there. I yelled for Jason again. Thankfully he found them drying on the airer that currently resided in the nursery, which had been doubling as a launderette for a while. I don't know what I'd have done if he hadn't. All of a sudden, it felt essential to get the smallest things right. Everything needed to be perfect and all I wanted around me right now were home comforts.

'Slippers!' I commanded. 'Where are my slippers? Oh shit, another contraction's coming and it's stronger!'

Once the second contraction had passed, I felt a pang for Mum, wishing she was here. I longed to hear her walk up the hallway, to see her enter my bedroom and put her arms tightly around me, drawing me into her chest as she told me it was going to be okay. She'd been through labour too; she would understand this pain. Did she go into labour early with me? Had she been frightened? Surely it was impossible not to be. I wondered about her caesarean again, and whether it was an emergency C-section; and whether this was why she'd stopped at one child. Would the same thing happen to me? I could hear her voice in my head – always so comforting and soothing, telling me that everything would be okay. For a moment I could almost feel her touch on my skin. I could smell her. Feel her breath and the brush of her hair on my cheek as she embraced me. I felt tears begin to well. But I wouldn't let them get far; there was too much to think about – like what was Jason doing right now? I looked at the bed and noticed he hadn't even gathered up my pillows or duvet ready to take to hospital. I thought he was on top of this?

As if he could hear my thoughts, he appeared at the doorway. Seeing my red eyes, he wrapped his arms around my shoulders and drew me into his chest to comfort me.

'Your mum would be so proud of you right now,' he whispered.

It turned out to be a long evening. I spent a lot of it pacing around the flat, or trying to watch some episodes of *Killing Eve* which wasn't exactly restful – not that it mattered, given I couldn't concentrate on anything anyway. Unlike Jason, who was gripped.

The next contraction came a few hours after the first, and then both of us forgot to check the time of the next couple, but they were certainly not frequent. The pain, though; it was so raw. Could I be further along than the timings led us to believe? I even put my phone onto the stopwatch setting alongside his, in case his was wrong. Was it really going to get worse than this? I couldn't bear it.

Jason was leafing through my Baby Group notes.

'It says you shouldn't go to hospital until the contractions are at least five minutes apart, or you will risk being sent home again,' he read out authoritatively. 'I'm afraid we've got a way to go yet, baby.' He gazed up at me. 'Fancy a game of Uno?'

'Uno?' I looked at him as though he were insane. 'Do I look like I want to play Uno?'

'Okay, well what about the playlist? We could go over the playlist?' He reached for his iPhone, taking it off the stopwatch setting. He was obviously trying hard to distract me from the fear of another contraction.

'Don't worry about the playlist!' I shrieked. The last thing I wanted to listen to was Salt'n'Pepa's 'Push It'. We had compiled it together over two months ago, when the birth felt like a distant diary date, a fun event, even, and we mistakenly thought Salt'n'Pepa might lighten the mood. It didn't seem so entertaining right now. All I wanted was a dark room and some pain relief.

The next few hours passed in a slow haze filled with toast and mugs of herbal tea. Jason gathered the last bits for my hospital bag and I spent much of the time standing by the window, leaning into the ledge and shifting the weight between my feet, as Maggie had suggested might help. After a few stretches, I gazed up and across at the backs of the houses on the street behind ours, noticing, as time passed, how lights were gradually being extinguished downstairs as the occupants took themselves upstairs to bed. I wondered how many women all around the globe, in different continents and situations, of different colours, religions and levels of wealth, were on the verge of this life-changing moment too. Whatever our background or circumstance, we were all together now, and we had to dig deep. I thought of Susie and wondered if she was still in labour. Everything had gone a little quiet on the WhatsApp thread. We hadn't heard any more about Susie after the 'fucking painful' message. Helen had responded:

Helen: Oh wow, good luck! But do you think you can spare any gory details until after we've all given birth? I'm getting twinges just thinking about it.
Hope it goes well! Xx

She had a good point. I was trying not to imagine what Lin had decided not to share. Helen was right; perhaps it was best to keep quiet until there was happy news to announce or a joyful birth story to describe. I wondered whose would be the first. A little bubble of excitement allowed itself to ripple through my veins; not long now until we would be meeting the bean. I wondered what it looked like – was it a boy or a girl? I was still leaning towards a girl prediction. With hair or without? All tiny, red and scrunched up inside of me. I stroked my belly and another contraction began to take hold. I pumped out hot breath and looked up to the heavens and prayed for our precious baby to arrive safely, before yelling for Jason to, 'Time it this time, for God's sake! They are definitely getting closer!'

After an aborted attempt to go to bed, by 3 a.m. the contractions were coming thick and fast – some every ten minutes – and I couldn't wait any longer. Jason helped me do up his largest hoodie over my pyjama top and we drove to the hospital, with me still in my slippers. It was agonizing sitting in the car and I adopted a position where I was practically kneeling in the footwell. I really hoped that we wouldn't be turned away – or pulled over by the police.

I spotted Lin waiting outside the hospital doors as we arrived. She was on the phone.

'Should we say anything?' Jason asked as we approached.

'No, we bloody shouldn't!' I yelled. The last thing I wanted was to bump into someone I knew when I was about to enter the transitional stage of labour. But she'd already seen us.

She was scrolling through her phone and whispered loudly:

'Hi guys, we have Charlie, our beautiful baby boy! I'm just making arrangements for the placenta tablets. You're up next then – baby's coming early. Good luck!' She looked at me and winced.

'All okay with Susie?' Jason asked, shifting the two pillows stuffed under his arm and setting down the wheelie case momentarily. I was annoyed he hadn't remembered to bring my duvet and the third emergency pillow, yet we seemed to have enough luggage to move in here for a week; something I hoped we weren't about to do.

'She's doing brilliantly, just, um, a long labour,' Lin sideways glanced at me and winced again. Noticing the fear in my eyes, she smiled sympathetically, but I had already clocked how exhausted she looked. To me, she looked like she hadn't slept for a couple of days and was in grave need of a strong drink.

I grimaced; another contraction. It was getting more intense by the second. I gritted my teeth through the pain. Now wasn't the time for small talk.

'Now, Jason. Let's go!' I commanded.

Jason turned pale and stuttered over his words. 'Well, congratulations – send Susie our best,' he muttered, before the doors swung open and we entered College Square Hospital.

Thankfully he remembered the way to the labour ward. I was so doubled up I was barely aware of our surroundings but at last I found myself by a bed. A curtain was swiftly pulled around us and I finally had a chance to bend over the side of something and concentrate on my breathing again – it was the only position in which I felt vaguely comfortable. I clutched my pillows tightly, breathing in the familiar smell of home to mask the clinical scent of antiseptic and starched sheets beneath it. I tried to focus on getting into some kind of rhythm with my breathing while I braced myself for the next contraction and the midwife went to get the gas. Another nurse came to check how things were coming on and, after managing to manoeuvre myself onto the bed, I felt as though she had crushed my soul when she told me I was only two centimetres dilated and we had 'jumped the gun rather' by coming in. I nearly throttled her. Luckily, they had a spare bed so she wouldn't send us back home tonight.

'Am I meant to thank her?' I scowled at Jason the second she disappeared behind the curtain.

'Well at least we can stay here,' he replied timidly.

'Whose fucking side are you on?' I retorted, knowing that the swear word was unnecessary, but it came out just as another contraction hit me like a landslide. 'You. Have. No. Idea. How. Painful. This. Is.'

The contractions continued, ever more frequent and when they checked again, I had reached seven centimetres. At first I thought they were having a wicked laugh at my expense when I was asked to get into a wheelchair. But no, they actually expected me to somehow get into one and sit still. I cautiously lowered myself into the chair the moment one contraction ended and was hurriedly pushed down corridors, skidding around corners, to one of the labour suites. Jason ran behind with all my belongings while I screamed at him: 'The pillows, don't forget ALL of the pillows! And the speakers!' If there was a time for 'Push It' to be played, it was now. It suddenly seemed like a good idea after all. An absolutely brilliant idea. I hoped he hadn't deleted it from the playlist. The gas had taken effect.

We reached the labour suite in the nick of time – the chances of an epidural or a birthing pool were blown. A monitor was put around my belly.

And then came the terrifying moment.

An alarm sounded loudly, a light flashed above the door and suddenly half a dozen doctors and nurses were around me, doing things with instruments and putting things I didn't understand on my bump. Jason was pushed to the back behind them. I grimaced loudly in the grip of shooting pains from within. A syringe was put into my arm, without any discussion. Sweat was pouring down my cheeks. I noticed Jason's ashen, shell-shocked face peering through, trying to make sense of what was going on.

And then it all seemed to go quiet.

CHAPTER TWENTY

Aisha

Suddenly the monitor beside me bleeped rhythmically and relief spread across the faces of the medical staff. A doctor called for everyone bar one nurse to clear the room and Jason appeared by my side, stroking my head. 'What happened?' he asked the nurse.

'Baby's heart rate slowed right down,' she said, not taking her eyes off the monitor, 'but it's all fine now, back up and beating as it should.'

I swallowed hard. That sounded serious. The pain of that last contraction had been unbearable. Did I do something wrong?

The nurse moved around to my other side now. 'Right Aisha, you're ready to push. On the next contraction okay, let's do this so you can meet your baby!'

It all happened so quickly. Just three strong pushes and then the sound of crying – high-pitched, weak, but a cry nonetheless – burst into the room. Sweat was dripping down my forehead and I gave a huge sigh of relief. Our baby was here – the bean was safe. Jason cut the cord.

'Well done, dear,' a kindly voice said, and I wasn't sure whether the comment was directed at him or me. 'Would you like to tell her the sex?'

A moment later, Jason's head was close to mine, his top was off and he was holding a baby against his chest. His hands were trembling and tears ran down his cheeks. It was a slightly blue, blood-stained baby with white bits all over it, but it came from my body and it was amazing.

'It's a girl! You were right. We got our girl!' he choked, as the tears fell thick and fast, setting me off too. A nurse came and helped him lay her across my chest. She was warm and slippery. And so tiny. I struggled to look down and take her all in. My hands were trembling too now. She had the sweetest little profile and dark hair, wet like a duckling. Her arms were held up, her hands almost clasped together in front of her face. I gently teased my index finger into her hand and her miniature fingers curled around mine. She was a miracle! I was overwhelmed with love and pride.

'She's beautiful,' I whispered, barely able to get the words out. My hands were shaking as I wrapped them around her tiny body. 'She's our Joni.' The name had been on our 'favourites' list for a while, a version of Joanne, which was the name of my late mum. It also meant God is gracious. And someone up there had been more than kind in granting us this bundle of perfection.

Jason wrapped his arms around us both. 'I'm so proud of you, Aisha,' he choked, kissing my forehead. 'You are incredible. And hello little bean,' he whispered, tears rolling down his cheeks. 'Or rather, Joni. I'm going to be the best father I can be. I love you both so much.'

Soon after, back on the ward, Joni had her first taste of colostrum; she latched on naturally and with ease. Even the midwife was impressed. I marvelled at how here she was, not even an hour old and already she was teaching me how to be a mother. I gazed at the side of her head as she suckled. I had so much to learn from her.

When I looked up, Jason was holding his phone, quietly videoing this tender moment.

'How do you feel, my beautiful wife and baby mama?' he asked, still recording.

'I feel so happy,' I said looking into the camera. 'And lucky. How do you feel, to be a daddy?'

He paused for a moment. 'I feel like the luckiest man on this planet.' And his eyes welled with tears again.

CHAPTER TWENTY-ONE

Lucy

Monday 24ᵗʰ May

The C-section appointment was at 8 a.m., which meant I wanted to leave the house by 7.a.m. – I couldn't bear the stress of being late. But Oscar was convinced it would only take thirty minutes maximum to drive from Clapham to College Square Hospital.

'Any earlier, and you'll have too much time to pace around and get nervous,' he said, and he did have a point. By 7.15 I was ready, so I tried to calm myself with a cup of camomile tea on the sofa as I read through some WhatsApp messages of luck from everyone in The Baby Group. Everyone except Helen.

Although he was the CEO of one of London's largest PR companies, Oscar was possibly the least organized person I knew. The result of having a PA for most of your working life. Plus a wife or a girlfriend and a teenage daughter. There was always someone – generally a female – to take care of things for him: his washing, the food in his fridge, his social life and his work diary. But when it came to taking care of me on the morning of the C-section, his disorganization surpassed itself. Although highly attentive to me when he was on the prowl for a blow job, or a home-cooked dinner, Oscar was not a practical guy.

Thankfully, where he struggled, I excelled. I guess that was one of the things that made us a good match. I had fastidiously packed my hospital bag two months ago, just in case the baby tried to catch me out. I had heard that they could come earlier if you were an 'older' mother. All I needed to do was collect a few of my toiletries together and I was ready.

But Oscar was still faffing about getting dressed at 7.20, and my blood pressure was beginning to rise.

Neither of us could have envisaged the broken-down lorry causing huge tailbacks on Kennington Road, nor could we have foreseen that a burst water main would prevent any way around it. The traffic chaos meant we didn't even pull into the car park at the hospital until nearly half past eight. I had called ahead to warn them we were running late, only to be told that we had missed our slot and would now have to be seen at the end of the surgeon's session, at around midday. We discussed turning back, but who knew what other disasters might befall us, so we ploughed on. Maggie hadn't covered how to handle stress like this – the stress of almost missing your own baby's birth.

I'd already decided that I didn't want Oscar beside me in theatre, for the birth itself. Even though he had come back into my life and we'd agreed to raise the child together, I felt I needed to do this on my own. I was concerned that his hand stroking mine as the operation took place – leading everyone in the room to wrongly assume he was the father – might be more of a distraction than a comfort to me. I'd made so many decisions on my own up until this point, I wanted to see it through by myself. At least Oscar had made that decision easier for me by making us late on this momentous day.

Yet I felt a deep unease. It was a strange feeling, to be bringing my baby into the world without knowing his paternity. I felt nervous and vulnerable.

When the time came to go into surgery, Oscar kissed me tenderly. 'You're going to be brilliant,' he whispered. 'I'll be here when you come out.' I breathed deeply, obeying the instructions to put my hair into the unsexy blue hairnet, pull up the compression socks and change into a scratchy medical gown.

It was time to meet my son.

As it turned out, about halfway through the caesarean, when I was squeezing the female anaesthetist's hand so hard her eyeballs appeared to bulge, I realized that all I wanted was to have Oscar by my side.

'Get Oscar! Please get Oscar!' I yelled. 'I need Oscar here, right now!'

I knew I could do it on my own – I could do anything on my own – so it wasn't that, but I wanted Oscar to meet my baby with me. Moments later, there he was, scrubs on, hairnet covering his bald head, which at least gave me some amusement through the surrealism of it all. He took my hand tightly in his, and whispered words of encouragement, telling me how well I was doing and how proud he was. He didn't let go until my baby was born. And the second thing I heard after hearing my baby cry was Oscar telling me he loved me.

The baby was apparently 'back to back' so it took some digging and delving to safely pull him out. And he was a big lad – a bonny nine pounds of baby. When the surgeon freed him from the safety of my womb and he appeared above the surgical sheet which was separating my eyes from the blood bath beyond, I lost it. I burst into tears and proceeded to shake and sob uncontrollably until he had been checked over, given a clean bill of health, and lain across my chest.

His features were scrunched up so tightly they were hard to make out, but he was real, he was breathing, he seemed healthy and he was safe. I was his mummy. I felt so proud of myself. I looked down at his little face, his tiny hands and feet, drinking him in. I wondered whether he had any of his father's traits, whoever that might be. Looking into his blue eyes felt amazing, magical, life-affirming, as well as life-changing. Even despite the missing piece to the puzzle, it was all the things I dared to hope it would be.

Despite the back-to-back position, it had been a relatively smooth procedure, the surgeon told me afterwards, as my little boy and I enjoyed our first cuddles. The bond between us was already so strong. I was so glad Oscar was there too, to bottle the moment and keep telling me it was real. After all I had been through with the abortion all those years ago, and dreaming of this day for so many years, I desperately wanted to feel complete. If this was a film, we would have just reached the conclusion: our heroine *could* have done this on her own, but it was twice as nice doing it with her love by her side. Yet it wasn't a film, and it was possible to feel simultaneously happy and sad.

It was early evening now and Oscar had popped out to get me some snacks. Although tired, I couldn't sleep. The baby was lying next to me in a plastic cot, wearing his first White Company babygrow – white with little yellow ducks embroidered on it – and he was looking at me and gurgling. He was little more than six hours old but already seemed so alert. Old beyond his hours, somehow. I wondered what was going on in his mind, and what he could make out of my face.

I ached to pick him up, but the burning sensation in my abdomen reminded me this was far from possible right now. Pressing my buzzer for the duty nurse, and then the agonizing wait for someone to come every time I wanted to hold him, or shift a pillow behind my back, bring more pain relief, or help me take a sip of water from the bottle that always seemed to be just beyond my reach, was becoming almost as painful as the wound itself.

He was woozy with sleep, now, and it made my eyes feel heavy at last. He already suited his name – Albert, after a great-great-grandfather I never knew. I had always loved the name, ever since I was a child and gave the moniker to my favourite teddy bear. I still have the teddy; it was currently propped up at the end of the cot at home, waiting to meet its name twin. He was to be Albie for short. No middle name, because in my family boys often took their middle names from their fathers. He had a downy covering of light brown hair on his perfectly round head. I wondered who he looked like; I couldn't see myself in him yet. I thought about whether he bore any resemblance to his father. But he only really looked like a baby. Or perhaps Winston Churchill.

I sent a message and a photo of Albie to The Baby Group:

Hot off the press – my baby boy is here. Meet Albie, 9lbs of gorgeousness. Mum and baby doing well.

As I pressed send, a big fat tear rolled down my cheek.

A nurse came to take my blood pressure and change my catheter. Having a baby was undignified however you chose to give birth. I asked her how long it might be before I could go to the bathroom by myself.

'We'll try to encourage it tomorrow,' she informed, 'but don't even think about it right now.'

I felt anxious about ever being able to get out of this bed. The feeling was beginning to return to my legs, thank goodness. But at this moment I was a very long way from being self-sufficient and that was a scary state for a control freak like me.

Much as we tried, breastfeeding didn't come easily to either me or Albie. With every attempt, even those supervised by the ward's breastfeeding expert, or a kindly midwife in the small hours of that first night, he seemed to get more flustered. From the word go my nipples were agony. At one point he somehow managed to draw blood, and he didn't even have any teeth. I wasn't sure how this was possible. We both became agitated, had a little cry, and gave up. The nurses wondered if he had tongue-tie and he became very distressed when they took him off to check. I waited in bed, the sound of his screams ripping my insides apart as he disappeared down the corridor with strangers, albeit helpful, caring ones who only had the best intentions.

Tuesday 25th May

My parents visited the next morning, just when I had managed to give him a small amount of colostrum administered via a miniature plastic syringe, after having spent the best part of an hour extracting a few meagre drops from the less painful of my breasts. It was excruciating and I was in tears throughout.

After staying with me at the hospital as late as he could last night, Oscar had gone home to rest and shower; there seemed little point in us both getting minimal sleep. I told him not to rush back as it would be easier for my parents to come when he wasn't there because it was still a little awkward between us, due to the fact that they didn't seem to want to accept that Oscar wasn't the father of this baby. Explaining to my parents that I had undergone IVF using sperm donated by an anonymous male, and that Oscar had agreed to bring up the baby with me, as if it were his own, had been difficult for them to process. Could you imagine if I had told them the full version of events?

When I saw Mum and Dad enter the ward, I thought

I had just about got myself together. They brought packets of fudge, a mini bottle of prosecco and a couple of books, none of which was what I needed right now. How would I have the time or energy to read a book, when I couldn't even feed my own baby properly? What I needed was a hug, but my parents had never been those kind of people. They were copers, not compassionates. I also wasn't prepared for their appearance to bring back such visceral emotions from the past. While I could see joy in their faces as they met their longed-for grandson for the first time, I felt the moment was tinged with anguish for them – and for me. It brought back some raw memories for us all. As they stood by my bedside, tears welled up in my eyes again and I couldn't hold them back. I sobbed and sobbed, every gasp pulling roughly at my C-section wound, giving me even more pain, my eyes all puffy, my nose running. Mum eventually passed me a tissue and I managed to get myself together. Mercifully, Albie remained asleep in the bassinet beside me the whole time.

Mum laid a cold hand on my arm when I stopped and muttered: 'I'm sorry, it's been an emotional day.' But mostly she and my dad just stood there, not knowing what to do or say.

Wednesday 26th May

I was discharged from hospital a day later. Although I had originally imagined I would bring Albie home on my own, in a taxi, the reality of that soon proved impossible, and not only considering I was not meant to lift anything heavier than the baby for the next six weeks and there was barely anyone around to ask for help, but because I cherished Oscar being there. It all felt so much more daunting than I had expected.

'How on earth do proper single mums cope?' I pondered, as Oscar gathered up the last of my belongings, ready to escort us back to the 'family' home.

'They have good friends, or perhaps a *boyfriend*, to help them out,' he replied stoically.

I was so glad to have him with me; I just didn't quite know how to articulate it. It had been an intense few days. 'Thank you. So much,' I said.

He acknowledged this with a smile.

Emerging from the hospital building, although I could barely stand up straight, I felt like a butterfly coming out of the chrysalis: brand new, on the precipice of a brave new world, but also exactly the same old me.

I paused, unsure whether I would need to wear my jacket. The temperature in the hospital ward had been tropical. Oscar reassured me it was only a short stroll to the car.

The London air around us was refreshingly familiar, the sky heavy with rain, yet the temperature mild.

As we drove home, Albie fell asleep. He looked so small, so vulnerable, encased in an additional two layers of cushioning inside his padded car seat.

The thought that he was completely dependent on me was overwhelming. If I wanted to jump out of this car right now and go meet a friend for a drink, he might well perish. Not that I was in any way capable of jumping out of cars. But the responsibility weighing down on me was huge.

London whizzed past the window, Waterloo, Vauxhall, Kennington, we stopped at the lights by Stockwell Tube and my mind flashed back for a moment. Back to *that* night. In the distance, I could see the pub, the one he and I had spent hours in, talking. Flirting. I looked across at Albie and for a fleeting moment I thought I recognized his face in that of my precious new boy.

CHAPTER TWENTY-TWO

Aisha

Monday 7th June

The first few weeks after having the baby went by in a flurry of guests, broken sleep and health visitor appointments. Thankfully, breastfeeding was going well and, despite a brief lull, Joni had already put on a few pounds in just over three weeks. She seemed to be hungry all the time, and I enjoyed being able to satisfy her – for two hours at least, until the next feed. We heard over WhatsApp the news that Will and Christian had welcomed their baby, a boy called Leo on the 22nd May, Lucy had had Albie on 24th May. So everyone had given birth now except for Helen, bless her, who was still waddling around nine days overdue. The Baby Group WhatsApp thread was alive with discussion about breast-feeding, the colour of poo, and unfortunately for Susie and Lin – colic.

I bumped into Susie on Monday afternoon in Boots – she

was stocking up on gripe water and Infacol, and had a bottle of Calpol in her hand.

'So much for being an earth mother then,' she smiled, embarrassed I had witnessed her with a basketful of drugs. 'Turns out that oxytocin can't cure everything.'

'Don't be ridiculous. Anything to stop them suffering, right?'

'Right,' she said. 'It's so much harder than I imagined.' Her eyes were sunken and she looked tired.

'I know,' I reassured her, glancing down at Joni, secretly glad I seemed to have a baby who was fairly contented, compared to Charlie. But I wasn't stupid enough not to know that that could change at any moment. I had only just got my head around what had happened in the delivery suite when her heart rate dropped. Things could happen so quickly when they're so tiny.

'Leaky boobs,' I said, holding up the box of breast pads I'd just put in my basket. 'I'm getting through an industrial amount of these pads right now. The glamour.'

She cracked a smile.

'Are you in a rush or do you fancy a coffee?' I asked. I'd been planning to get a takeaway from Starbucks to drink on the way home – I was making the most of being able to consume caffeine again – and Susie looked like she needed some too. I thought she might appreciate the company.

She looked at her watch, then to baby Charlie, sleeping peacefully in his pram, and nodded gratefully. 'Ironic that he sleeps when I go out. Why can't he do it when I'm in bed too? It's a conspiracy,' she muttered. 'Let's do it, I've got a couple of hours before Lin will be home. It was her first day back at work today and she's missed him like crazy.'

We walked with our strollers to the nearest coffee shop, a cute French café on the edge of Clapham Common, and took the window seat, nursing steaming hot mugs of frothy coffee. Joni was asleep again, and Charlie had woken but was happily cradled in Susie's arms, staring at a black and white image of a butterfly on a fabric book she had managed to prop up next to him. They looked sweet together so I captured the moment on my phone and sent it to the rest of the Baby Group with the caption, 'Susie and I bumped into each other in town – aren't these two adorable'.

We treated ourselves to slices of carrot cake and soon the colour returned to her cheeks.

'It's funny,' she said, leaning towards me, conspiratorially, 'I thought that I was going to be the one fixated on homeopathy and doing things nature's way, but I've been the opposite. I've got a secret stash of pain relief at home, and I had a can of Coke this morning – my first in two decades. I had a McDonald's yesterday and I've been bingeing on Mini Eggs for energy. I'm too ashamed to tell Lin.'

I shrugged. 'Nothing wrong with the odd can of Coke or the Golden Arches, and who doesn't need Mini Eggs in their life? Don't beat yourself up. How are you finding the placenta capsules by the way?'

'Lin's been the one necking most of them,' she chuckled. 'I can't bring myself to tell her that the thought of it makes me want to vomit.'

'Is she buzzing around like a toddler full of sugar?' I smirked.

'To be honest with you, I'm so riddled with tiredness, absolutely everyone looks like a Duracell Bunny compared to me,' she replied.

'Anyway, do you want to hear a funny story?' I leant in. 'I was feeling so pasty last week, I fake-tanned myself while Joni was snoozing.'

'Fake tan?' she said. 'You're lucky to have gorgeous olive skin, you don't need it.'

I pushed up my sleeve. 'Being half Indian helps, but this is pale for me. Besides, I needed a boost.' I looked across at Joni, her little face poking out from under the white bonnet given to us by Jason's parents, and felt glad that she couldn't know I was talking about her. 'Anyway, Joni ended up waking and I gave her a cuddle forgetting the tan was still wet on my skin. I didn't notice, but a couple of hours later, there was a huge brown splodge on her cheek. When Jason got home, he asked if it was a birth mark. I felt so guilty.'

Susie started to laugh. 'That's too funny.'

'Look, you can still see it.' I pointed to the area. 'It won't come off. And, typical, the health visitor was coming the next morning.'

'Did she notice?' Susie asked, her hand across her mouth to stop any crumbs of carrot cake from escaping as she giggled.

'Of course she did, so I had to come clean. She gave me a painful lecture about the types of cleansing products that are safe to use on newborn skin. I felt like I was in detention at school.'

'They can be so preachy, those health visitors. Mine always eyes me with suspicion, like I'm depressed or not coping as I should. Although sometimes I think she's onto something.' Her voice trailed off.

'Mine's just the same,' I reassured her. 'But you could try talking to her about how you're feeling, if you're worried. I'm sure she'll have some good advice. And I'm always here, that's what we all joined The Baby Group for isn't it? To help each other get through this?' I ate the last bit of carrot cake. 'As for me, I might go the whole hog and give Joni a summer shimmer for the next visit. Perhaps try some Sun In in her hair – that'll give my health visitor something to *really* worry about,' I said, and we both cracked up again.

Just then we were disturbed by a loud noise from Joni's nappy. Even the people at the next table turned to look.

'Oh great – poo-mageddon again!' I exclaimed. 'Off to the bathroom for me, I might be some time. I'm going in…' I grabbed the nappy bag.

'Don't,' Susie cried, holding onto her middle, 'I can't laugh because pee comes out!'

And we both roared with laughter, clutching our bellies and trying not to follow in Joni's footsteps by having a little 'accident' in a busy café.

As I walked home, I felt buoyed. Finally, this maternity-leave lark felt as though it was going to be fun. I was glad to have made some new friends in The Baby Group. We'd only known each other for a matter of weeks, but we had already shared so much. I hadn't even had a chance to tell Tara the full birth story yet – she was so busy herself with two toddlers – but I'd discussed everything with The Baby Group. Sometimes Susie and I would be WhatsApping each other at 2 a.m., offering comfort and support in the small hours when it felt like we were the only people in London who were awake. It was only Lucy who seemed to have withdrawn slightly from the group. I had messaged her once to ask how it was going, but she'd only sent a short reply that all was fine.

Susie had mentioned that Lucy was having a tough time breastfeeding, so later that night – it must have been about midnight because I had just finished giving Joni a dream feed – having noticed Lucy was online, I decided to message her separately again.

Me: Hi, are you up?

Lucy: Yes, just about. You ok?

Me: Yes, all good, just given Joni her dream feed. How's it going with you two?

Lucy: It's tough, to be honest. Feeding is hard. Whatever I do, he just cries and cries.

Me: I'm sorry. Have you tried a bottle?

Lucy: He won't take it.

Me: Is Oscar able to help?

Lucy: He's in the spare room. He's in a busy period at work so I'm trying not to disturb him.

Me: Two words – nipple guards. Meant to be good?

Lucy: Maybe. Anyway, I'm going to try to get some sleep.

Me: Sleep well. Maybe a coffee next week?

Lucy: I'll give you a shout in a couple of weeks. I don't want to bore you with my negativity.

I paused for a moment. Her tone seemed quite cold. Had I said something to upset her? We had been getting on so well. Meet up in *two weeks*? Two weeks was basically an eternity when you're on maternity leave. I switched off my phone and placed it on the bedside table next to me, then I turned the light out. I lay in the darkness, thinking. I hoped she was okay.

The following morning, I showed Jason the thread. He brushed it off.

'She was probably having a bad night. You said yourself that she's quite stuck up. She's high maintenance. Bit of jealousy too, perhaps,' he said.

'Jealous?' I asked.

'It wouldn't be hard to be jealous of my beautiful wife and her brilliant boobs,' he smiled. 'You have taken to motherhood so naturally, I'm proud of you.'

'But why would she brush me off like that when I was trying to help?'

'Don't read too much into it. Besides you've got other friends – Tara, Susie… Just give Lucy a wide berth perhaps.'

'Okay,' I muttered, 'but you're right, it was probably just a bad night.'

CHAPTER TWENTY-THREE

Lucy

Tuesday 8ᵗʰ June

I read through last night's WhatsApp exchange with Aisha. I had been purposefully keeping my distance from The Baby Group. I couldn't face them right now. I had been thinking too much, worrying; afraid of what I might say if we did meet up. Now that Albie was actually here, it all felt very real. That, plus the fact that things seemed to be going so well for the others, especially Aisha, when things were going far from smoothly for me. And Albie was struggling so much in the feeding department, it broke my heart that I couldn't satisfy him easily. Although I was happy to have him here, it didn't stop me feeling like a failure at the same time.

Albie had eventually taken the bottle last night, thank God – a reprieve from his tiny mouth gnawing at my battered nipples and listening to his high-pitched hungry screams. At one point I had to leave him lying on my bed, his arms and legs waving in the air, like an overturned beetle. I just needed a moment to take a few deep breaths; to walk downstairs, grab a glass of water and a digestive biscuit and compose myself before going back into battle.

Oscar had moved into the spare room on the floor below our bedroom for the week because he was finding it hard to cope at work, thanks to the broken nights. And he wasn't the one up every two hours. Reality had set in, and I worried whether Oscar's promises about being ready for all this were going to be broken. Nobody – not even Maggie – said it would be this hard.

I had wanted a baby so badly for years, but in my dreams it was easy, natural. People without degrees, helpful partners or management roles had babies and they all seemed to cope, so why couldn't I? I knew now that I had imagined motherhood through rose-tinted glasses. I felt anxious a lot of the time and wondered if Albie and I were bonding well enough; if it was normal to feel this sad sometimes. I mean, I knew I loved him, I loved him more than anything in the world, but sometimes I wanted it to be just me again; to go out and meet a friend for dinner; to go to the corner shop and get a newspaper without careful planning and my heart beating so fast. I was okay when I only had myself to look after. A lump came to my throat.

Oscar told me it would get easier. 'This will soon be a distant memory'. He even made me laugh one day when he got home from work early and found me in tears, yellow poo splattered on the wall beside us, like thick emulsion paint. Two soiled babygrows in a heap on top of the nappy bin and a peppering of poo over my top.

'Someone had curry for lunch then?' he remarked, smiling. 'I did warn you to go easy on the spice.'

His comment made me laugh so hard, it turned into hysterics and soon I had tears rolling down my cheeks, until I wasn't sure if I was laughing or crying any more because I was such a hot, out-of-control mess.

'I can't keep up with the washing!' Was all I was able to mutter when I managed to compose myself.

'I'll take over, you clean yourself up and take some time out,' he commanded, taking off his smart blazer, which looked so out of place in this environment, and rolling up his sleeves. Albie cooed innocently and waved his legs in the air, happy for the attention.

'No, baby boy, I'm not a fan of the korma either,' I heard Oscar coo back as I made my way to the bedroom to change.

When he had bathed and dressed the baby, they both came and joined me in the living room. I inhaled the top of Albie's head – he smelt divine again.

'I'm sorry,' I whispered. 'It's just *so* hard sometimes.'

'I know, my darling, it *is* hard, no one dares tell you that before you have them. But exploding poo is all part of the joyous parenting experience,' he smiled. 'Been there, got the soiled T-shirt.' The creases beside his eyes appeared; they comforted me. Oscar's lovely, kind and capable face. 'Don't put pressure on yourself to be perfect,' he continued. 'Perfection is futile right now.'

Gradually, as Albie had started putting on weight, I didn't feel so guilty every time I gave up on my breast and forced him to take the bottle. And I didn't freak out so much when we resigned ourselves to having a day at home, covered in poo. I clung onto Oscar's notion that this was normal; that 'this too shall pass'.

That evening, when I was sat with Albie snoozing on me, absent-mindedly scrolling around Facebook on my mobile and feeling pangs of jealousy as I saw photos of Katie on holiday in Mykonos with a group of girlfriends, the caption 'Mums on the loose!' beneath it, my phone lit up with a message. Although I had previously deleted the number, I knew who it was immediately.

'We need to talk. This has gone on too long. Call me. Please.'

CHAPTER TWENTY-FOUR

Aisha

Thursday 24th June

Thursday 24th June

Now that all the babies had safely arrived – finally a whole two weeks late, but just missing being induced, a bonny baby girl arrived by home birth for Helen and Ian – I got on the Baby Group WhatsApp thread and suggested a trip to the pub. I thought that wetting the babies' heads and chatting about our feelings with the other new parents could be fun. I was genuinely pleased when there was uptake, especially from Lucy.

Me: How about seven on Wednesday at The Crown?

Will: Count us in!

Lucy: Great. I'll see if Oscar can come too. Might help with the baby wrangling. x

Me: Yes, why not. Although I'm considering leaving Jason at home with Joni so I can escape for a couple of hours. Literally dying for wine and girlie chats!

Will: Ahem!

Me: Sorry boy chats too :-)

Susie: That's a bloody great idea, I'm going to try to leave Charlie with Lin. Had a horrific night last night. I can barely see straight and I really need WINE!

Helen: You make me laugh. See you there, I'll bring Ian to carry my wine glass, while Maddie (hopefully) sleeps soundly. It will be our first social outing! Hope you're all ok. xxx

Susie: Lin wants to come too, so that means the Devil Colic Child will be there too. See you Weds. Goodnight to all!

Wednesday 30th June

I was looking forward to seeing Lucy and meeting Albie, but I wondered how she was going to be. Had she even realized she had been a little off? Or perhaps I had said too much when we spoke the last few times.

When we got to the pub, Lucy did seem hesitant about coming over to me. I was stood with Susie and Lin; we had taken possession of one table and were hovering beside another where a couple were just finishing their drinks, so we could commandeer it and push them together.

'What's your tipple this evening then?' asked Lin.

I barely heard her, I was still thinking about Lucy and whether it was going to be awkward.

'Aisha?' she said again, more loudly. 'What are you drinking?'

'Oh sorry, miles away. I'll probably have red wine – shall we all take it in turns to get a round?'

After chatting to Helen and Ian first, then Will and Christian, Lucy finally greeted me with a stiff hug, and said she was sorry for 'being short over text the other night'. It was evidently on her mind too. Jason was right, she could be a bit stuck up – it was likely that she had never had to struggle with anything before in her life, so a baby's unpredictability was probably testing. I couldn't blame her for that because she seemed to be having an especially hard time feeding Albie, but I still felt a little cautious around her, now that I'd seen her more prickly side. Lucy had come without Oscar or Albie, and seemed relieved that I was also alone, quipping: 'I'm glad I'm not the only mum-on-the-run this evening!'

'Oh, Jason decided to come in the end, he's following a few minutes behind with Joni – we forgot the nappy bag so he had to go back. Rookie error!' I joked, hoping to make her feel better if she thought that we were all making mistakes and learning on the go.

When he arrived, Jason headed straight to the bar to join Ian and Will. I followed him to retrieve the pram and manoeuvred it between chairs and tables to join our make-shift 'buggy park' in a corner of the pub. For a moment I had a pang to go out somewhere on my own too, unencumbered by the amount of stuff – and by that I meant the physical paraphernalia, as well as the emotional baggage – that came with a baby. Sometimes I missed our past life. It used to be so easy to pop out to this very pub with girlfriends or for a cosy after-work dinner with Jason. I had taken such things for granted for the last twenty-odd years of my life. It wouldn't be that easy again, not for a long time. I looked across at Joni and felt guilty for even thinking this, my heart so full of love for her. It was okay, I told myself, I could wait.

As I parked up, Christian and Lin were pushing together the two small tables to make one we could all sit around. Susie was gathering some extra chairs.

'Where's Leo this evening?' I asked Christian.

'Babysitter!' he replied. 'The perk of not being able to breastfeed.'

'Lucky you,' muttered Lucy.

Susie pulled out a chair for me to sit next to her and caught my eye. 'How's the, um, "birth mark" doing?' she asked, indicating the inverted commas with her fingers before gesturing to the pram where Joni was lying, her eyes open and fixated on the ceiling lights.

'Totally gone, thankfully,' I smiled. 'Naughty mummy.'

'Phew,' Susie breathed and turned to ask Lin to get two bottles of red wine from the bar, rather than one. 'Don't know about you, but I'm in the mood this evening.'

'Birth mark?' asked Lucy, startling me. I hadn't realized she had heard. She pulled out the chair on the other side of me and sat down.

'It's nothing,' I replied. 'Just an accident I had with some fake tan.' It felt like something had shifted between Lucy and me and I didn't feel like sharing the moment with her. 'Sorry I won't get to meet Albie this evening,' I said. 'He looked so cute in the photo you sent.'

'No, he's at home with Oscar. We thought that getting me and my boobs out of the house might help him to feed from the bottle more readily this evening – out of sight, out of mind? Oscar's going to try anyway.' She paused. 'He's been amazing, all things considered.'

'He's still not taking the bottle easily?' I asked. She shook her head in response.

'I'm sorry.'

If I wasn't mistaken, her eyes were filling with tears and they looked red. She took a large sip from the glass of red wine in her hand. She didn't seem her usual bubbly self.

'I just need to go to the bathroom, excuse me a minute.' She knocked back another gulp of wine and edged out of her seat.

Lin returned from the bar and sat down opposite me.

'So how are you finding motherhood, Lin?' I asked, wondering if I should go after Lucy. I'd give it a few minutes then if she didn't come out I'd go and see if she was okay.

'I'm loving it,' she smiled, squeezing Susie's arm. 'I'm just so proud of them both. I mean, it's a rollercoaster all right,' she glanced sideways at Lucy, who was on her way to the Ladies'. 'Nothing can prepare you. The lack of sleep really gets to you, and his colic isn't showing any sign of improving – yesterday, the doctor said it could last until he starts solids – but, on balance, we definitely won't be putting Charlie up for adoption. Will we?' She nudged Susie with her elbow.

'No, definitely not!' Susie smiled.

'The only downer is that I've had to go back to work,' she said, turning to face Susie and smiling doe-eyed. 'I just want to be around them all day.'

'That's lovely to hear,' I cooed. It was nice to hear some positivity; it had felt as though we mainly used WhatsApp to discuss Colic problems so far.

'Has anyone even thought about work?' I asked, just as Helen plonked a bottle of white wine in a chiller in the middle of the table.

'Evening ladies and gents,' she announced, before glancing around at our drinks and noticing we were all nursing glasses of red wine. 'Oops, looks like this bottle is all for me then. Perk of formula feeding! Just going to quickly check on Maddie.'

And she popped over to her pink Bugaboo, peeked in and replaced the pink muslin canopy quickly and delicately, creating a cosy tent for the sleeping baby inside. She made an 'okay' sign with her hand and rejoined us, unscrewing the top from the wine bottle and charging her glass.

'It feels so weird to be out!' she exclaimed. 'But Ian is currently boring Jason with the football results so some things don't change,' she rolled her eyes.

Lucy had come back from the toilet and took her seat next to me again.

'That's them gone for hours then,' I said, reaching for my glass and taking another small sip.

'He used to play at Bristol,' Lucy muttered.

'Yeah, that's right,' I said, turning towards her, 'Jason, you mean?'

'Um, yeah,' she said, seeming a little flustered. 'There was a photo, in your flat – the team.' She was right, there was a framed photo at home of Jason with the Bristol Uni football team, just after they won the universities league. He had never allowed me to take it down. She must have noticed it at the breastfeeding class; I was amazed she remembered.

'Where did you go to uni?' I asked, glossing over the fact that she had been stalking our photos instead of concentrating on the tutor – maybe if she had paid attention, she wouldn't be in such a state with feeding now. I berated myself for bitching, even if it was inside my head.

She looked at me like I had asked her a very personal question.

'London,' she replied, fixing me with an intense gaze, one that made me refrain from asking any more. 'I'm just popping out to give Oscar a call – to check on Albie.' She stood up.

We stayed in the pub for a couple of hours, ordering chips to wash down the wine, and for a blissful time it felt liberating to be out of the house, socializing, like normal people.

I was a little annoyed that Jason didn't make any effort to socialize with the wider group – he stayed up at the bar with Ian for nearly the whole time. Once I glanced over and caught him looking at Lucy, but I guessed he was only watching out for me, after the text weirdness the other night. Later, I saw his eyes follow Helen to the Ladies', as she went to change Maddie. In her little denim skirt and pale pink sweater, you'd never have known she pushed a baby out just two weeks ago. She looked like a Barbie. I hated myself for feeling a twang of jealousy, insecure about my own looks post-pregnancy.

It was 9.30 when I noticed Joni stirring and decided it was time for us to leave; I didn't particularly fancy breastfeeding her in the pub, which was now getting louder as people enjoyed a mid-week night out. Jason was nursing a new full pint at the bar.

'You stay,' I insisted, thinking that I shouldn't be too harsh, at least he was getting on well with the dads. Will and Christian had joined the guys and they were huddled together laughing about something.

Soon after I had finished saying my goodbyes to the women, Lucy reached for her coat too.

'I'd better get going as well,' she said, waving to the others. 'Duty calls – looks like Albie needs me.'

As we prepared to go our separate ways outside the pub, Lucy touched my arm. 'How about that coffee,' she said, more as a statement than a question. 'This Friday any good?'

'Sure,' I smiled. Maybe I had judged her too harshly. At the end of the day we were all coping in our different ways.

CHAPTER TWENTY-FIVE

Lucy

Oscar had called four more times while I was in the pub. After an initial panic about where to find things, I thought he would manage on his own. Apparently not. I had to put my phone on silent, not wanting to cause a scene in front of the others, and besides, Albie would probably be suckling away peacefully any minute if he persevered. Things could change so quickly with a baby – Oscar needed to keep going with the bottle. But then he sent a text:

ANSWER YOUR DAMN PHONE!

Swiftly followed by:

He won't take the bottle and I've tried three different teats. It's been an hour. He's in a state. Shall we come find you in the pub or will you come back?

Bloody hell. This is what I went through every day. Couldn't he just let me have a few hours' peace? I messaged him back:

Okay, I hear you, I'll head back now.

I saw Aisha was getting ready to go home too so I told her of my plan to leave and took the opportunity to ask her about going for a coffee.

As she stood up, I noticed how slim Aisha's tummy seemed to be, just weeks after giving birth. How did she manage that? I was still finding it difficult to do up the pregnancy jeans I'd been wearing in my third trimester. Helen looked amazing this evening too, as though her size six body had snapped back overnight. I felt a twinge of jealousy. My C-section scar was still sore and my blubbery stomach felt as though it would never be flat again.

Joni was awake in the pram beside her. She had slept quietly for the whole evening thus far; she was so well behaved. I was glad I sat next to Aisha this evening but I couldn't help wondering if I had messed things up; she seemed a bit uneasy around me.

When we were outside the pub, Aisha said: 'She can get fractious at this time of the evening, especially when she's tired and hungry. I'll walk with you a little bit, if you like, Joni will probably drop off.'

'It's okay, it sounds like Albie needs me. I'll run ahead.' Her home was in the opposite direction anyway.

'I hope he gets back on the bottle okay,' she said sympathetically.

Once I was alone in the street, I had a chance to send the text. It was time.

CHAPTER TWENTY-SIX

Lucy

Oscar phoned again as I neared our street.

'What's taking you so long?' he bellowed, before I could speak.

'I'm coming as fast as I can!'

'Hurry,' he replied. I could hear Albie screaming blue murder in the background.

'Okay!' I shouted over the din, 'but give me a break – this is the first time I've been on my own for more than an hour and a half in four fucking weeks!' As I hung up, I shocked myself at how angry I sounded. All the secrets and lies of the last few months were taking their toll.

Albie was in a terrible state, I could hear his cries from down the street. When I got home, Oscar was pacing around the room, trying to contain the purple-faced baby in a badly made swaddle. An open bottle of red wine was on the table.

'I was calling non-stop. None of the teats worked. He wants *you*,' he said sternly, handing him over. 'I'm not sure if I can do this all over again.' His words stung and I almost told him the thing I had been keeping from him for over nine months. But I stopped myself, knowing I would instantly regret it.

'I'm sorry,' I said, taking Albie into my arms and feeling his warm little head settle into the nook of my neck. The light covering of downy hair on his crown was damp, his face was red and scrunched up; he'd got himself into such a state. He stopped crying for a moment at least. 'I honestly thought he'd take the bottle if there was no other option. I thought perseverance might help.'

Oscar shook his head and avoided eye contact. 'He's only tiny, Lucy,' he sighed. 'He needs his mama.'

I felt like a bad mum.

'I'm doing my best,' I said. 'I feel shit enough as it is.'

'It's my turn to go to the pub now,' he declared.

We stared at each other in silence. His words rolled around my head. *I'm not sure if I can do this again.*

I didn't think Oscar was being serious about going out, but soon realized he was, as he strode down the hallway to retrieve his coat and shoes. He shut the door without saying goodbye, clearly desperate to get away from the wailing baby. I wondered if he would come back. Maybe it was best if he didn't. I'd pushed him too far this evening. Perhaps it would be better if I just raised Albie on my own; perhaps I didn't deserve a good man like Oscar – maybe I didn't deserve to be a mother at all. Not after what I had done. My chest felt tight.

As the door closed I poured myself a glass of water in the kitchen and sat in my usual place on the sofa, pulled down my top and undid my bra strap, ready to smother my nipple in a thick coating of Lansinoh cream and brace myself for Albie's hard little tugging mouth. I was grateful that Oscar had left a half-drunk glass of red wine on the coffee table, and I soon polished it off and poured another.

I took a deep breath and readied myself for the feed and the searing, hot pain – which I was prepared to go through because it was worth it for the little bundle in my arms. I pulled the breastfeeding cushion into place on my lap, lay Albie down on top and tried to focus between gritted teeth, flinching with the shooting pain as he suckled.

When Albie had settled and appeared to be drinking smoothly, I stared ahead and went over the conversation in my mind, fear beating a drum inside me.

CHAPTER TWENTY-SEVEN

Aisha

It was past midnight when Jason got home. I was sitting in bed having just given Joni her dream feed and she was fast asleep in the 'Cocoonababy' beside me. I had started to flick through the Gina Ford book Tara had given me, but was too tired to take anything in. The routines seemed baffling.

'Hello, wife,' he said, sinking onto the bed beside me. He hadn't yet taken off his coat or shoes. His breath smelt of beer.

'Hello, hammered husband,' I said, noting a wild look in his eyes.

'Not hammered, just missing my beautiful wife,' he replied, running his hand down the side of my face and kicking his trainers off his feet. 'I love you so much, you know,' he said. 'You and Joni, you're my absolute world.'

I smiled. It was nice to hear he loved me, even though he was drunk.

'I'd be lost without you, I love you so much,' he continued, soppily. 'You're so beautiful.' He brushed a strand of hair away from my face and tucked it tenderly behind my ear. He looked at me, doe-eyed. 'My gorgeous, hot wife.'

I hadn't heard him speak like this for ages, and I certainly didn't feel particularly beautiful, let alone hot in my loose-fitting breastfeeding nightie. But it was quite sweet to be on the receiving end of such flattery. Jason had looked handsome in the pub this evening, as he bonded with the other guys. I was proud he was mine.

'You're *really* drunk,' I said. 'You'd have to be, to find this milking cow attractive.'

'Maybe a little tipsy… I'm sorry it's so late, but I enjoyed toasting our beautiful little bean's head,' he replied.

'It's not a bean any more,' I reminded him, gesturing to the cocoon and its softly snoring contents. 'That's Joni. Did you stay at the pub?'

'I went on to meet a couple of guys from work. They were at one of the bars on the high street, so I joined them for a bit.'

He wriggled out of his jacket and dropped it onto the floor.

'I love you so much,' he said, moving closer to my face. 'Do you love me?'

'Of course I love you,' I replied, slightly confused by his need for reassurance.

'Do you love me for all my faults?' he continued.

I looked at him, puzzled. 'Are you trying to tell me something?'

'Just that I love you, I love you so much,' he said again.

Perhaps he was trying to make light of the fact he was blatantly drunk – and horny.

'For all your faults,' I said.

Then he held my head in his hands and we began to kiss, gently at first and then with more urgency. I could smell cigarettes on his breath; he occasionally succumbed when he was drinking. But I was glad he had made an effort with the dads from The Baby Group, and I couldn't begrudge him a few extra pints this evening, he'd been so attentive to us all week.

Jason flung the duvet back and placed his hand over my nightdress, on the top of my thigh. I felt self-conscious and also nervous about what he was going to find under there, in a region I had successfully avoided thinking about, let alone touched, in any way other than a medical one, since giving birth. And it was still fairly early days to be having sex again. I was worried about how it would feel to have him inside me. I stiffened slightly.

Before I could decide whether this was a good idea, Jason was already pulling his jumper and T-shirt off over his head.

'Baby, just go slowly, okay,' I urged, holding onto his shoulders as he pulled me on top of him. If I'd known this was going to happen, I wouldn't have put my breast pads in. I pulled them out and tossed them onto the floor quickly, all the while trying not to think about which colour of Sainsbury's finest big granny knickers I was wearing under my nightie this evening. At least I had weaned myself off the gigantic sanitary pads by now. 'I think it will be all right, at least I hope—'

He silenced me by sticking his tongue into my mouth again. 'Oh Aish,' he moaned between kisses, 'I've missed you. I've missed you so much.'

'I've missed you too, baby,' I whispered self-consciously. I felt as though I had completely forgotten what to do during foreplay, let alone how to make love or talk dirty.

I glanced towards the cocoon. At least Joni was asleep – she shouldn't see this, it could scar her for life.

It didn't matter that I had regressed to a virgin because Jason was in the mood to show me what to do. His lips and hands were everywhere, as I prayed he wouldn't squeeze my breasts too hard because milk was certainly going to come out. My nipples tingled with delight – and a little engorgement. He took one into his mouth and sucked.

'Mmmm,' he moaned. 'Your tits are amazing.'

'Just lightly.' I took his hand in mine and slowed the pace, guiding him away from my breast and across my stomach. Luckily I had only just fed her, so I didn't think there was too much danger of spurting milk as we got it on, but it felt pretty strange being groped in an area that was currently being used to keep our child alive. I struggled to put an image of a cow's udders out of my head.

He slipped his hands under my nightie and pulled my knickers down. Things down there felt better at least and my breathing slowed. He entered me gently, cautiously, unsure how this was going to feel for either of us. It must have taken all of his willpower to move so slowly. My back arched as I felt him inside me.

'Remember, don't come,' I whispered, thinking of Maggie's warning that a woman can be especially fertile in the weeks following childbirth – and 'Irish twins' was the last thing either of us needed right now, especially me.

'Don't worry,' he panted, 'I won't. God I want you so much. I fancy you so much.'

It only took a few gentle thrusts before he was withdrawing again, this time to come. It was all over within minutes – which, to be honest, was a relief. It was hard to feel properly invested in a lengthy shagging session when I knew Joni would be wanting another feed in about two hours, which meant only a small window for sleep even if I dropped off immediately.

'Aisha,' he said between rapid breaths, his eyes clamped shut, his arm wrapped around me. 'I love you and Joni so much. I do, you know. I really hope you believe me.' And then he promptly fell asleep.

Meanwhile I got out of bed, went to the bathroom for a quick inspection down below and hunted for my breast pads and a fresh crop top to keep everything in place overnight. As I lay there in the darkness, watching his chest rise and fall, and listening to Joni breathing steadily on the other side of me, it occurred to me that my body was doing an amazing job keeping everyone in this household going right now. And of course I believed Jason loved me and Joni – why would he doubt that?

CHAPTER TWENTY-EIGHT

Aisha

Friday 2nd July

I met Lucy in the same French café Susie and I had gone to a few weeks earlier. Luckily Joni was less of a fidget than Albie seemed to be; she had been content to snuggle into my chest for the best part of an hour, transfixed by the black and white pattern on the wallpaper behind me, as I'd one-handedly managed to scoff some scrambled egg and toast.

Albie had been unsettled, crying quite a lot and not taking the bottle well, and now he was back in his pram, grabbing for the string of toys stretched across the top just out of his reach. How frustrating it must be to be a baby. Lucy had disappeared to the counter to order another coffee. She could have called over a waitress, but she seemed agitated.

I half wanted to pick Albie up and give him a cuddle, but my hands were full with Joni as I gave her a quick feed. My hormones were out of control at the moment – if I looked at any baby for long enough, my eyes pooled. I was in tears watching a Pampers commercial the other morning, while Joni dozed in my lap. I kept looking from the screen to her and back again – marvelling at her precious vulnerability, and the fact she is so blooming cute. You just can't appreciate it before you have one of your own.

Lucy came back to the table, just as I was quietly finishing the feed. 'Meant to ask if you wanted one too?' she said loudly, putting a hand on my shoulder.

She took me by surprise, coming up behind me so quickly, and somehow I managed to spill the glass of orange juice I was holding in one hand – thankfully cold – down onto Joni.

I automatically held her up in front of me, as far away from my white T-shirt as I could safely reach without losing my grip of her – stupid colour to wear when you're a mother of a tiny infant. It had missed her face but gone all over her little pale-yellow onesie.

'Oh my God, I'm so sorry!' Lucy exclaimed, more loudly than was strictly necessary, as I drew a few glances from other tables. 'I didn't mean to make you jump.'

'It's fine, don't worry, I'll just grab a wipe.'

I jumped to my feet and dashed to retrieve my nappy satchel from the buggy, parked out of the way, on the other side of the café. Thank God I'd remembered a pack of wipes and a change of clothes for her today.

The nappy bag had somehow got its strap tangled with the frame of the buggy and I struggled to free it while holding Joni with one arm, conscious that if orange juice transferred onto this T-shirt, I was unlikely to ever get it off, and I didn't have a change of clothes for me too.

I yanked the strap again but failed to free the bag. This time I turned for help and noticed Lucy look up. She was the closest person to me and had two free hands, unlike most of the others.

'Take her for a second, would you?' I called, pleadingly, to Lucy from across the small café.

Lucy hesitated and for a moment I actually thought she was just going to leave me hanging, drawing unwanted attention from a number of nosy bystanders.

'Lucy,' I said again, 'help me out?'

'Of course, sure.' She finally came over and I handed Joni to her.

'Just don't get too close,' I warned.

She put her hands under Joni's tiny armpits. 'There's no babygrow stain I haven't seen in the last twenty-four hours, believe me.' She held her out at a safe arm's length.

Joni gurgled in response.

I untied the bag and, realizing a wipe wasn't going to do the job, took her off into the baby changing room.

When I returned, only Lucy and one other table were left in the café. Admittedly, it had taken a while to do a complete strip-down, change her nappy and re-dress.

'So sorry again,' she said when I finally sat down again.

'It was an accident,' I laughed awkwardly.

We fell into silence.

'Albie seems to be taking the bottle now, finally,' she said eventually, making us both relieved to have something to talk about.

'Oh great, I'm happy for you,' I said. 'What did you do? Did Oscar giving it to him help?'

'He just got there in the end,' she sighed. 'It's a relief. Oscar has been trying, but it's not been straightforward. Maybe Albie senses something is wrong…'

'Wrong?' I probed her this time.

'Well not wrong, exactly. I guess I'm just scared. I'm worried that Oscar's not ready to be a daddy again.' She paused, her head hung, avoiding eye contact. 'I'm not sure he and I can do this together.'

'I'm sorry, Lucy. It's hard enough without this extra worry. Maybe Oscar just needs more time to get used to being a father again?' I offered. 'I guess we have nine months of intense training, whereas the men's lives only properly change once the baby arrives. They have to catch up with us.' I peered across at the pram. 'Aw, look at him though; so handsome. He looks so much like him.'

Something I said seemed to stop Lucy in her tracks. After that, she didn't seem to want to talk any more.

'His lordship clearly isn't going to sleep, so I might see if the walk home sends him off. I'd better get going,' she said.

It felt as though Lucy was keeping secrets – teasing me with bits of information, the odd cry for help, but never giving away enough for us to have a proper conversation about how she was feeling. I suppose I'd only known her for a few weeks and perhaps she didn't find it easy to open up, yet I had a hunch there were layers upon layers to be pulled back. I wondered if Lucy had many close friends. She hadn't mentioned any – she had barely even spoken of her family, come to think of it.

Perhaps she needed some support right now. I resolved to give her the benefit of the doubt and make an effort. We might be new friends, but we had already shared so much. I decided to plan something nice for Lucy, mulling over the idea of organizing a small girlie surprise dinner for her, without babies, in the coming weeks. Perhaps some prosecco and company would help to cheer her up.

CHAPTER TWENTY-NINE

Lucy

Aisha's slouchy white T-shirt had been pulled down so she could feed Joni, revealing a hint of thin bra strap and bare shoulder, which somehow managed to look sexy as her baby suckled contentedly. I felt a desperate stab of inadequacy. She could be a model in an advert for breast-feeding that wouldn't look out of place in any fashion magazine. Even Joni was making the cutest little sighs. Aisha seemed to have everything. Everything I wanted. It made my insides ache.

There was one moment in the café when I was holding Joni – Aisha had thrust her into my arms unexpectedly – when I looked at the baby's face and, for a fleeting second, my mind flashed back. The memory began spinning around, faster and faster, until I almost felt dizzy. For a split second I was unsure what I might say or do next. I looked down at Joni, so pure and innocent, and imagined what would happen if I took her. I had an acute sensation that I actually wanted to cause Aisha some pain. Luckily for her, she quickly took Joni back and hurried off to the loos. The spell was broken. For now.

CHAPTER THIRTY

Aisha

Thursday 5ᵗʰ August

In no time at all I had been a mother for three months. Time seemed to pass in a regulated haze. Everything seemed to need measuring – from keeping track of how many hours' sleep I got last night, to how much expressed milk to freeze, to how many weeks old and how many pounds Joni had put on. The remembering of digits was endless – and a sure way to make a mother feel hopeless, when you couldn't always remember them. Most of the time it was hard enough to keep track of which boob I'd last fed her from.

But the last few weeks had been magical because Joni had started smiling properly. Not just the dozy, blissed-out, milk-drunk smiles of the early days, but proper, 'I know you – and I love you,' beams. Seeing her blue eyes open and sparkle, and then her whole face light up into a smile, revealing a little dimple on one cheek, when she woke up or saw me enter a room was all the reassurance I needed to know that I was doing a good enough job as her mummy.

It felt as though we were beginning to understand each other. I hadn't really got what Maggie was going on about in The Baby Group when she described the different cries a baby gave – one for hunger, one for tiredness and another when they were really irritated about something – because all baby cries had sounded the same to me before I had my own, but now I knew. Most of the time I could understand Joni and it made it easier to give her what she needed, when she wanted it. I also knew her favourite breast to feed from and the way she liked to be held. I knew how to rock her to sleep. And I learnt that she loved to play peek-a-boo on the changing mat after bath-time – she found it so amusing when I popped up from behind the towel, breaking into giggles so cute and infectious, I could feel rushes of oxytocin wash through me.

Part of the reason I was having such a blissful time with our baby was because things with Jason had also improved. It felt as if we had overcome the issues with him not being ready for all this and he was now fully engaged with Joni. Jason and I felt more in tune with each other than we had in months – it reminded me of the heady, loved-up days we had in Hong Kong. Whereas I used to sometimes dread him getting home from work because his mood-swings made me feel anxious, now I couldn't wait to hear his key turn in the lock. He would arrive sporting surprise bunches of tulips, or my favourite chocolates for 'no reason'; he'd sometimes send me a romantic message or cheesy poem on WhatsApp during the day and tell me how he couldn't wait to get home and kiss me all over. It was so lovely. I felt truly loved.

Although he was still putting in the extra hours where he could, I understood why. In fact it got me thinking differently about Jason's motivation for all the overtime and late nights he did at work during my pregnancy. He must have felt such a pressure to earn more money once he knew we were to become a family. He had told me that his request for a pay rise had been declined; maybe it had dented his pride more than I realized. It can't have helped when my dad kept sending us a few hundred pounds by bank transfer. I didn't have a big issue with it – it was Dad's version of a baby shower after all – but Jason had taken it personally; he saw any offer of help as a slight against his ability to provide for his family and it took me a while to convince him that we shouldn't just send the money back. But now I saw things differently, I understood that his strong need to provide for his family was as innate as my desire to carry our child.

Because I was awake so much at night – Joni was still asking for a feed every three hours on average – I'd taken to sleeping when she did in the early evening, knowing I'd be awake again at eleven-ish to give her a dream feed and then every few hours through the night. According to Tara, it was a good idea to start getting into some kind of routine about now. Jason had considerately started sleeping on the sofa in the living room or in the nursery to allow me to feed her without worrying about waking him up. Or he would use the opportunity to work late again. We both agreed that he might as well use this time to clock up some overtime, and that we could take turns with the night shifts over the weekends. It felt as though we were really sharing the load.

But one evening, when I began to fill him in on my day as I often did when he'd been on a long work shift, he appeared distracted.

'Joni loved sitting on my lap on the swing in the park today,' I told him.

'Sweet,' he said, not taking his eyes off the TV and shovelling some stir-fry into his mouth.

'And I successfully managed the routine – she took her naps like clockwork. I just hope this will eventually translate into sleeping for longer stretches at night,' I went on.

He didn't register what I said, making me feel like the world's greatest baby bore.

'And then she did some one-handed cartwheels all around the playground.'

Nothing.

'I was thinking, Jason, that I would like to sleep on the sofa tonight,' I continued, more loudly. This wasn't something I had said before, so it at least got his attention. 'Okay with you?' I added, although, from my tone, it was pretty clear I wasn't going to take no for an answer.

'Are you feeling okay?' He momentarily looked up from his dinner.

'I'm just tired,' I said. 'The nights of broken sleep are catching up with me.'

'Sure,' he shrugged, as if it were no biggie. 'Although I'll have to be up and out early tomorrow.'

I had read about the fourth trimester and, although

coming to the end of it, I knew my hormones might have had something to do with me feeling sensitive today. But Jason definitely wasn't engaging with me like normal and I wondered why.

That evening, when I made up my bed on the sofa in the living room – Jason having already gone to bed, in anticipation of getting some shut-eye before Joni's night feed – I noticed he had left his phone on the coffee table. Ordinarily I would have just moved it into the kitchen and put in on charge for him, but this evening something compelled me to take a look.

I scrolled through his WhatsApp messages. There were several work threads to do with applications and technical terms I couldn't understand. Plus a thread with Peter, in which Jason had been querying the overtime he was to be paid this month.

There were some chats with his mum and sister, mostly containing photos of Joni, and their cooing comments back. Jason's enthusiasm to pass on some of Joni's developments with them was encouraging; it showed he was genuinely embracing being a new dad.

I moved to his text messages. There was nothing of interest, except one that he had sent to an unknown number, just a series of digits against which there was no name.

Okay, this evening. Let's talk.

That was all it said. It had been sent a week ago and whoever it was intended for had not replied.

I tried to brush it off, but there was something about this mystery message which made my heart rate quicken.

Then I was distracted by an alert on my own phone. It was from Will. He had noticed an advert in the window of a local pottery shop about sessions for 'baby imprints' and discounts for groups. He posted a photo of the ad to the group.

Will: Could be a fun activity to do together – create crockery for ourselves or gifts for relatives?

Susie was the first to respond:

Ooh yes, have been meaning to create some imprints – they look so cute. Count me in if we can make it Tuesday to Thursday – we're having a long weekend away! Xx

We had asked Tara to be Joni's godmother and she had accepted, so this appealed to me as the ideal little gift for her.

Me: Sounds good. Joni and I would love to come x

Lucy: Sure. Lx

Helen had gone strangely quiet on the thread and was the last to respond late that evening with the final yes. A date was set for the following Tuesday.

In the end, I didn't sleep any better on the couch as I would have done in bed. I still found myself waking every few hours when I heard Joni stir and Jason clank around in the kitchen making her bottle. It was as though I was tied to Joni with an invisible string. It wasn't easy, but I resisted the temptation to get up and see whether Jason needed any help; he would have to work things out for himself.

But when he left the house at 7 a.m., I crept back into our bed to be close to Joni.

Later that morning, on a call with Tara, I mentioned the text message.

'Honey, it could have been to do with any number of dramas at work,' she reassured me. 'It might even have gone to a wrong number, because of the lack of response. But if you're that worried, why don't you just ask him?'

'And let him know I've been snooping on his phone? No, I couldn't. He'd be so cross, and rightly so,' I replied. 'But I suppose you're right, it's probably nothing.'

'You said things have been so much better recently – one off-evening coupled with sleep deprivation doesn't help perspective, believe me,' Tara continued sympathetically. 'So please don't over-think it. What I would prescribe, is some pampering time. It's so hard to ever relax properly when you're in the same house as your baby, so why not book yourself a spa treatment somewhere lovely, when Jason is around to look after Joni one Saturday? You bloody deserve it. Seriously Aish, if you're not careful you'll turn into a martyr otherwise.'

I remembered I had a massage voucher given to me by my agent as a baby present, at The House of Elemis day spa in town. As luck would have it, they had an appointment free on Saturday morning. If there was a woman in London who deserved a massage right now, surely it was me, I told myself as I booked myself in. But that night I struggled to sleep. The text played on my mind. Call it female intuition, something didn't feel right.

CHAPTER THIRTY-ONE

Aisha

Saturday 7th August

At 5.30 on Saturday morning, unable to get back to sleep after Joni had been awake for the past hour, I meticulously prepared a list for Jason and put it on the kitchen table. Last night, he'd only seemed to be half listening as I briefed him to use the freshly expressed bottle of milk within the hour and to remember to take another out of the freezer a couple of hours later.

Right on cue my boobs tingled; the thought of Joni being hungry made my breasts fill rapidly. I took a deep breath and tried to stay calm. I knew that Jason was more than capable of keeping our baby alive, so surely nothing could go too wrong in just half a day. Could it?

More pressing was a serious concern about how I was going to get through a massage in about an hour and a half's time with rock-hard breasts. The thought of it didn't feel very relaxing at all.

I distracted myself from worrying about Joni and opened up my laptop for a quick scan of my emails. After leaving me to enjoy motherhood for a few months, my editor seemed to think it was okay to start emailing me about work again. Such is the life of a freelancer – no one expects you to stay out of the game for long, and they don't seem able to leave you alone, even if you wanted to. There was an email about a new book project. The deadline for initial thoughts was in a month's time; I was going to have to start carving out some time for it in the evenings if I had a chance of getting the commission. I sighed. That meant I was going to need to count on improved support from Jason if I had a hope in hell of pulling off being a working mum. Either that or we would have to start looking into childcare – although the thought of dropping Joni off at a nursery at such a tender age felt unbearable, not to mention impractical as I was still breastfeeding and intended to keep it up for at least six months. We would need to discuss other options, all of which were bound to be expensive. I closed the laptop and left the house, leaving Jason muttering to Joni about a trip to the park.

The Tube journey from Clapham Common to Oxford Circus should have taken thirty minutes maximum. Sometimes, if you timed it right at Stockwell, it could be done in twenty. But everything seemed against me today. There was some issue at Stockwell, meaning the station was closed so I had to continue to Elephant and Castle and then get the Bakerloo line to Oxford Circus. I kept looking at my phone to check the time. I was going to be late, no question.

When it turned eleven o'clock, the time of my appointment, I was only at Charing Cross. The Tube was busy and hot; it was making my heart beat faster.

When I finally surfaced at Oxford Street, I was a whole ten minutes late for the appointment already, and it was still about a ten-minute walk to the Elemis spa. I checked my phone, half hoping Jason had been frantically trying to call me, so I had a legitimate reason to explain why I was late – maybe they would take pity on a frazzled new mum. It didn't help that my breasts now felt like watermelons. I felt another surge of milk, just thinking about this. I was glad I was wearing breast pads because they would certainly be leaking any moment. I stood in the middle of a crowd of people waiting to cross the road. Everyone looked so purposeful. Eyes fixed ahead or focused on their phones. People rushing along the pavement. Why was everyone so busy? Shoppers and tourists were moving around as though they didn't have a second to waste. I had been living a relatively sheltered life in recent weeks, pottering around the flat with Joni and straying no further than the Clapham area, from coffee shop to the common; from one supermarket aisle to the next.

I had almost forgotten about the world beyond, the always on the move, hectic pace of city life. It had not slowed at all. I felt disorientated, like I didn't belong here any more, like I didn't know who I was. I felt sweat appear on my forehead and my breathing quicken as I debated sprinting down to Elemis to see whether anything could be salvaged of my appointment, or whether to just call them and cancel it. I looked across the street to the big store opposite – if

I cancelled, I could spend a whole hour browsing Topshop instead. At any other time of my life, this would have been my idea of heaven. Not any more. I didn't know what size I was now, and it seemed pointless picking out clothes that would be suitable for breastfeeding when I'd only be doing it for a limited time. And I couldn't think of a single impending event that I needed a dress for. I had lost my former identity. The only thing I knew for certain was that I wanted Joni. I needed to feel her warm body next to mine. Only she could provide the comfort I craved in this moment.

A suited man pushed past me briskly, nearly knocking the handset from my palm.

'Hey!' I called out, but he had rushed off without even noticing.

All I wanted to do was get home and cuddle my baby. Ouch – another shooting tightness in my boobs. I tried to stop thinking about Joni, but I couldn't. There was no way these mammaries were going to last an entire massage, I'd be paranoid about spurting milk before the lights went down and that wouldn't be enjoyable at all. For anyone. I called the spa and cancelled the appointment. Thankfully they didn't charge me for wasting their time – they took pity on the new mum who sounded utterly lost in her home city.

Realizing I now had absolutely no reason to be in the centre of town, I decided to call it a day. I waved at a black cab and within seconds I was being driven back to Clapham. The traffic was heavy so it took longer than it would have done by Tube but I was quite happy to sit there, feeling like a voyeur and marvelling at how London life was carrying on while I felt so disconnected from it.

When I reached the flat, I was surprised to see Lucy standing in the street with her pram.

'Aisha!' She seemed startled to see me too. The cab had pulled up beside her, a few doors down from our place, and I got out to pay the driver through the passenger window. Perhaps I had given her a shock.

'Lucy – hi – I haven't forgotten we're meeting, have I?' I asked.

'No,' she shook her head, 'I was just passing. I was on my way to Boots.' She paused. 'My... steriliser broke, and I was going to get a new one. And then I thought I'd see if you were home.'

'Don't get a new one – we have a spare,' I offered, remembering the pressure I had put on Jason to order all the items from Maggie's list, forgetting I'd already bought one online with money sent by Dad. I noticed that she looked nice, her hair neat and with subtle make-up on. 'Come in for a cuppa if you like, Jason's home with Joni. Would you believe I was meant to go to a spa today but,' I felt a little embarrassed saying it, 'I chickened out. It was so busy in town and I missed Joni. I just wanted to get back to her. How silly is that?' My voice trailed off.

'Not silly at all, I can't imagine anything worse than being in the middle of town right now,' she said, making me feel better. 'I'd bubble wrap myself some days, if I could.' She smiled, but didn't move.

'So do you want to come in for a cuppa?' I asked.

'Perhaps I could pop in quickly, just to pick up the steriliser…' She seemed to falter. 'Then I'd better head off.'

The flat was disarmingly quiet when I opened the door. I'd half expected Jason to fail at keeping Joni's routine, and that, unable to resist the urge to play with her in any waking hour, she'd be cooing on her jungle gym when I got home.

'Where's Joni?' I asked when he came down the stairs to greet me.

'Sleeping soundly, as instructed,' he said proudly. He kissed me tenderly on the forehead. 'She's just fed. Come and see. You're back early?'

When Lucy appeared behind me at the door too, he seemed surprised.

'I just bumped into Aisha as she got out of the cab,' Lucy said quickly, taking the words out of my mouth.

'I said Lucy could borrow our steriliser. We don't need two. Okay with you?'

'Yeah, of course,' Jason replied.

'Great. Please stay for tea,' I said, rattled by Jason who was not being particularly friendly towards Lucy.

As he was asleep, Lucy left Albie in his pram by the front door and I made us tea in the kitchen. Jason didn't stick around to say more than 'Hello'. But I knew he could be funny about people and as my first impressions of Lucy hadn't exactly been overly positive, perhaps he was clinging on to that. He could be quite protective.

And maybe he was just being sensitive, leaving us to it when our conversation turned into a full-scale mum-to-mum chat about breast pumps and when it was safe to stop sterilising all the equipment that went with it. Poor Lucy told me she had been suffering from mastitis too. No wonder feeding had been so painful for her recently. The extra make-up today was an attempt to make herself feel better. 'Believe me, I'm tired and pale underneath,' she confessed.

I had just offered to crack open some Hobnobs when we were distracted by the sound of Albie beginning to stir downstairs.

'I'll head off.' Lucy stood up. 'I'm sorry I'm not the best company today. But I'll see you next week, at the pottery shop.'

'Yes, such a cute idea, it will be nice to do something crafty. I'm really looking forward to it.'

'I'm sure you'll show us all up with your artistry!' she teased and moved towards the stairs.

'Oh – don't forget the steriliser!' I exclaimed. 'I'll just grab it for you.'

CHAPTER THIRTY-TWO

Lucy

Tuesday 10th August

In the pottery shop, I focused on choosing my colours, opting for a blue, green and white combo for a plate for Oscar's birthday, and then I got to work on my design. A hush fell as everyone concentrated, broken only by noises of frustration when something went wrong with their brush stroke, or they struggled to get a good baby hand or footprint onto their 'masterpiece'. The babies were remarkably well behaved.

'Oscar's going to love that!' Will exclaimed as I somehow managed to cajole Albie into producing two reasonably recognizable little blue foot prints on the plate.

'I think he will,' I smiled.

The truth was that Oscar had been sleeping in his office on and off over the last week and I was having serious doubts about whether we could get through this rocky patch. I was doing my best to give him some space, so he might come around, but it was hard. It was taking all my energy not to cave in and tell him everything. There had been a couple of moments lately when the secret had risen inside me like a towering wave and I had wondered, if I chose to surf it, whether I would come out by the shoreline, or drown. It felt as though I had partially lost him anyway. Did I have much more to lose?

I noticed Aisha was quiet today; she seemed as lost in thought as I was for much of the morning. Joni was asleep in her pram for a lot of the time. I searched Aisha's face for clues, but then checked myself – just the fact she was here was a good thing. She was concentrating intently on the three bunnies she was painting; putting us all to shame with her artistic talents.

Susie, Will and I were distracted for a while by gossiping about Helen, who had politely declined the pottery invitation, choosing WhatsApp to tell us the news that she and Ian were currently 'on a break' and that she and Maddie had moved back to Windsor to live with her parents for a while. She didn't explain anything more. It had come as a shock to us, as they had seemed so together, so perfect.

'I can't even imagine them arguing,' Susie observed, to which we all agreed.

The mystery of their break-up brought it home to me that none of us really knew what was going on in each other's relationships. What a shock they would get if they knew the truth about me. I glanced around the table, which was now awash with painted baby footprints, Wet Wipes, spilt paint, and smudgy plates. I shouldn't even be here.

When we left the pottery shop, I decided to go for a walk.

Aisha had left early and gone to meet Jason. I'd thought about trying to persuade her to go for a spontaneous lunch with me instead, but had chickened out. My insides were churning. Would that be the last time I saw her?

I needed some air and Albie always slept better and for longer when we were outside. I headed up towards the common, and before long he was asleep in the cosy pram, oblivious to it all. I stopped for a moment and lowered the canopy to look at him. A peacefulness had spread across his features, so innocent, so unaware of his importance in the world; the pure, beautiful baby at the heart of this mess. Our umbilical-like bond tugged at my heart; a love I'd once wondered if I would ever feel.

It must have triggered something because my mind began wandering. My thoughts turned back almost twenty years, to the first baby I was pregnant with.

I had been at university for almost a year when I discovered I was pregnant. I fled back home to get some space; work out what to do next. How could I expect my gorgeous boyfriend or university friends to have the language or life experience to understand that kind of thing? And then I became too ashamed, too afraid to tell anyone else in case they judged me and hated me as much as I hated myself for either getting pregnant in the first place or going ahead with the abortion. But in moments when I least expected it, I could still see it. I could see the clotted blood so clearly.

'It's time to move on, get back on track and forget the past. It's for the best,' Mum told me the night after I had the abortion, bizarrely in the same London hospital that I was born in. Her arm was hanging loosely around my shoulders; she seemed relieved.

'There's no point dwelling on things,' echoed Dad. Then they shut the door on me in my childhood bedroom, my grief so raw and palpable, my eyes heavy with tears and red from all the crying. Who could do that to their own daughter?

The only person I confided in was Katie, who had been shocked, but vowed to support me whatever I decided to do, although she too had leant towards the feeling that perhaps a termination was the most 'sensible' choice.

I can't pretend to know what losing a baby later in pregnancy, or at full term, must be like, but even so, at ten weeks, she was very real. I don't know for sure that my baby was a girl, but I'm as sure as I can be. I felt it. She was strong; a cheeky one. She didn't want to go so soon, before she even had a chance at life. I know, because she was inside of my body. But I took her future away. I felt there was no other option. If I didn't terminate the pregnancy then I'd have to drop out of uni, and I hadn't even completed my first year. I'd end up living back at home, I'd be a drain on my parents' lives and finances for the foreseeable future. My dreams would be cut short. I didn't believe I had any other option. I was so wracked with shame and guilt. My mother even made the appointment at the hospital for me. Little did I realize then that I'd end up dropping out of my university course anyway.

The day after that, my boyfriend came from uni to visit; he thought I'd been in hospital for suspected appendicitis.

That was the story Katie and I made up. I was still in shock and I looked awful, and I wanted to tell him the truth so desperately, but I had been warned by my parents that it wasn't a good idea. It was better to get on with my life rather than risk what his reaction might be.

'It will be okay, Luce,' was all he could say. 'At least you didn't have to have it taken out.'

If only he knew the irony in those words.

I searched his face for some comfort, for him to somehow ask the right question so that I would have no choice but to tell him everything, but found none. He didn't know how to deal with me, and I didn't know how to let him in. I was too scared. Things felt awkward between us for the first time ever. He stood by my bed in silence. My hand lay there on the duvet, aching to be held. He must have thought this was a gross overreaction for suspected appendicitis. But something between us had gone. We had been together for nine months – the same amount of time that it takes to grow a baby – and it had felt so intense. At first it was about his good looks, but our bond quickly deepened and I thought I had found my soul mate. Yet now we didn't know how to connect right now. His expression was fearful when I asked him to give me some space to rest and I'd give him a call when I was back on my feet again.

'Are you breaking up with me?' he asked solemnly.

'I guess I am,' I said, my eyes full of tears. It was the last thing I wanted in my heart.

He left.

He tried to contact me a few times after that, but I ignored his texts and calls. I pushed him away because it seemed the best option for us both. After a few weeks the calls stopped. I suppose his young ego prevented him from chasing me too hard. We were only 19 after all – there would be plenty more Miss Rights out there for a guy like him.

How I wish I could turn back time.

I went back to uni a month after the abortion, but I couldn't cope. I was unable to simply move on, it was too painful. And my ex couldn't understand why I wasn't able to be 'just friends'. Instead of finding the strength to return his calls, I became more isolated and drifted further away from my social group. I even found it hard to be around Katie because she was the only person who knew my secret, and neither of us were equipped for the level of 'adulting' the associated emotions required. I couldn't blame her for that; I was naïve too. She tried to be there for me, but I found it hard to understand my own mind until a long time later. As the days passed, it felt more and more impossible to ever explain to anyone why I was feeling so low.

So, after a few weeks, I dropped out and moved back home to London. It was easier to just disappear and move on without explanation. 'Ghosting', they call it now. I didn't even say goodbye to my tutors or all of my friends. Only Katie knew the real reason and although she begged me to think again, I had already made up my mind. The pain of what had happened felt too much to bear. It had been relatively straightforward to cut ties back then, before social media had really taken hold and we became used to recording our daily life. And there was no one I would miss more than him. At the start of the next academic year, I enrolled on a marketing communications degree in London.

As the years passed, no Mr Right came along for me; no matter how hard I looked, no man lived up to my first true love. He invaded my dreams and infiltrated my thoughts almost every day. The pain of terminating a baby made with a person I loved so much didn't dull as the years passed.

It's a decision I always regretted; always wondered: 'what if I'd told him I was pregnant? Would things have turned out differently?' For years I toyed with finally sharing with him the secret I'd been cradling for so long, but he had blocked my phone number when we split up. I hadn't found any way to contact him since.

Until that night.

My relationship with my parents had never been the same since. As I grew older, I learnt how to keep secrets from them – it was much easier to deal with life on my own than to share my problems. I've always felt alone in my life choices and I struggled to make friends or hold down relationships for a long time, because I didn't find it easy to open up to people.

Until Oscar.

Just before Oscar and I officially got back together when I was pregnant, I told him about the abortion so he understood the significance of me expecting a baby again. But there the story stopped; I didn't dare tell him any more because we were in such a good place – I didn't want to rock the boat, and I was fearful of Oscar's reaction.

I was already nervous about whether Oscar was really on board with a baby arriving in our lives; I didn't want to do anything to risk losing him for a second time. Oscar was understanding and said he hoped the baby would help give me closure on what had happened all those years ago. He didn't put two and two together like I feared he might.

Although a secret this big tortured me day and night, no one suspected anything.

I often thought about my girl, the precious 'daughter' I lost. She would have soon been turning 20. A year older than I was when I got pregnant. I wondered if we would have been great friends. I pictured her with dark brown hair, like her dad, and milky-white skin, like mine. Her eyes were green. She was so beautiful, a real head-turner.

And then the tears would well up in my eyes once more as I tried to picture the sun on her face, illuminating her freckles, her hair messy, sunlight dancing in her eyes, her infectious smile, but I couldn't. I could never get that far. Because there was a blinding, bright light that started to bleach out her features and then her entire face was gone and she disappeared as if she was a star going super nova. It hurt me physically when she went from my mind.

But sometimes when she disappeared, there was another face left in her wake. His face. He had the same green eyes as her. My first true love.

I wondered if Albie would look like him too.

CHAPTER THIRTY-THREE

Aisha

I had missed several calls from Jason during the pottery class. Then he had texted:

> Are you at home this morning? We need to talk. I can meet you by the bandstand on Clapham Common in 45 minutes. Please meet me there. Jx

It was now just gone 1 p.m. when I approached the bandstand area of Clapham Common. The coffee I had picked up en route was still piping hot, so I put it in the cup holder on the side of the pram and concentrated on tightening my pelvic floor, thinking I'd do my abdominal exercises all the way to the bench by the side of the bandstand and hopefully by then the coffee would be cool enough to drink.

It wasn't like Jason to have free time during the day, but the fact he did – and that he wanted to meet up with me and Joni – gave me a spring in my step. This was the new Jason

I'd seen over the past few weeks. Perhaps he wanted to take us for lunch. He seemed really invested in putting more into our relationship.

As I neared the bandstand, I saw Jason's familiar figure walking towards me. When he saw me, his pace seemed to slow. I lifted my hand and smiled. As he got closer, I realized that he didn't seem to be smiling back. His expression was hard to make out but, if anything, he looked stressed. I hoped something bad hadn't happened.

As he approached us I could see he was sweating. He looked hot and panicky and it wasn't a particularly warm day.

'Aisha,' he exclaimed when he reached me, 'I'm so glad you could come.' He was shaking and there was an urgent tone to his voice.

'Baby, what's up, are you okay?' I asked. My first thought was his parents or sister. 'Has something happened?'

He took the pram from my hands, and steered it towards a bench – one of those in a circle around the bandstand area. We sat down.

'There is something I have to tell you,' he said slowly and gravely. He looked at me with a fear and sorrow in his eyes that I had never seen before. It scared me. What was going on?

'I've made a terrible mistake,' he began, his voice faltering. 'There is no easy way of saying this.'

I let out a short burst of sound – an involuntary gasp.

He continued: 'I bumped into an old girlfriend on the Tube last September. A few drinks led to a one-night stand. Aisha, I bitterly regret it. It was one night of madness; we only slept together once. I can barely remember the details because I was so drunk. I'm sorry. So desperately sorry.'

A burning heat moved upwards from my chest to my face and I felt my cheeks flush and my heart pound. 'Jason, what? You're joking, right? This isn't very funny.'

If only it was an unfunny joke.

'There's more. She got pregnant. She's had the baby now and we have taken a paternity test, but I don't have the result yet. I'm really scared, Aisha. I'm petrified I could be the father of this baby.'

With tears in his eyes and shaking hands, he told me that he couldn't keep it a secret any longer.

I listened in silence. The fact we were stood here in such a familiar spot suddenly felt utterly surreal given the enormity of what he had just said.

'Do I know her?' I asked, as calmly as I could.

'I'm afraid so,' he bowed his head. 'It's Lucy.'

'Lucy from The Baby Group?'

His facial expression told me the answer.

I was floored. 'Seriously? No, I don't believe you. It can't be. Lucy and I, we, we're friends.' The words hung in the air, sounding ridiculous and completely at odds with what he had just said. 'It can't be true.'

'I'm sorry Aisha.'

It had taken less than two minutes for Jason to deliver the words that would change our lives forever. For a moment I sat there, glued to the bench, feeling numb. I couldn't look at him, so I put my head in my hands and desperately tried to collect my thoughts, wrap my mind around this shocking revelation. I wanted this to be a dream.

When I did steal a look at him I felt nauseous. He already looked different, unfamiliar.

Jason's eyes were fixed on a piece of hard gum on the floor. He stared and stared.

An anger simmered inside of me.

'You *seriously* think you're Albie's father?' I asked pointedly, barely believing the words coming out of my mouth.

'I don't know. I think there's only a slim chance. But she's a psycho Aisha, I don't know what she's trying to do – to me, to *us*. I'm petrified. She's not right in the head. I couldn't handle it any more – the guilt was killing me, killing our family. I realize this is a huge thing to tell you. I'm so sorry.' He turned to look at me. 'Are you okay?'

Was he having a laugh? Of course I wasn't 'okay'. When I failed to reply he tentatively put his hand on my shoulder. I recoiled. I didn't know him any more and I certainly didn't want him to touch me. It felt as though a crushing weight had descended on me.

My brain was still struggling to compute what I had been told. 'But Lucy told me she and Oscar went through IVF,' I said. 'Was she feeding me all of these lies to cover up your torrid affair?'

'It wasn't an affair. It was one night of insanity, I promise you,' Jason said. 'And she did have IVF, the...' He paused. 'The thing with us happened the night before.'

'I can't believe you'd do this to me – to *us,*' I said. 'How long have you known her for?'

'We dated at university, in the first year and only for a couple of terms.'

That made her comment about Bristol University when we were in the pub fall into place, plus her interest in the Bristol FC photo in our flat. The fact she had been there, in our home, stalking our photos, made me feel sick. I did vaguely recall him mentioning a Lucy when we had talked about past lovers over the years, but I'd never needed to give her any real thought.

'But she got pregnant,' he continued. 'She went home and had an abortion. She thought I didn't know, but one of her friends told me. I didn't know what to do – we were only 19. We split up and that was it. Life completely moved on.'

'Moved on until you found yourself in bed with her again?'

'Bumping into her, after all that time, it caught me in a weak moment. I thought the past had been laid to rest – it had for me, but clearly not for her. When I told her I had known about the abortion, she took it badly.'

'I'm failing to see how this ended up in making a baby.'

'We went to a pub and got drunk, so drunk that my memory of the whole thing is a bit hazy; I think I might have passed out. After that, I cut off all communication. I blocked her. After her reaction to the abortion comment I thought she seemed vengeful, crazy.'

'And then she turned up in our Baby Group.' I spat the words out; this was like something out of a horror film.

'I was so shocked when I first saw her there. And at the same stage of pregnancy as us. I put two-and-two together.' His head was hanging so low it was almost in his lap.

'I freaked out, panicked, big time.' His words then became peppered with sobs. 'Honestly Aisha, I'm furious with myself, for keeping all of this a secret from you; I know I should have come clean.'

My mind was ticking over, trying to piece together the dates. This would have been at exactly the same time I discovered I was pregnant.

He seemed to read my mind: 'That day, when you came to work to tell me you were pregnant…' His voice trailed off, like he didn't have the guts to finish the sentence.

'Tell me Jason,' I pressed. 'You owe me the truth now.'

'That was the morning after it happened. I didn't have the heart to be so callous as to wipe the joy from your beautiful face with this dirty news. Not that day, and then there was never the right day.'

So many things clicked into place. He had fed me so many lies. I felt like the world's greatest mug for not noticing or confronting him about anything, even when Jason and I were so obviously drifting apart during my pregnancy. In the weeks after Joni was born he had been so much more attentive and kind. Now I knew why. His guilty conscience was catching up with him.

He looked at me pleadingly. 'I would do anything – *anything* – to turn back the clock. I love you both so much,' he wept. 'I've tried to show you that. I know I struggled when you were pregnant and wasn't there for you. But you and Joni are the most important people in the world to me. I'd be lost without you.' He looked like a broken man.

We were soon both in floods of tears. I used the last of the tissues in my pockets.

We were interrupted when Joni woke. At the sound of her first cry Jason went to reach for the pram, but I instinctively knocked his arm away, accidentally sending my coffee cup, which had remained in the cup holder, falling out and onto the ground.

'Get off!' I snapped, finding some kind of other-worldly strength from within. I stood up and gripped the handlebars, releasing the brake. 'Don't touch my baby!'

A few people turned to look at us with concerned expressions. I didn't care.

'Please, Aish, wait. Can we talk?' he said, moving towards us.

But my disbelief had turned to anger. 'You lying shit! Just leave me alone.'

I didn't want to hear any more right now and somehow I summoned the energy to get away from him, not noticing or caring in which direction I was travelling, my feet barely touching the ground. Anywhere to get him out of my sight. I felt so stupid – like a fool for not acting on the sixth sense I'd had that something wasn't right; that he was keeping something from me. But I never expected this.

CHAPTER THIRTY-FOUR

Lucy

Thursday September 10ᵗʰ, last year

I'd always considered myself a person who disliked surprises
– loathed them, in fact. From surprise birthday parties – my
worst nightmare – to opening gifts I knew I'd never use, but
was too polite to ask for the receipt for. I was much better if
I could prepare for something. Only some carefully planned
days could occasionally turn into extraordinary days, when
you least expected it. And that is what had happened.

As if going through the IVF process as a single woman
wasn't gruelling enough, the element of surprise it had
involved had made me anxious all month. I had pretty much
cleared my calendar, aware that I might have needed to attend
the clinic for a blood test at a moment's notice, ready to
undergo IVF at exactly the right time. I had one good-quality
frozen embryo and had opted for a natural cycle.

My consultant was happy with my progress that month

and I was ready for the embryo transfer. I decided to wait until the last minute to book the day off so there was less likelihood of anyone knowing what I was doing. I even turned down the opportunity to chat to the clinic's in-house counsellor because I felt so in control of my emotions and had made peace with the knowledge that I was in the hands of fate now.

When the day drew near, I booked it off work, claiming a family matter had arisen.

The day before the transfer, I left work early to pick up some treats to keep me going after the procedure, so I could rest at home and hug my belly in peace, while eating cake and drinking herbal tea.

As I walked to the Tube, taking a detour through Green Park because it was such a nice evening, I noticed a couple kissing on a bench, their legs wrapped around each other, oblivious to the constant stream of commuters marching past them. They were young and looked so loved up, so *fertile*. I thought about how IVF couldn't be further removed from love-making. What a clinical way to make a baby, stripping away the romance and leaving the stark reality of a scientific experiment in its place. The whole thing was about as unsexy as a wet espadrille. So I put in my AirPods, put on a relaxing playlist and decided to think about sex as a way to somehow beautify what was going to be happening between my legs the next day.

When thinking about sex, I always fantasized about the same person; in fact it wouldn't be inaccurate to say I had thought about him at least once every day in the twenty years since we'd broken up. Jason Moore, my first love.

Sometimes, if I was in the right mood, I could drift off and, for a split second, be back in the past. I could remember exactly what he looked like – or rather, had looked like then. The way he had smiled, how he had closed his eyes when he kissed me – I could picture him clearly. For flashing, brief moments, I could feel the same skin-tingling, intoxicating sensation of being with him, and what it was like knowing that he wanted to be with me.

Jason was my university sweetheart. I was head-over-Timberlands for him then, and no one had lived up to him since, no matter how much I had wanted myself to fall in love. And believe me, I had *really* wanted to love like that again. Over the years, I had tried so hard to find someone to replace Jason. But no one came close. Oscar got warm, but when he told me he didn't want any more children, I knew I had to move on; I had to take control of my desire to become a mother. So there I was, single and trying to make a baby on my own.

I'd read enough features in women's magazines to know that nothing hurt as much as the first time you fell in love; I was not stupid – and I was not overemotional. I just thought I would have been over him by now; that the years would have blurred the depth of feeling, and that other people would have filled the void, ideally by being better than him. But the truth was, I hadn't experienced the kind of madness that came with true love – the utter insanity when you would do anything for five minutes in the company of that person, even if it meant flying to the other side of the world – since Jason.

So when I saw him that Thursday, it was the shock of

my life. I was snapped out of my daydream by an *Evening Standard* vendor pushing a copy of that evening's paper into my palm. The sun was still high in the sky and I decided to buy myself a cupcake from Lola's near the Tube station as a reward for tomorrow. Despite a little apprehension – because the appointment had the power to change my life forever – I was in a good mood. I had a strong feeling of hope in my heart, like it was going to be okay.

I was sat on the Tube reading the paper, the red velvet cupcake encased in a little box in a paper bag between my feet, with my beloved cross-body Gucci bag on my lap. At each stop there was the bustle of passengers coming and going, bobbing up and down as they moved in and out of seats around me. I couldn't explain why I chose that moment, but I looked up from the paper for a second and that's when I clocked him sitting directly opposite me. I knew that face. I knew it so well. A moment of recognition and then I averted my eyes, looking back down at the printed paper in front of me. My body reacted immediately, suddenly feeling very hot and tight around the chest, my breathing quickened and my heart rate sped up. Was I imagining this? I swallowed, but the thumping in my heart only grew stronger. I glanced up again, fleetingly, to double-check. He was engrossed in his laptop – he had become that guy who worked on his laptop on the Tube. But I'd have recognized his face anywhere: the angular, chiselled features but soft, green eyes. The thick mop of dark brown hair, although it was styled in a sensible neat crop then, rather than the longer, grungy look of 2000. He was still good-looking.

I panicked and moved the newspaper higher, hiding behind it like a comedy spy, lowering it occasionally, just to triple-check it wasn't a dream. Perhaps I was having a sugar dip; sugar dips could do strange things to your vision. I reached for the Lola's bag, pulling it on top of the Gucci, wondering if I could grab a piece of icing off the cake and eat it, to sort me out. I felt sick. This wasn't a dream or a sugar dip. Maybe it wasn't even a coincidence. Perhaps it was meant to be; maybe this was our moment.

As the Tube began to slow down, ready to approach the next station platform, my mind raced. Should I make eye contact? Perhaps I should get up, leave the train at the next stop? Maybe I could move seats? But I felt paralysed, as though I was glued to the fabric beneath me. The doors opened and closed at Kennington. A few people got off, emptying the carriage further, making it easier for him to spot me. I thought how I might wobble if I stood up, so I stayed put. So did he. He had barely looked up from his screen. He had to be well versed in this journey because he knew which station we were at instinctively. As we gathered speed again, my breathing felt a little more under control; it must be his usual route. I stole another glance. It was 100 per cent Jason. He had his laptop screen down then, and was looking above me at some advert, probably about teeth whitening or dating. He seemed lost in thought. Maybe he had noticed me. I was both willing him to look down and praying he didn't. Perhaps he wouldn't recognize me. My hair was much longer when we were at uni and I obviously looked older now. I closed my eyes and took a deep breath. It was only ten minutes ago that I was imagining having sex with him. It was too much of a coincidence for us to be here now, not even a metre apart. Perhaps if you thought about someone enough, your mind played twisted tricks and made you believe you'd conjured them up, like a hologram. I slammed my eyes shut. I really should get a grip and say hello.

The Tube had slowed into Stockwell when I tentatively dared to open my eyes. My stop. Though my heart was desperate for him, I felt too nervous to approach him. I was too self-conscious to do it in a public place and fearful of what his reaction might be. I resisted the temptation to glance at him one last time – the face I hadn't seen for two decades. I stood up, holding on to the handrail for support and quickly disembarked the train without looking back. Would I regret this forever? A part of me thought I might. But it was too late now.

The platform was mercifully quiet at that time, just ahead of rush hour, so I was able to make a quick dash through the walkway on to the adjacent Victoria line platform. I moved as fast as I could, without looking back. I found an empty bench-seat and sat down, relieved there were two minutes before the next train so I could steady my breath, get my head together. I was just thinking that a mouthful of cake would help get me back on to an even keel when I felt a light tap on my right shoulder. It was Jason.

I let out a startled little gasp as I turned and saw him.

'It's you, Lucy, isn't it?' he asked.

Any concern a nearby woman may have felt, was satiated by the fact that I quickly rose and greeted Jason like the long-lost friend he was.

I smiled, uncertain whether my voice was going to work. 'Yes, Jason, it is.' I said his name as boldly as I could, trying to mask the fact that my cheeks were flushed and my legs felt like jelly. I wondered if he knew I'd spotted him in the carriage. Did I sound surprised enough? 'Wow – it's been a long time.'

'I'm so glad it's you,' he enthused, green eyes shining. 'It would have been embarrassing if it wasn't,' he stuttered slightly, indicating he was nervous too. 'Crazy. It's been so long. It's good to see you.' We looked at each other in awkward fascination for a moment. I wondered what to do or say next.

'So, what have you been up to?' he offered tentatively. By now a train had been and gone and the platform had cleared around us.

I smiled. 'In the last twenty years? Quite a lot. Like you have too, I'd imagine,' I replied.

Little did he know that I knew a bit about what he'd been doing from a number of Google searches. I was still barred from his social media, from when I broke up with him. I estimated that he'd come back from Hong Kong about eighteen months ago. He was probably still in that phase when you came back to London and felt like a tourist – a time before you remembered that Londoners generally didn't talk to each other on the Underground. Even if you spied an old friend sat in your carriage, your first reaction would have usually been to avert your eyes or get off – just like I did – so this was unusual. I mentally weighed up whether or not to say, 'I'm so sorry, but I'm in a mad hurry,' and leave the station to get a cab the rest of the way home. Any more small talk could have got painful. But something made me want to stay there. To drink up the beginnings of wrinkles around his eyes, the jawline that was a little softer; to bank the memory of his face for a little longer.

As another train pulled in and I began to walk towards the edge of the platform, Jason stayed with me, seeming keen to continue talking.

'I don't actually need this line,' he confessed, as we watched the Tube doors open and close. Something stopped me from saying goodbye and jumping on. I was intrigued.'

We both remained rooted to the spot, neither wanting to be the first to break away, like there was an imaginary pull between us.

'Do you fancy going for a drink?' he asked. His features lit up expectantly. Looking at his face, for a moment I forgot everything – I felt 19 again. 'I've had a shitty day at work, and I'd love to hear what you've been up to. There's a lot to catch up on,' he smiled. 'A quick drink?'

I knew I wasn't meant to drink ahead of the transfer, and I knew I should have headed straight home to put on slouchy clothes, relax and watch something on *Netflix*, in preparation for tomorrow, but I had thought about this guy too much in the last two decades to let him slip through my fingers and disappear into an Underground tunnel. I wanted to find out more about him. Maybe it would help me lay the past to rest? Maybe if we talked, it would help me move on. I felt like I was in a TV drama with no control over the plot.

'Just one drink, then,' I grinned.

We exited Stockwell Tube, walking in silence for a few minutes, towards the first pub we came across, The Pilgrim.

As we sat down at a table, I remembered the cupcake.

'Fancy a cake?' I offered. 'Although it's probably slightly battered by now.'

'Was it meant for someone special?' He had presumed incorrectly that women didn't buy themselves cupcakes.

'Nope – just me.'

'You're celebrating something? I could help you celebrate if so?'

'No, it's fine,' I said, clocking the gold wedding band on his left hand and experiencing a sick-to-the-pit-of-my-stomach feeling, to see it in the flesh. 'When did you get married?' Somehow it sounded accusatory.

'A few years ago, in Hong Kong,' he replied. 'We met there, although we're both British.'

'Expats,' I said carelessly; again it sounded disparaging. I smiled weakly.

'We moved back a year and a half ago,' he continued.

Hearing him use the term 'We' so many times, felt like punches to my heart.

'Are you married?' he asked. 'Kids?'

I thought it was pretty obvious by the lack of decoration on my wedding finger. 'No. Not yet. I'm in a relationship but we're not at that stage,' I lied. I immediately thought of Oscar, and how a large part of me wished we were still together; if the circumstances had been different with him, maybe I wouldn't be sat here right now. 'To be honest, I don't see marriage as the be all and end all. I think children are more of a commitment. But I'm not at that stage either, yet. I always knew I'd have my children late – when I'm ready.' I looked up and caught him looking fondly at me. I'd just told two whoppers because I didn't want him to wonder why I was still single at 38; he might have wondered what was wrong with me. I knew it was pathetic to feel so insecure.

He appeared to be grinning.

'What?' I asked.

'You're just the same,' he smirked affectionately.

'What do you mean?'

'You know what you think. You always did.'

'Well, at 38 I would hope so,' I remarked, relieved that I had sounded so convincing. 'What about you – any children?'

'I'll get us another drink before we get into this one,' he said, looking strained.

When he returned with two more large glasses of red wine, he paused. 'I don't want this evening to become about my problems.'

'Problems?' I examined his features.

'The kids thing… We both want it, I think. But I'm scared. I'm worried about whether it will happen, and if it does, if I will be good enough.'

'Good enough? Of course you're good enough,' I said.

'But to be a father,' he replied. 'Do I have what it takes to support a family – both emotionally,' he paused for a moment, 'and financially. The responsibility scares me.'

His phone rang and he picked it up and looked at the screen.

'Talk of the devil,' he said, before stopping the call and replacing his phone, screen down on the table.

'Do you need to call her?'

'Later,' he said.

'Of course you're enough,' I told him, surprised about the extent to which he had opened up so quickly. 'She married you, didn't she? For better, for worse. I'm sure she doesn't care about your earning potential when it comes to having a child. It's love that really matters.'

'I know,' he nodded. 'I need to "man up" I guess.' He coughed, a little embarrassed. 'Thank you for the pep talk. Let's change the subject.'

It was almost like old times except, of course, for the great stomping elephant in the room: the reason why we split up all those years ago. I ached to bring up the subject of us.

'My turn to get a round,' I said, pushing out my chair and picking up my bag. I knew it wasn't a good idea to be drinking, but I didn't feel drunk; two or three glasses of wine between old friends couldn't hurt.

When I returned, the corners of his mouth turned up. 'Anyway, what we *haven't* discussed yet is why you so cruelly dumped me all those years ago?' he said, as if he had read my mind. He looked at me intensely. I took it as an acknowledgement of how much time had passed, and what we once meant to each other. I thought I saw a flicker of longing in his eyes.

'Still scarred, are you?' I replied wryly, calling his bluff.

'It came out of the blue, took me a while to get over you, if I'm honest.' He propped his elbow on the back of his chair and leant his cheek into his hand. 'First love – cuts the deepest…' He stared at me in wonderment, like he once used to.

'I do have an answer to your question though,' I said,

starting the sentence before I knew how it was going to end. And then it was left there, resting for a moment in the air between us, like a ring of smoke from years gone by.

He fixed me with those eyes. The eyes I wanted to dive right into and lose myself in, never to re-emerge. I could have swum in those eyes forever. No life jacket needed. A warmth filled my cheeks. I almost wanted to cry. I took a deep breath.

'It was complicated,' I began. 'We were young.'

'Only 19,' he said. 'We knew so little about life then.'

'I knew what it felt like to be in love though,' I replied. 'And I really did love you.'

His phone rang again, but he immediately turned it off.

We both looked at each other in silence for a few seconds. I mean, really looked.

He slid his hand around my neck and pulled me into his chest. I hoped he would stop this line of questioning because it felt so good to be held and I desperately wanted to kiss him. For us to forget about everything and everyone else, just for a moment. He smelt nice, comforting – a faint woody cologne and washing detergent.

'It's okay,' he whispered, his eyes gleaming. 'Let's not get into it.' And he stroked my hair.

After that, the following hour seemed to pass in a flash. Glasses charged, we started to talk about some of the fun times we had had at uni, the freshers' parties, the time we had drunk so much peach schnapps we couldn't get out of bed for forty-eight hours, and then we moved on to our work, families and the few mutual friends we were still in touch with – he remembered Katie and was interested to hear what she was up to in Oxfordshire. All the while we stole shy, fleeting glances at each other as we covertly weighed up the passing of time and what had once been between us.

So much had changed, yet so much was exactly the same.

He still had a face that smiled entirely, his eyes as engaged as his mouth, his lips plump and wide, and the little gap between his lower front teeth that used to bug him when we were young made him even more handsome. He laughed easily – the infectious delight he took from life. It wasn't hard to imagine that many women had fallen under Jason's spell during the last two decades. I couldn't help but feel honoured he still remembered me; that I held a special place in his heart.

I found myself fighting an impulse to sink into him, to let him wind an arm around my shoulder again, to pull me close and kiss me. He felt so familiar yet I didn't really know him at all. But the chemistry was still there, I couldn't be imagining it. Surely he felt it too?

Jason had just returned from the bar with a bottle of red wine – we had drunk at least a bottle and a half already, in single glasses, and now there was no mistaking it, we were drunk. As he sat down and faced me, I got the feeling he felt the attraction too. There was something familiar between us, but also illicit; a thrill in our behaviour but also a feeling that we were doing nothing wrong. That it was natural and right that we were together right now. It was as if, in that moment, we existed in a parallel world. That's how I justified the feelings I was having towards a married man, anyway. The wine was slipping down far too easily, and I'd noticed Jason down a large shot at the bar. He seemed intent on getting drunk; I sensed an underlying recklessness to his actions. I wondered if there was more to it; if he was happy in his marriage.

Under the table, Jason put a hand on my knee. I could see that he was drunk, his eyes less focused as they rested on mine for a moment too long. Eye contact is such a powerful thing. This time I didn't look away. I wished I'd worn my new Michael Kors dress, the one I was saving for an exciting date – the kind that hadn't been on the table for quite a while. The dress had been hanging in my wardrobe unworn for weeks. If only I had known about this evening. I couldn't take my mind off his hand; I ached to feel his soft fingers on my warm bare skin. I was sure I didn't imagine his hand move slightly higher, to rest on my thigh. I didn't dare move my leg for fear he might take it off. I longed to lace my fingers with his. I think I said something about my job, how I got passed over for a promotion recently, so perhaps his gesture was meant sympathetically, perhaps it was totally innocent. But it didn't feel innocent. Every touch felt electrifying. I wanted his fingers to gently ride up the inside of my leg, and stop around my crotch. I wondered what it would feel like if he was to part my legs a little and just hover there a moment, pushing his index finger into my jeans. All I wanted to do was lose myself in him. I felt my eyes glaze.

Jason broke my thoughts by coughing, then he got up and excused himself for the Gents'.

I can't have been imagining the sexual tension between us. Perhaps Jason needed to splash cold water over his face. I metaphorically did the same, running my fingers through my hair, sitting up straighter and moving my head from side to side in an effort to sober up. I tried to focus on the food menu that lay untouched on the table. Perhaps something to eat would help.

I pulled out my phone and checked the time: 10 p.m. We had been drinking for over five hours, it was no wonder I felt drunk.

There was a message from Mum:

Are you watching Channel 4? There's a programme about PR. X

Mum would be irked by the lack of response, so I quickly replied, telling her I'd find it on catch up and would call her tomorrow.

There was another message, from Katie:

Loads of luck for tomorrow. Hope it all goes well. Call me after. Much love x

I wondered what they'd say if either of them could have seen me now. On the way to being plastered with an ex-boyfriend. *This* ex-boyfriend in particular.

I felt a little disappointed that Oscar hadn't messaged me. Not that he knew why tomorrow was so important, or because there was any reason for him to contact me, but hearing from him still had the power to brighten up my day. I missed him a lot.

I put all thoughts of tomorrow – and Oscar – out of my head.

Jason returned to his seat and placed two tequila shots on the table.

I pushed mine away. 'I've never been good with tequila,' I said.

'Remember that cheap stuff they used to serve at the campus bar?' He smiled. His brow was slightly sweaty as he downed his shot followed by mine.

Then I can't even remember what we were talking about because my mind was too focused on how badly I wanted to kiss him. The alcohol was making me feel reckless. As if reading my mind, he put his hand back on my leg, only this time he squeezed harder, and then he slowly walked his fingers up my thigh. I didn't want him to stop, but something made me put my hand on his, to slow him down as much as anything.

'You okay?' he asked, turning to me, his eyes glassy.

'Yes, fine,' I answered, my insides full of excited butterflies.

How could I say that it felt amazing, that I was fantasizing about what I'd like him to do with me in the corner of a busy pub on a Thursday evening? Although I was worried about what might happen if he did go there – if I'd be able to stop him, and how I'd cope afterwards. I thought about what was going to happen tomorrow, how I would be lying on the bed in the clinic, my legs in the air, having a tiny embryo placed inside me. I should be at home, getting ready for bed. I shouldn't be pissed in a pub, fantasizing about letting an ex-boyfriend finger me.

I pulled out my phone again, although I already knew what time it was.

'It's late,' I sighed, barely able to look him in the eye. I wanted him so much. Just the lightest brush of his arm was doing all kinds of things to my insides. I hadn't felt this sexually alive in a long time. Maybe I should leave now, go home, eat toast and drink lots of water before sleeping the alcohol off. My gaze lingered on his lips again.

'I don't even have your number,' he said.

I unlocked my phone and opened a blank new contact page.

'Here, put in yours,' I replied as if this were as normal as an exchange with a new work contact.

He added his name and number. Just 'Jason'. He hadn't needed a surname in my address book then, and he didn't need one now.

'I'm not ready for tonight to end – are you?' he asked, delighting me as much as terrifying me, that yes, he did seem to be thinking the same.

'I really *should* be going home, I've got lots on tomorrow, but…' I allowed myself to look fully into his eyes and let him reach into mine. 'I'm really enjoying your company.'

I think that was the moment we both made the decision.

'Let's get some air,' he suggested.

It was still fairly warm outside, when we stood on the corner of the main road, just outside the pub. I felt exposed out there. Where I could have imagined us kissing in our discreet corner of the pub, now we were out in the open the spell was broken. What if someone either of us knew saw us? He was married, after all.

'Which direction are you heading, we could share a cab?' he suggested.

'I'm Brixton. You're Clapham, right?' He'd already described where he lived to me earlier.

'Perfect, we can get a cab. I think there's a taxi rank this way.'

'Taxi rank?' I smirked. 'Which London do you live in? Everyone gets Ubers, I haven't heard of anyone seeking out a "taxi rank" in years,' I giggled.

'Oh really, Miss Lucy Raven, well maybe I'm just a proper old-fashioned gent,' he grinned, tipping an imaginary bowler hat.

'Hmm, gent? Local scallywag, more like,' I retorted.

'Let's see about that,' he replied, and then he peeled off down the street and leapt up into a pirouette under a street light. It was quite skillful, considering how drunk we were. I chuckled. He had always been a funny guy. The orange glow of a free taxi came into sight and he caught the driver's attention with a whistle.

The next thing I knew, he was putting a hand on my back to guide me into the black cab, and then it was as if destiny was controlling what would happen next. It was so easy, so natural, so right and so totally wrong at the same time. He took my hand and squeezed it tightly. Every touch felt charged. We kept turning to look at each other, lust in our eyes; weighing up what would happen next without needing the words. The cabbie would definitely have assumed we were a couple. Why should he have noticed that only one of us was wearing a wedding band?

My insides yearned for Jason; I was aching for him. This feeling, it was more than just lust. I was familiar with lust and its heightened senses, but this was lust mixed with rekindled love. A sensation that was impossible to rationalise, but was tipping me into insanity and making me willing to take such a huge risk on this night of all nights.

I unlocked the door to my flat with Jason standing behind me. I could feel his breath on my hair, one hand touching my waist. A hurried goodbye in the back of a taxi didn't seem right, not with our history. It made sense to invite him in.

The second the front door closed behind me, before either of us had even spoken, in the darkness of my hallway, he turned my face towards his, cradled my head in both hands and leant forwards. Suddenly his tongue was in my mouth, swirling around mine passionately and it felt electric. Our bodies were pressed together. At first I was taken aback by the urgency, but I happily gave into it. Kissing him felt familiar and right. Once a good kisser, always a good kisser. He smelled good. His lips were soft and warm. Our noses gently brushed one another. Occasionally we broke apart to look at each other, eyes shining with longing. His hands were running up and down my sides. Then they were on my breasts, holding them through my jumper, while his mouth worked its way down my neck, to my collarbone, kissing me all the way, breathing deeply. He lifted my jumper slightly and pressed his body into my bare stomach, then his hands slid further under my jumper and I gasped as he pulled down my bra until one nipple popped out of the cup and my flesh was pushed upwards. He lowered himself and put his mouth around my exposed nipple, whipping it into a solid peak with his tongue and then he did the same with the other.

I reached down and ran my hands under his jacket pulling his shirt out of his trousers, then working my way to the front, running my fingers over the clasp of his belt and reaching down to touch his cock through his trousers, feeling the hardness I knew to expect.

'Not yet,' he whispered into my ear, having worked his way back to standing, pressing his erection into my body, thrilling me.

I was moaning with longing, I couldn't help it.

'But I want you,' I found myself whispering, this time taking his head into my hands and pulling him into my gaze. He looked at me and smiled.

'I know,' he said. 'I want you too.'

I knew it was wrong. I knew he had a wife. And I knew full well that I was meant to refrain from sexual activity just before the embryo transfer. I also knew this was likely to end up hurting me all over again, and possibly harder than before – because this time, at this moment, I had even more to lose. I knew that we couldn't make the past right, whatever happened. Yes, I knew there were thousands of reasons why this was a bad idea and very few arguments to say it was a good one. But cupid was sat on my shoulder firing arrows all around us, like an Instagram filter come to life, making everything look perfect. He was goading me on. I couldn't say no.

I had rarely felt so drawn to someone, not since Oscar. I was still mourning what Oscar and I could have had. It was so serendipitous that Jason was back, right here, in my – slightly blurry – sights, on this night of all nights. Maybe I had to go through everything with Oscar to find Jason again.

'I've thought about you so much,' I said. It came out louder than intended.

He didn't answer and for a moment I thought I'd said too much; ruined it all. Admitted something that might send him running for the door.

But instead he said nothing, he just lifted me up into his strong arms, and carried me towards the sofa.

'Not here,' I uttered, as he gently lowered my feet to the ground. Instead I took his hand and led him to my bedroom.

And there, we couldn't hold out any longer. I sat on the edge of the bed as he pulled my jumper off over my head, unclasped my bra so it collapsed in submission around my torso and when I had flung it onto the floor, he pushed me backwards into the duvet, pinning my arms above my head and encouraging me to keep them there before getting to work on my nipples again, expertly caressing them, massaging my naked breasts and hard nipples and running his fingers over my stomach towards the top of my jeans. They hovered there just long enough for me to feel ready to give him anything he liked. I tried not to think of tomorrow, my legs in stirrups and the face of a consultant very close to where his was now.

At last he expertly unbuttoned the fly with a single flick and pulled my jeans down my thighs, taking my knickers with them and kissing my exposed skin as he went.

And then he was inside me, filling me up as he thrusted deeply, the weight of his body on mine. His eyes were scrunched closed as we rocked backwards and forwards together, moaning with ecstasy, making love.

It must have been nearly sunrise when I woke up. His eyes were heavy with sleep as I planted a light kiss on his shoulder. I was nearly dropping off again myself when his head turned, he opened his eyes and looked at me – he looked into my soul – and we shared a moment. We acknowledged what had happened. I felt that life would never be the same again.

'Morning,' he said, his eyes smiling as much as his lips. 'How are you feeling?'

The truth was, I had a banging headache. 'I've felt better,' I mumbled, my voice still hoarse with sleep. 'My head is killing me. What about you?'

'The same. What a night.' He planted a kiss on my forehead. 'You were so naughty.'

'Me?' I scoffed, jokingly. 'I think you were just as naughty, from what I recall.'

I rolled over to face him. He paused. He looked as though something was weighing on his mind.

'What are you thinking?' I wondered if the adultery he'd just committed had hit home yet – and how it might make him feel. Perhaps he was still drunk.

'Actually, I was thinking about you,' he said. 'About how we broke up. When you went home with appendicitis. Do you remember?'

I nodded. 'Of course I do. But why are you thinking about that now?' My heart quickened. I was too hungover for heavy chats this morning.

'We touched on it last night; the reason you broke up with me,' he said.

'It was so long ago, Jason. I really don't want to go there again.' Not today, not now.

He continued, seemingly on a mission to get something off his chest: 'It wasn't your appendix, was it? You were pregnant.'

He must have seen the expression on my face change immediately to one of horror as the colour left my cheeks. He stopped. A few seconds passed. But then he continued, undeterred. 'You were pregnant with our baby,' he said it almost matter-of-factly. 'Tell me what happened, Lucy? I really want to know.'

'It sounds like you know already,' I replied, partly still in shock at what he had revealed. 'I'm not sure I want to go into this right now. In fact, I really don't feel up to—'

'You aborted our baby.' He said the words in such a cold, unemotional way.

I felt a strong impulse to cry but did my best to fight it. I took a deep breath. Although floored that he knew all this, perhaps he did deserve an explanation.

'My emotions were all over the place,' I began. 'My parents believed it was the best option, so I went along with it. I couldn't fathom bringing a baby into the world. I had no idea how it would work. Jason, we were still teenagers. But it hurt, it hurt so much when I went through with it. I've never got over it.' My head hung down. The fact I was naked now felt dirty and cheap. Anything but beautiful or sexy. The idea that his lips were clamped onto mine just a few hours ago, it seemed like a very wrong and distant memory. I pulled the duvet up around me and my fists clenched around it.

We were both silenced now.

'It's a decision I've regretted ever since,' I added after a few seconds. I breathed out, my head pounding. I fought back tears again. Once the floodgates opened, I wasn't sure how they would close. I really didn't want to cry. Not naked in bed with him.

He reached for my hand and squeezed it. 'I'm sorry,' he said. 'I'm so sorry I couldn't help you. I could have been there for you if I had known before, but I only found out when it was too late. I was young and scared. It must have been so hard.'

I moved my hand away from his. *I could have been there for you.* Did he have any idea what that meant?

It was the best but also the worst thing he could say.

'But if you knew – why *weren't* you? I've lived with the guilt of terminating our baby, of you not knowing, of betraying someone I loved, my friends, of hating my parents, of dropping out of a university I loved… The list goes on. And it doesn't get any easier with time, I assure you. If anything, it has got harder as I've come to realize the full implications of what I did. And all this time, you knew. Who told you?'

'It doesn't matter any more,' he said.

Tears filled my eyes and I closed the lids for a moment to try to hold them in.

'I'm sorry, Lucy, I shouldn't have said anything. It was a bad idea. I shouldn't have found you again.'

'Found me?' I said, in a tone that was half way between laughter and yelling. 'Now you're telling me you *found* me?'

'I looked you up, you're easy to find online. The PR company has your profile on its site.'

'You stalked me yesterday?'

'I wouldn't put it quite like that.'

'Why did you find me, Jason?'

'I was intrigued. But, like I said, I can see now that it was a bad idea.'

He was getting out of bed as he said this, searching out his clothes which were scattered all around the floor. He put on his boxers and collected the other items. His nakedness now seemed sordid.

'I can't believe you've done this to me,' I seethed, barely able to get the words out, my head felt so muddled – a combination of the alcohol still in my system and how horribly wrong this morning's post-coital chat was going.

'I'll go, I can see you need to be alone,' he said, already half-dressed. He just wanted to leave.

After I heard the front door close, I lay there in shock, unmoving, lost in thought I looked around the room, only my own clothes strewn across the floor now. I began piecing together the events of last night and how it felt to have Jason's body pressed into mine; I could still smell him, feel his warmth on my skin; I could still taste him in my mouth. There was a fug of him all over me, the sheets and in the air. The smell of sex enveloped my body. I could remember us having sex, him on top of me and then him rolling me over so I could ride him. My breasts beating against his chest as he firmly held my hips and took me fast and furiously; filling me up, squeezing my bottom in his hands. We were consumed by lust and lost in each other's bodies. I had a vague recollection of things slowing down and then him rolling off me and passing out. I couldn't be sure whether or not he came, but I'd hazard a guess he did. I knew we hadn't used any protection because I didn't have any in the flat.

How could he? Jason had sought me out and slept with me knowing such a big secret – a secret that had haunted me for the past two decades. I tried to blink back the tears from the corners of my eyes, but they continued to fall. It felt like they might never stop, dripping onto the pillow no matter how fast I tried to wipe them away. I felt so used.

I must have cried myself to sleep, because when I woke up again, I was lying diagonally across my bed, and there was a streak of light across the duvet as daylight leaked from the gap in the middle of the curtains. I guessed it must be around eight. My head was throbbing. I was alone. My heart unbearably heavy. The events of this morning filtered back into my consciousness.

It must have been soon after sunrise that he left and the weight of his flesh moved away from my bed, his hands ceased to hold me, his gaze gone. All that was left in his wake was a shattered memory of what might have been.

Oh fuck. Oh fuck, it was today. The Day. The one I had been counting down to for the last year of my life. I held my stomach, lacing my fingers across my middle and tears prickled at my eyes again. Had I completely ruined my chances by having sex last night? Sex that I could barely remember because I was so drunk, and now bitterly regretted? My head hurt with the vice-like grip of a grade A hangover. My mouth was dry.

I must have sobbed for at least the next ten minutes.

Slowly, my breathing began to steady and I collected my thoughts again. I had to think straight. My appointment at the clinic was at two this afternoon, and now it was still early. There was time to get myself together. I just needed more sleep. I'd weathered hangovers worse than this before – sleep and water would help. I knew I couldn't let myself miss this appointment.

I tried to placate the nagging voice in my head with the reasoning that so many women were well and truly trolleyed when they got knocked up – and many more only realized they were pregnant after weeks of getting pissed and having sex. In fact they didn't even know for sure when they conceived. And *they* went on to have perfectly healthy babies. Having sex wasn't a crime anyway. Could it really be that bad? Perhaps I had doubled my chances of a successful pregnancy. Maybe there was a silver lining.

For the next hour I drifted in and out of consciousness, desperate to shake off the pounding headache, but refraining from taking any medication because of the slim chance that I might be pregnant – or that I could be pregnant again by the end of today.

I tried to piece the evening together. I was absolutely certain we didn't use any contraception because I had none in this flat. Could I be pregnant? Should I still go ahead with the transfer? My hand hovered over my phone as I considered calling Katie. She would be shocked yet intrigued to know that I'd seen Jason after all that time. It could have been a cute, romantic story if it wasn't such a disaster at the same time. I decided against it – it all felt too emotionally raw – and instead raced out of bed to find my laptop.

Jason left so early I didn't even have a chance to implant his features on my mind once more. He had certainly changed in twenty years. His skin was now slightly lined around the eyes, his nose a little wider perhaps, but he still had the same square jaw, dark eyelashes, thick hair, and the traces of the deep tan he must have got from spending all those years in Australia and Asia. I thought about how there was once a time when I had woken up half naked next to him regularly. Back when my body had been lithe and pure; when my heart had been full of hope. My fertility hadn't even crossed my mind back then. I'd taken every morning with Jason for granted, sometimes rising before him and heading out to the uni campus, not giving him a second glance as I dashed out of the door because I felt secure in his love for me. I had barely slept in my allocated room in our student halls because I was always with him, squashed together in his single bed, sleeping entwined. I fell in love with him so fast and hard.

By the time I was ready to leave the house for the IVF clinic I was feeling a little stronger. Jason was the only man to have ever got me pregnant and, devastated as I was, after what he had told me this morning, I wasn't going to let him ruin my second chance at becoming a mum.

CHAPTER THIRTY-FIVE

Lucy

Tuesday 10th August, present day

I walked halfway around Clapham Common, but couldn't face going the long way back so decided to take a short cut on the path that went through the bandstand in the middle.

When I approached, my attention was caught by a couple on one of the benches to the right. The woman had spilt a cup of coffee everywhere.

And then I recognized them. It was Aisha and Jason, and they didn't look happy.

Certain they hadn't seen me, I spun around and walked, or rather ran, in the opposite direction. I didn't care that this was taking me further away from home, I'd jump on a bus at the other end to be sure not to bump into either of them. My heart was racing fast. It didn't look like they were having a cosy chat. I felt sick. Was that the moment – could he have told her?

When I reached home Albie was awake and in need of

a bottle. It was a welcome distraction to cradle him in my arms and watch him make cute raspberry noises as he played with the teat of the bottle.

I kept my phone in sight on the kitchen island next to me and when it pinged it made me jump. I had a sense of dread. I still didn't have his number saved into my phone, but I recognized the digits immediately. It confirmed my very worst fear. Just two words:

She knows.

For a moment I tried to carry on as if everything was normal, but my hand was trembling as I lifted the bottle to Albie's lips again. He was playing me, and clamped his mouth shut. Milk splattered everywhere.

I hurriedly cleaned Albie up and tried again, holding him closely on the sofa as he polished off the bottle of milk. I didn't take my eyes off him as he contentedly gulped it down. I was literally clinging on to him as though our closeness would give me strength. As I stared at his tiny features, an overwhelming love washed over me; a love for Albie more powerful than I had felt since he was born. It was so strong it almost hurt, like someone was twisting at my heart, wringing it out. I couldn't love him any more if I tried. I kissed his forehead.

'I love you so, so much, my little man,' I whispered aloud. 'But what the hell is Mummy going to do now?' I paused, my eyes pricking with tears, just as Albie let out a little gurgle. 'Oh you think so, do you? You think Mummy should do that? I think you could be right.'

When Jason and I took the home DNA test in his flat, that morning when Aisha was supposed to be at the spa, although we didn't know the result yet, I achieved a form of closure. I realized that I didn't want Jason in my life. But that Aisha deserved better than him. I think I realized then that she should know – whatever the result happened to be. But it didn't surprise me that Jason may have reached the same conclusion and, naturally, he was determined to get to her first.

The reality was that if he did turn out to be Albie's father, Jason might have to be in my life. I knew the chance was slim – 'negligible' was the word the consultant had used when I first discovered I was pregnant and came clean to the clinic about what had happened – but soon we would know for certain and I would have to deal with the consequences.

I was pretty sure that Aisha would never want to see me again; she must be feeling so betrayed, not only by Jason, but by someone who had come to be her friend. I wished I'd never joined the stupid Baby Group. At first I did it to put the frighteners up Jason. His face was going to be a picture when he saw me. But I hadn't properly considered Aisha. She was *so* much more than I expected; a really lovely woman – she was kind, warm, clever. I liked her, and genuincly felt we had become friends. She made it all so much harder. She didn't deserve this.

But most of all, I was terrified about what it might do to Oscar and me. There was now a large risk that he would find out – perhaps Jason would tell him next, out of spite – and Oscar might want to leave me. And if the baby did turn out to be Jason's, well that could tear Oscar and me apart forever. It felt as though we were hanging on by a thread as it was. The thought of losing Oscar was now my biggest fear. Oscar was Albie's daddy in every practical and emotional sense and the thought of losing him too much to bear.

Albie seemed to sense something was up because he stopped feeding momentarily and looked up at me. If I wasn't mistaken, his blue eyes had started to lighten slightly. In some lights they were a clear azure – coincidentally the same colour as Oscar's. They were not turning green, like Jason's, as I had once imagined. His forehead was crumpled and he had a puzzled expression, which also reminded me of Oscar.

'I love you so much, little angel,' I whispered, as he suckled away happily again. 'I'm so sorry for this mess. But whatever happens, it will never change the fact that I am so lucky to have you.'

When Albie had finished the bottle, I burped him and set him down on his play mat, rattling the jangly toys above his head and enjoying watching his face light up as he gurgled excitedly, trying to reach them. His blue eyes were still sparkling as he lay directly underneath a spotlight on the ceiling. I tried to view them purely as Albie's eyes, the windows into the soul of my precious baby boy. I vowed to live in the moment with him for as long as life would allow us.

CHAPTER THIRTY-SIX

Aisha

After an immediate burst of anger towards Jason, it quickly fell away and was replaced by pain. The pure, visceral, searing pain of realizing that my world had been rocked to its core and everything had changed in a heartbeat.

Joni was sound asleep in the pram, so I turned my back on Jason, ignoring his loud, desperate pleas for us to talk, and started walking as briskly as I could to nowhere in particular, just anywhere. Eventually his cries stopped. He didn't dare follow me, judging correctly that it would cause the most almighty scene if he did.

Although I was in a daze, barely registering where I was going, my feet and mind seemed to lead me towards our street on auto-pilot. Once I found myself standing outside our flat, I wondered about not going in. The sun was beating down and I'd forgotten a large muslin to cover the pram. I hadn't been planning on staying out for long, but nothing about today was normal now. I decided to go inside, hoping Jason would at least be sensible enough to stay well away and give me some space.

Alone in our flat, the building suddenly felt unfamiliar and cold. I left Joni sleeping in the pram downstairs, blissfully unaware of the bombshell her daddy had just dropped, while I went up and wandered from room to room, barely able to focus on finding the muslin, I had been so blindsided by Jason's news.

How could he have done this to me – to *us*? To *our* little bean, Joni, who we created out of love and I grew inside of me. I felt nauseous. Everything we had felt like a lie. It was as though a trail of falling dominoes – one for each day of my life – had been set in motion and I had no idea when its path of destruction would end; whether it would be today, tomorrow, or never. I bit my quivering lip.

Was I a single mum now? I took a deep breath in an attempt to hold back my tears. Not right now. I had to think.

Still on automatic, I went to the bedroom, and pulled out the spare baby-change bag. I needed some time to get my head around what to do next. I began filling it with a few essentials: the big muslin, a couple of babygrows, some nappies and a pack of wipes; and then for myself, a couple of spare tops, my skincare products, a hairbrush, and a few pairs of knickers. Then I moved to the kitchen and loaded up on baby bottles, formula, the sterliser and some Tupperware containers useful for any eventuality. Travelling with Tupperware would at least give me some comfort. Even in the face of earth-shattering news, Joni would still need taking care of, so certain aspects of life had to carry on as normal.

Suddenly I felt unsteady on my feet. I had barely eaten all day – my hope that Jason planned to take me for lunch laughable now. The optimism I had felt was a joke. God, I felt so stupid. My phone pinged and a message appeared on the Baby Group thread. It was from Will – a picture of a dribble bib and a caption:

Missing in action. Does this belong to any of you? It was left at the pottery shop. Thanks for coming along. Hope the gifts go down well! Wx

I recognized the bib as belonging to Albie, but wondered whether Lucy would respond; whether she had any idea that I knew and, if so, if she felt any remorse for the hurt she had caused. The thought of her and Jason in collusion made me feel like throwing up. I realized my hands were trembling as I held the phone. The Baby Group were the last people I wanted to see or hear from. I doubted whether I would ever be able to see them again, especially Lucy, after what she had done to me. I had unwittingly found myself at the centre of a storyline even a writer on a soap opera might find a little far-fetched.

My mind wandered back to the day I told Jason I was pregnant, when I turned up at his office because I couldn't reach him on the phone; how he had sobbed, it was almost uncontrollable. I went over and over that memory for clues. I wished I hadn't buried my suspicions that something wasn't right. Maybe if I had put Jason on the spot, or given him an opportunity to open up, he would have told me everything. I wished he had. I wondered how Jason had been able to live with himself for so long, and especially that day, when it should have been momentous for us, finally finding out we were having a baby. I thought of all the times Jason and Lucy had come into contact with each other. Jason's offish behaviour when he left the Baby Group sessions made perfect sense now. Knowing what an enormous secret they shared not only made me feel sick – but such a pitiful fool.

There was a noise from downstairs as Joni woke. I dashed to her and when I stood above the pram and her eyes met mine, her whole face showed she was eager to play. She looked so innocent and happy, so completely oblivious to what had happened today, it broke my heart. I shoved the bag under the pram and we left the house again.

I called Tara and explained in as few words as I could that I needed to come and stay with her tonight, that I was desperate. I could tell she wanted to ask me what had happened, but all she said was, 'Of course, I'll be home in ten minutes. You can stay as long as you need.' As I put the phone down a tear rolled down my cheek.

CHAPTER THIRTY-SEVEN

Lucy

Thursday 12th August

Over the next two days I barely left the house, partly because Albie had come down with a shocking chesty cough, but mostly because I felt so anxious. All I could think about was whether or not I should contact Aisha, and the test results. I just wanted this to be over, but I was also fearful of what would happen next.

I wondered if a one-night stand could be classed as an affair. More specifically, whether Jason had called it an affair, seeing as we had known each other for so long and he had admitted he came to find me. Deep down, I knew that what Jason and I had could not be classified as an affair. I felt pretty sure he would describe it to Aisha as his 'biggest mistake'.

I wondered, if the truth hadn't come out, whether the secret would have killed Aisha and Jason's marriage eventually, anyway. However you looked at it, there didn't seem to be an uncomplicated outcome.

For me, it was more than a 'one-night stand'. Jason had been inside my head for over twenty years. And in my mind we'd been having an emotional affair since that evening over a year ago, because he had taken over my thoughts so regularly. As painful as it had been the following morning, I could never regret the sex we had because, one way or another, the course of events over that twenty-four hours gave me Albie. So something went very right. But I needed to know the truth now, for Albie's sake.

Things had gone quiet on the WhatsApp thread and in light of what was going on, I didn't feel inclined to make the first move. Aside from the note about the mislaid dribble bib – to which I did not respond – and a couple of exchanges between Will and Susie about suspected hand, foot and mouth disease after a session at a soft-play centre, there had been no suggestion of meeting up. I stayed mute and so did Aisha.

Aisha played on my mind; her face haunted me. She would be devastated, and the last person she would want to hear from was me. Everyone in The Baby Group was going to hate me, that was a given.

Then a really terrifying thought hit me: perhaps Aisha would want to confront me. Every time the doorbell rang, my heart rate sped up and I peered through the security camera, wondering if it was her, come to let rip. Once or twice I'd seen a stranger standing on the doorstep and hadn't opened the door, worried that she or Jason had sent someone to confront me on their behalf. I missed a couple of Amazon deliveries as a result.

I began to live in fear of what would happen next and it

sent a feeling of perpetual sickness through my body. I felt anxious most of the time, but was becoming adept at hiding it. Conversely, during the past two days, when I had successfully managed to internalize, things were better between Oscar and me, and he was back staying in the house every night. The only difference he did pick up on was that I had lost my appetite and the desire to cook. Personally, I wasn't too worried about this side effect because it finally gave me the opportunity to drop some of the postpartum pounds I was having trouble shifting. But my disinterest in food began to be noticed by Oscar and one evening he cottoned on to something.

'I'm thinking of making a noodle stir-fry for dinner tonight, but are you still on a diet?' he called out, wok in hand, as I sat in an armchair giving Albie his bedtime bottle. 'You should eat properly you know – you need the energy.'

'I had a massive sandwich as a late lunch,' I replied. It wasn't true. But didn't everyone have secrets, tell little white lies to cover up the truth sometimes? It had become second nature to me.

'Where did you go?' he asked.

'What?'

'To *eat*,' he said, 'Where did you go to eat the sandwich?'

I looked at him blankly.

'Earth to Lucy… Is there anybody in there?'

'I was here,' I answered breezily.

'Where did you hide all the bread then?' he retorted, opening the lid to the bread bin and finding nothing inside it. 'I'll just have a sandwich myself, if you're not eating with me.'

'Sorry, I must have finished it,' I said.

He fixed his eyes on me. He knew I was lying; that I was up to something.

'Lucy—' he started.

I stared down. 'I need to put Albie to bed. Let's talk after that. Perhaps you could pour us a glass of wine each?'

I knew I needed to let Oscar in, but I was so scared it would end up with us having a fight – and worst case, that he would leave us. He would be flabbergasted by this news.

Once Albie had drifted off to sleep, I stayed in the nursery, sitting in the darkness on the bench seat by his cot for a while. The rhythmic sound of his breathing soothed me. I knew my behaviour must seem strange to Oscar; I'd practically become a recluse. Perhaps I hadn't been hiding things as well as I thought. But I needed him now, more than ever.

As if Oscar was reading my mind, Albie's door opened a little and a shaft of light from the landing created an orange pathway on the carpet. Then Oscar's tall shadow filled it as he stood in the doorway. He had two glasses of red wine in his hands. His silhouette looked big, strong, sensible, and dependable; all the qualities I loved in him.

'What's going on, Lucy?' he asked solemnly. 'I can see you're not yourself. Please talk to me.'

I didn't reply. Where would I even start?

Oscar came and sat next to me in the dark. He passed me a glass of wine and I took a much-needed sip.

'I never should have joined that Baby Group – you were right,' I muttered after a few seconds passed. 'It's brought back memories I wanted to forget.'

'Memories?' he asked. 'What do you mean?'

We sat there in the shadows, talking for the next hour – somehow it was easier that way, close to the baby at the centre of all this, without the intensity of Oscar being able to read every expression on my face.

I told him about the night with Jason, and about what he had told me in the morning.

Oscar took it all absolutely calmly, saying, 'Keep going', in appropriate places.

Of course, I spared him the hottest parts, about how electrifying the sex had been and how consumed with lust I was from the first touch of Jason's hand on my leg. But I also told him how things had ended. How Jason had revealed he knew I'd had an abortion all those years ago – that he'd known at the time, and just hadn't told me. How I felt that if we had talked, maybe I wouldn't have felt pressured to go ahead with it. How, after dropping that bombshell, he had left, only to completely blank me two weeks later when I tried to reach him on text to tell him I was pregnant. How he had blocked me from all of his social media accounts, callously cut me off. How it stung then, and that it still hurt me now.

'So how did you find out about The Baby Group?' Oscar asked. 'If Jason had cut you off?'

'I'd been googling him and found a photo on the society pages of a Hong Kong online magazine. It was a wedding photo of a couple who were obviously somebodies in Asia, and on either side of them, so the caption said, were friends Jason Moore and girlfriend, Aisha Chandra. I recognized him immediately. And I knew Aisha was of Indian descent, so there was no doubt it was her and her surname gave me another name to search for. Her Instagram account appeared immediately: "Aisha Chandra. Children's book illustrator and lover of vintage finds, London". It had to be her. Then I saw the latest photo on her grid.' My heart leapt into my mouth at the memory. 'A photo of a baby scan, and underneath it the caption: "Baby Moore, due early June". From there, it wasn't hard to find which Baby Group they had joined because I knew they lived in Clapham. At least now I knew why Jason cut me off. He must have panicked.' I paused for a moment; revisiting all this was painful. 'I'll understand if you need to go somewhere,' I said hesitantly, turning to Oscar. 'I won't blame you if you want to leave.'

But Oscar didn't flinch. 'This is quite a story. I want to know everything,' he said.

'You need to understand what it meant to me when I saw Jason on the Tube that day, and I'll come onto that,' I said, feeling calmer now that he wasn't running to pack a bag. 'I wouldn't have approached him, it was him who came up to me, it was him who suggested we went to the pub, and it turned out that he had purposely found me that day. He must have followed me from work. We got really drunk; we were catching up on twenty years, and I can't even really remember leaving the pub. But he came back to mine and… we got physical. It was consensual, of course. But he was really pissed – much drunker than me; he'd been doing shots on top of all the wine. I know we didn't use any protection. Deep down I think it's unlikely Jason is Albie's father – even the IVF doctor told me the likelihood is 'negligible' – but on that night, you and I weren't back together, and a bit of me still wanted to believe Jason was the only man who could get me pregnant.'

Oscar had finished his glass of wine while I was speaking, and now he took mine and drank that too. I carried on. Oscar had to know this, even if it meant the worst. In a strange way, however awful this was, it was almost a relief to be talking to him. The words were spilling out like water from a broken tap. I didn't want any more secrets; I hated them.

'In my mind, after Jason cut me off, I wanted to get him back,' I said, between pauses to blow my nose and wipe the tears from my eyes. 'I wanted to test him. As time moved on, I still couldn't let it go. Then I had this twisted idea that if I joined the same Baby Group, when Jason saw me he would put two and two together and believe he had fathered my child. And then, in one way or another, it would ruin his marriage. I wanted him to feel some of the pain I had endured over the past two decades. At the time, when I signed up to the group, you and I had only been back together for a few months and deep down I was nervous about our future. You had made it very clear you didn't want a family with me not so long before, and having a baby felt like the biggest need in my life. I had to prioritise myself and Albie ahead of anything.'

I slid my eyes towards Oscar to gauge his reaction. He looked shell-shocked.

'Lucy, I hear you, but don't try to blame *me* for what you did. You might have destroyed a family. Possibly two.'

That last comment really stung because he was clearly referring to us.

'I managed to convince myself that joining their Baby Group was the best way to see Jason again. But once I was in the class, I knew it was a terrible, terrible mistake. He was so filled with venom towards me. The pain he caused me when he told me he'd known about the abortion all along came flooding back and it hit me hard. But as I became friends with Aisha – with his wife – the secret, as well as my baby bump, grew bigger and bigger. I knew she didn't deserve to be treated this way; that she deserved better than Jason; but I couldn't see a way out.'

I hung my head low in shame. Sometimes I questioned my own sanity; saying it all out loud, it sounded like the doings of a mad, vengeful person. Was that what I had become?

It seemed absurd to think I could ever have been in love with Jason and built him up to be some kind of Adonis in my head, when the person I needed the most was right here under my nose all along. Oscar.

'I wish I'd never joined that group because, if I hadn't, none of this would have happened and I wouldn't have had to unearth "that night" again.' The dragging weight of the past made my head feel heavy and my eyes fill with tears.

Oscar had now finished my glass of wine. 'Let's move downstairs and get another,' he whispered. I felt relieved he wasn't exploding with rage, but his calmness was unnerving.

I walked down the stairs behind him and sat at the breakfast bar. I watched his back and arms as he refilled his glass and poured another, purposely keeping his body turned away from me, perhaps as a means of disconnecting for a bit.

I wondered what he was thinking. I felt such enormous love for him. If anyone was worth fighting for, it was Oscar.

When he joined me on a stool at the counter I continued: 'When you told me you didn't want children, I had to split up with you,' I said. 'Having a baby has been one of the biggest desires in my life, and in my late thirties it became an obsession. I couldn't imagine a future with you without children.' I paused, pondering for a moment whether to go on.

'Well Lucy, you got your baby.' He turned his face away from me, so I couldn't read his expression.

I swallowed hard in an effort to compose myself and continue. 'Jason was the only man to have got me pregnant naturally, albeit twenty years ago. Subconsciously, when I was with him that evening, my body reawakened. I had imagined seeing him again so many times in my head over the years, and now it was really happening. Childhood sweethearts, reunited. It was such a romantic notion. But it was a baby I longed for, it wasn't him. I know that now.'

In sentences punctuated with tears, I described how I had lived with the grief and guilt of terminating that baby for so long. It felt as though only now, now that I had become a mother again and held my own child in my arms, I could process the emotion I had blocked out.

'After that night with Jason, when I had IVF the next day, it gave me a renewed hope that motherhood could be a reality for me. And coupled with seeing Jason, the timing of it so uncanny, I had the romantic idea that fate had brought us together and maybe we *were* meant to be together after all, whether or not he was the biological father of my baby.

I thought we might have a chance of the future we lost twenty years ago. But I was so wrong.' I stopped, took a deep breath and dared to reach for Oscar's hand, 'It was only ever you, Oscar. You are the one I love more than anything.'

'Jason must have been petrified when he saw you there, in The Baby Group,' Oscar said, almost comically, allowing my hand to gently rest on his for a few moments before he moved it. 'But Lucy, if you felt all this, why did you continue going to the group?'

'Because there was no return. You can't just turn up like that and then just casually disappear in a puff of smoke.'

'You *can* if you want to!' Oscar snapped, startling me.

'I had made a good friend there,' I mumbled. 'Getting close to Aisha made everything a million times harder. Some part of me thought we could be friends – as mad as that sounds.'

Then I told him how Jason had confronted me in the hallway when I'd gone to the Ladies' during one Baby Group session before he made a swift exit, and then he texted me trying to arrange a time for us to talk. I put him off. I was scared of Aisha finding out. At first he had warned me off – he had ordered me to 'Stay away from his wife!', and then he had started demanding a paternity test. He was threatening. I was terrified – not only for my own safety, but for Albie too. I told Oscar that Jason and I had taken a DIY paternity test and the results were expected in a few days. Although my instinct was that Jason had not fathered Albie, I knew that we all needed to know the definitive truth.

'But whatever the result,' I reasoned, 'the big – and most important – thing I've realized since having Albie, is that it doesn't matter who the real father is. We will probably never know who Albie's real dad is because I opted for an anonymous donor. But actions are more important than biology. Oscar, you are more of a father to Albie than anyone could ever be. He is so lucky to have you in his life.'

I stopped again to catch my breath and simultaneously try to read Oscar's face. Tears bubbled to the surface. I felt desperate. Desperate for him and any reassurance that he still cared about me and Albie. My voice faltered as I went on: 'Please believe me when I tell you that I didn't mean any harm. Please believe that I love you, Oscar – I love you with all my heart, and I can only imagine Albie and me growing old with you.' My voice trailed off into little more than a quiet whisper as I uttered, 'I am so sorry.'

This time the urge to cry was too strong. As tears spilled down my face, Oscar got up and pulled me into his chest. He didn't say anything, he just held me tightly.

I'd gone to the precipice of losing him and it was a terrifying place to be.

CHAPTER THIRTY-EIGHT

Aisha

Tara had proven to be a hero friend. Adept at multitasking, she had opened the front door to me with one hand and put a glass of red wine into mine with the other. Then she had taken the pram and picked Joni up, planting kisses on her cheeks. She'd literally scooped us both up that day.

'You and Joni will stay here until you're ready to leave,' she'd commanded. 'I've sent Hugo away for the night to give you some space, but he agrees with me that you should stay as long as you need. We've got every type of baby para-phernalia you could possibly need – that's if you don't mind Joni dressed in boys' clothes. This is the twenty-first century. And you can borrow anything of mine.'

I had cast an embarrassed look down at myself, taking in my denim jeggings, black espadrilles and gingham smock top, barely able to remember getting dressed that morning, it already felt like a lifetime ago. The scarf I had wrapped around myself in case I got covered in paint at the pottery class, or needed to breastfeed, was clashing badly. Things had really slipped in the fashion department.

'How do you do it?' Tara had commented, seemingly oblivious to the hot mess before her. 'No matter what happens, you always look bloody beautiful.'

I'd been relieved when her youngest, three-year-old Dexter, appeared between her legs, causing a distraction just as my eyes were prickling with tears.

'We'll get the kids down ASAP and then talk. We're going to take good care of my friend Aisha and baby Joni, aren't we Dexter?' she'd said to the little boy who was blowing raspberries at us both. 'Our friend needs lots of cuddles.'

When she'd looked up again, tears were streaming down my cheeks. Like flowing rivers, they would not be stemmed.

'Oh my darling Aish.' She had lain Joni back into the pram for a moment and wrapped her arms around me in a big bear hug. 'It's fine, let it out. You and Joni are safe here.'

We had stood like that for at least a minute, both afraid to draw away from the warmth of each other, because then one person might be expected to say something. It wasn't easy to find the words, for either of us. But that was the beauty of being with Tara, we didn't need words. Another few seconds had passed until Dexter had given Joni a prod in her pram and she had made her presence known.

'Thank you,' I had mustered, as my breathing steadied. 'Oh Tara, it's so bad – I don't know what the hell I'm going to do.'

The last two days at Tara's had been exhausting physically as well as emotionally. I'd been through the whole spectrum, from crying uncontrollably for hours in the middle of the night, often with Joni on the boob, to feeling quite numb when thinking through the logistics and resolving there was no option but to make Jason move out. The fear that a call could come at any time to reveal the outcome of the paternity test also left me in a permanent, sick-to-the-stomach state of nervousness.

At the same time, Joni had decided to land the worst bout of sleep regression on me since the one she'd had at three months. Maybe she had a sixth sense and was feeling the same separation anxiety from Jason that was also waking me up in a hot sweat several times a night. There were moments of physical pain, deep within me, as I yearned for Jason – the old Jason – and our former life, which I had always believed was happy. I now knew we had been living a partial lie. I fluctuated between feeling incredibly stupid for not listening to my intuition a year ago and raging with so much fury, both for him and Lucy, that I wanted to explode.

The first morning at Tara's, I was so tired from the broken night's sleep and all the crying, I could barely see through my puffy, bloodshot eyes when I woke up. For a few precious seconds I woke to the blissful sounds of my baby, and then the horror of what had happened hit me full on.

Much as Tara's spare room was a lovely place to be, it was also the last place I imagined we would find ourselves during my maternity leave, when I should be enjoying these moments with Jason. I had received a barrage of frantic texts and missed calls from him during the first evening, but aside from sending him one text back, to let him know that we were safe and that I'd tell him when I was going back to the flat, that was the only communication we'd had. Words seemed futile right now; there was nothing he could say to make it better.

Now, after a second night at Tara's, I was ready to go home. I didn't want to see Jason, but I wanted to be back in the flat, for practical reasons as much as anything else. Joni and I needed our own clothes and things around us. I texted Jason to tell him I was coming back, and that he needed to go. I might not have been able to control the past, but it was my turn to call the shots now.

CHAPTER THIRTY-NINE

Lucy

Friday 13th August

On the night of my revelation, Oscar and I had got ready for bed in silence. We had drunk plenty of wine and were emotionally wrung out. I barely slept. On the one hand, the fact we were sleeping in the same bed had given me hope. But on the other, I knew things were far from resolved. When Albie woke in the night and I brought him into our bed to comfort him, Oscar silently moved to the spare room.

In the morning, when Albie stirred, I lifted him out of his cocoon on the bed next to me and took him into the spare room to see if Oscar was awake. The bed was empty. My heart sank.

I heard the noises downstairs so I followed them, Albie in my arms. Oscar was making breakfast in the kitchen. He was wearing his dressing gown and nothing else.

'Hello,' I whispered tentatively.

'Morning,' he replied in such a monotone way I couldn't second-guess his mood.

'Is everything okay?' I asked. Albie gurgled hungrily.

'Lucy,' he replied, turning to face me front on, 'I've always loved you and since you've become a mother, I love you even more. You're an amazing mum.' He smiled at Albie and right on cue, Albie cooed back. 'I've developed such a strong bond with Albie and I can't imagine not being here to see all the firsts in his life. But I really wish you had told me all this before.'

The 'But' floored me.

I looked into his eyes. 'I know, I wish I had too. But—' A pause. 'Can you forgive me?'

I was petrified of his answer. My question hung in the air. The suspense was almost too much to bear.

'I've been awake half the night thinking things through,' he sighed heavily. 'I'm going to stick by you through this, Lucy,' I sensed there was a caveat coming, 'because I love you, and I'm in this forever. But you must never keep secrets from me. I'm not going anywhere right now, but I don't want any more surprises. I mean it.'

I moved across the room towards him, still holding Albie close for reassurance, relief washing through every part of my body. 'I promise. No secrets. I'll always be yours. Thank you, Oscar. I love you so much,' I whispered in Oscar's ear. It quickly became moist from my tears.

Then his mouth gently touched my skin and I knew it was going to be okay. For now.

CHAPTER FORTY

Aisha

When Joni and I got home, the place felt empty and cold. On my request Jason had moved out, no discussion, he knew better than to question me right now. Even here, it felt as though Lucy was haunting me; I remembered how I had caught her looking at our photos when she came here for the breastfeeding class. I bet she was desperate for a nose into our personal life. It sickened me to think of her here, pretending to be so innocent.

I took down all the photos of Jason from the flat. My eyes lingered for a moment on the Bristol FC photo, the one that had caught Lucy's attention that evening at the breastfeeding class. It would have been taken around the time they had dated. I couldn't bear to look at any part of him – the lips that had kissed hers, the hands that had been all over her body, the legs that had led her to wherever it was they had sex. Maybe it was in a hotel room, in a car, her place, don't tell me in was in our bed – it could have been anywhere. It was so seedy. I didn't want to know the details, yet I had a morbid fascination with thinking about them together. The thought of them having sex repulsed me, but I couldn't let the image go. Fleeting scenes as if from a film flashed through my mind, much as I tried to push them away. I wondered whether it had been passionate. I always thought that Jason and I had great sex – it was regular, it wasn't over in seconds, we could tease each other for hours if we wanted, there was dirty talk and sometimes role-play, pre-baby of course, and generally we both came. He satisfied me. But it was apparently not enough for Jason, he clearly wanted more.

The feeling was no better when I left the house. Every paving stone on the streets of Clapham reminded me of her, as did the smell of coffee outside Starbucks and a sign for the nearby yoga studio. I couldn't bear to go near the church hall where we had met at The Baby Group, taking the longer route around it to Sainsbury's, rather than be transported back to the time Jason had sat in the same room as Lucy, both of them holding this big smutty secret between them. I wondered if it had excited them at all. It certainly helped to explain Jason's weird behaviour at the session he came to. How Lucy had showed off with her speciality salads. Who was she trying to impress really? I wondered if Oscar knew about Jason too. I doubted there was any truth at all in her IVF and anonymous sperm donor story. How could she have been such a lying bitch?

I decided to try to make life as normal as possible for Joni, so that afternoon I took her to the playground on Clapham Common. But as I pushed her on the swing I momentarily froze, imagining I'd seen Lucy out of the corner of my eye, appearing behind me with Albie. When I turned it was just a stranger. I thought about spending a few more days away from the area to escape this feeling – to escape *her*. I considered booking me and Joni a flight to Dubai to stay with my dad, but he had moved in with a woman I had only 'met' on Skype and I decided I'd feel even more alienated over there, without Tara or my flat in easy reach.

I told Dad about Jason on the phone, and his reaction surprised me. Where I'd always got the impression Dad was slightly disappointed with Jason – that he thought I should be with a wealthier man, who could keep me in the luxury in which he had kept Mum – there was genuine sorrow in his voice. Once again I was hit by the physical pain of missing Mum. I felt sure I would have confided all this in her, and wondered what her advice might have been.

'Whether or not he's the father of that child, he's still the father of yours, Aisha,' Dad said. I sensed remorse in his voice. 'Does Joni deserve to lose him from her life as well, over a foolish mistake? We men all make mistakes. We're not as together as you women.'

I wondered if this was his way of saying sorry for his lack of engagement in my own life. Whether he was a keeper of secrets too. I got the feeling he felt guilty, although he couldn't articulate it.

Saturday 14ᵗʰ August

The next day, after a better night's sleep, I was feeling stronger. And as each day passed, it started to take less and less time to root myself back in reality when my eyes opened each morning.

I felt resolute that I was the innocent party here and I wanted Jason out, for the time being at least, whatever the result of the test. How could I trust him again after such a huge betrayal? Perhaps I would be fine as a single mum. Tara had done a good job of drilling some courage into me; sending me regular texts of support and pictures of affirmations about finding inner strength and believing in myself. She was helping to reassure me that I had done absolutely nothing wrong, and time would help me to decide where my life was going to go from here, but not to make rash decisions or invite Jason back in before I was ready; to focus my energy on Joni.

Still, wherever I went, I kept feeling Lucy's toxic presence. Occasionally I'd get a waft of that sickly sweet rose perfume she wore and I would turn sharply, my heart pounding, expecting to see her standing behind me, only to discover she wasn't there at all, it was simply my own shadow.

That night, when she was asleep in her cot beside me, I tortured myself by staring at Joni and wondering whether she looked like Albie at all. Whether she could feasibly be his half-sister, based on their looks, as that was all I had to go on.

There was a similarity in their looks, well, as much as babies all look the same to some degree. But if you looked closer, they both had the same shade of brown hair and what you might describe as strong features. It gave me goosebumps.

I wondered how many times Lucy had done the same, and remembered how I had caught her looking at Joni so closely once in the café. I thought about the moment I had thrust Joni into her arms that time when I was trying to untangle the nappy bag. The fact she was someone I had considered trustworthy, that she had held my baby in her arms, made me shudder. How could she have been so brazen? Now it explained so much. She was scheming for certain, I just wondered how far she was planning to take this car-crash situation.

CHAPTER FORTY-ONE

Lucy

It was Oscar's birthday when I decided it was time to start going out again. I hadn't heard a thing from Jason so I imagined he had decided to focus on his own family unit until we had the paternity test results, which we were due to receive any day now – or he was plotting my slow, painful death. Either way, it didn't seem fair that Oscar should also become a recluse because of this. He was my rock. I made a reservation at his favourite Michelin-starred restaurant in London, and surprised him with the news the day before. He was delighted and seeing Oscar so happy made my spirits lift too.

I had hoped that we might have the test results by now – so Oscar and I would have some concrete news to celebrate – but when I called the company first thing that morning I was told nothing was on the system yet and that we should get it by email 'in the next couple of days'. The wait was excruciating.

Mum and Dad had offered to come and babysit. This was a first, and I wasn't going to turn them down. They even volunteered to stay the night so we could have a little lie-in the next morning. Recently they had been more attentive; they clearly approved of Oscar and me being together. Finally, I seemed to be getting things right in their eyes. I prepared thoroughly for their visit, labelling Tupperware boxes in the fridge, organizing bottles of formula and leaving out Calpol, just in case – nothing was going to cut short our first proper romantic evening since the baby was born.

We decided to walk to the restaurant. It would take about thirty minutes, but although cold, it wasn't raining and would give us an opportunity to chat, like old times. Both of us were keen walkers and we had spent many of our early dates strolling home from restaurants or bars late at night, talking ten to the dozen. Because of the clandestine nature of most of our early date nights, Oscar being my boss and all, it had been safer to take the streets under the cover of darkness, rather than be spotted by someone from work on the Tube, and Oscar had been too afraid to use his Uber or company taxi accounts in case his PA had clocked he was coming to my flat so often. So, walking it had been, sometimes stopping on a dark, empty side street, or behind an inviting bush, for a snog.

Oscar's hand reached for mine as we left the house and our shoulders visibly dropped – Albie was asleep and it felt so nice to escape the confines of baby land together. It felt liberating. Oscar asked me if I was feeling okay and I told him the truth: it had been a stressful few days and I was nervous about the test result, but I didn't want it to overshadow our evening together.

We had a brilliant time and that night Oscar and I had sex for the first time since Albie was born. It was slow and tender. He spent ages sucking my breasts and caressing my thighs until I begged him to take me fully. When he did, it was intense and sensual. He quickened and slowed the pace instinctively, just as I needed him to, bringing me close to orgasm several times. We came together. I felt like I'd come home.

'I love you so much,' he breathed, his eyes shining.

'I love you more,' I said, lifting my head to kiss his lips, while he was still inside of me.

Afterwards, when he went to the bathroom, two big, fat, round tears rolled from the corners of my eyes, tickling the side of my cheeks as they began to dissipate.

In the darkness, as Oscar slept, I rolled onto my side and thought about Jason for a while. I thought about how different Oscar was to him – in looks, personality, sexually, everything. But I didn't wobble; it made me feel calm and happy. Just by being himself, Oscar was perfect and our little family was complete. Almost.

CHAPTER FORTY-TWO

Aisha

Sunday 15th August

Jason had obediently given me the space I requested and stopped the relentless calling, bar one text to deliver the news that the test results had not yet arrived and he would let me know the moment he found out. I was in the kitchen making soup and toast for myself and some baby rice for Joni – I had reverted to creating myself five-minute maximum student-style meals in Jason's absence; there never seemed to be enough time or inclination to do more – when my phone began ringing on the kitchen counter. I saw Jason's name appear. I froze, barely able to catch my breath.

I wanted to know the result and at the same time, I didn't. It would mean more heavy conversations, more decisions – possibly even bigger ones. Plus Joni was hungry right now and I was just about to eat, myself. By way of a distraction, I'd begun reading up on weaning, and looked forward to the coming weeks when I could introduce baby rice and a few pureed solids to some of her meals. Jason didn't know about any of this. He had asked to see her, but I'd said no. I didn't know how we'd manage it, and although I knew how hard this must be for him, not seeing her for almost a week, I wasn't ready yet.

I reached for a tea towel to wipe my hands, which were covered in avocado mush, but missed the call. Shortly after a text came through.

> Hey. Can you talk? I don't have the results yet, but I'm wondering if I can come over please? I'm desperate to see Joni and you. I know I don't deserve either of you, but this separation from our baby, it's killing me. Jx

I realized I was holding my breath, thinking the text was going to be the test result. I felt desperate. Half of me wanted this horrible mess to just go away, to forgive him and try to get back to normal. But the other half wanted him to stay away. Jason's text was all about his own feelings – what about mine? I wasn't sure if he realized quite how betrayed and angry I felt. And he hadn't just let me down – he'd let down 'our baby' as well. How I wished there was a Gina Ford handbook for discovering your husband's been unfaithful. But there was no manual to tell me what to do.

I sat down at the kitchen table, giving myself some time to consider my response. Sitting here took me back to that day when I returned home from the spa and found Lucy outside our flat, how I had merrily invited her in and let her borrow our spare bottle steriliser. The idea of this now seemed absurd and I wondered the real reason why she had been standing outside our house that day. Was something still going on? Now I thought about it, it was very suspicious that she 'just happened' to be walking past on a day when Jason knew I was supposed to be out; she was wearing more make-up than usual yet she had seemed out of sorts. And then a piece of the jigsaw puzzle slotted into place. Well, how would you feel if you had just taken a DNA test to decide the paternity of your child? That must have been the day they did it. I was conveniently out of the way. That meant they would have done the test in front of Joni too. They had made a fool out of me. My blood heated up.

What a fool I had been. An anger bubbled to the surface as I began questioning how many other times they had deceived me. I wondered why Lucy had been in the same Baby Group as us. Surely it wasn't a coincidence. But what did she want from all of this? Was she trying to steal my husband? Why did she want to cause me so much pain? Before I realized what I was doing, I banged my fist against the table in frustration. It made the soup bowl shake and some of it splashed over the edge.

Joni looked up at me from her baby seat by the table. She looked worried.

'I'm sorry my darling, I didn't mean to scare you.' I undid the clasp and picked her up, cuddling her into my chest. There was nothing more comforting than her warm body; she reached for my hair with a podgy avocado-smeared hand and tugged it.

I tried to keep positive. To focus on the facts. There were plenty of blanks I would need to ask Jason to fill in when the time was right, but for now, I wanted to believe it was just the 'one night of madness' he told me about. Joni pulled my hair again.

'What is it, little one?' I asked. I was losing the plot now, thinking a three-month-old was trying to tell me something. I looked into her eyes. So far Jason had agreed to abide by my wish for space, but perhaps it was unfair to deny Joni the chance to see her father. I had to think about what was best for her too; she was the innocent party in all of this.

I texted Jason back:

OK, but I'm not ready for you to stay long. You could come tomorrow, for an hour at 2 p.m., to spend time with Joni.

No kiss at the end.

Thank you. I'll be there then x

I had completely lost my appetite now. I gave Joni some more of the mush, which she appreciatively gobbled down, and then laid her onto her jungle gym in the front room for a kick-about, which would hopefully wear her out ahead of bath time. I returned to the kitchen and poured the soup down the sink and put the toast in the bin. I flicked the kettle on before wandering from room to room as my mind raced with what Jason might say tomorrow, and all the things I wanted to say to him. I went into the bathroom to run the baby bath for Joni; while the water ran into the little plastic bassinet, I stared at myself in the mirror for a few minutes. My face was bare of make-up. I looked weary. There were bags under my eyes, and the last week had taken the colour from my skin. There was a degree of leanness to my face that I hadn't seen since pre-pregnancy, but it wasn't a good thing. I looked older. For a moment I thought about what I might wear tomorrow when Jason came around, but then decided against making any effort – why should I hide the battle scars of the last week?

That night, I woke to the sound of Joni crying. It was a loud, urgent kind of cry. Her forehead felt hot and clammy. I lifted her out of her cot which was now in the nursery and brought her into bed with me. I looked at my phone: it was only 1 a.m., she shouldn't be hungry. She looked so small on the side of the bed where Jason should have been sleeping. She also looked under the weather. Her cry turned into a whimper, as though she couldn't muster enough energy to keep it up. She was waving her arms around though, as if trying to tell me something. She seemed to be in discomfort and her nose was runny. Was she okay? I felt panicky and alone. Without Jason here, there was nobody to confer with. I thought about who else might be awake and sober at this time of night – the other women in The Baby Group, of course. My finger hovered over the icon for the group – a picture of a baby bottle, which Lucy had uploaded when she set it up. Little did she know then the battle she'd have with baby bottles as she tried to get Albie to take one. I felt nostalgic for a moment, despite the fact she had duped me. I wondered if any aspects of our 'friendship' had been based on truth.

I decided not to send a message to the group. Instead I scooped Joni up and padded into the kitchen to give her some Calpol for her temperature – it was probably nothing more than a summer cold. The weather had turned unseasonably chilly in the last couple of days. I also gave her half a bottle of milk to wash it down. She drank it hungrily, so I gave her some more; perhaps she was a having a growth spurt.

I reflected on the camaraderie our Baby Group had shared and wondered whether I would see any of them again. Now this had happened, I couldn't imagine ever meeting up with Lucy in a café for a catch-up.

I decided to let Joni spend the rest of the night in bed with me. Co-sleeping might not be Gina Ford's style, but tonight it felt as though we needed to be extra close to one another.

Once the paracetamol took effect, she was soon asleep again, her arms up by her head in submission, her legs splayed like a little frog. She made sweet snorting noises that melted my heart. In the last week or so she had begun to look more like Jason. My heart ached for him to be here with us.

I looked across at Joni again. Despite her presence, sometimes I felt so desperately alone, it was suffocating.

Monday 16th August

I must have eventually fallen asleep because the next thing I knew, I was woken by Joni stirring at 6 a.m. I was feeling tired and jittery in anticipation of seeing Jason again. I busied myself on a mission to clean the flat. Joni seemed grumpy, clearly the broken night of sleep had been tough on both of us. At one point, when I found myself spraying the bathroom mirror with deodorant instead of glass cleaner, I realized that maybe this wasn't such a great idea and I needed to slow down. So when it was time for Joni to have her late morning nap, I decided to take the opportunity for a rest too, putting my phone on silent but setting the alarm for 1.30 p.m. so we would be ready for his arrival. I put Joni down in the nursery so I could sleep more easily in the bedroom, without fear of disturbing her.

I woke abruptly to the sound of the alarm. I must have been straight out the moment my head hit the pillow because I felt groggy from a deep sleep. The flat was silent which was great news because it meant Joni had been down for a full two hours, meaning she had hopefully slept off whatever had kept her awake in the night and would be in a good place for Jason's visit. I got up and ran a brush through my hair and changed my top, thinking I'd put on a bit of make-up and make myself a strong coffee before waking her. I was feeling nervous about seeing Jason.

When I entered the nursery, which was only tiny, I knew immediately that something was very wrong. It was the total silence at first and then my eyes confirmed the worst. Joni was not in her cot.

I struggled to breathe and a bitter chill rippled through my whole body, turning my face ashen, my heartbeat fast.

Her Grobag was still there, but it was unzipped. I ran to the side of the cot, lifted it up and shook the material, although it was plain that she wasn't in there. It still felt slightly warm.

My chest felt tight, my stomach knotted, as I jolted into action, dashing from room to room calling her name 'Joni! Joni!' I knew it was futile because she was barely five months old – she could only just roll, there was no way she was capable of climbing out of her own cot. I returned to my bedroom, to double check I hadn't absent-mindedly brought her into bed with me. I dramatically flung back the duvet and threw the pillows off the bed, I even stooped down to the floor and looked underneath the bed, but she was not there. The flat felt disturbingly empty and cold.

Where the hell was she?

I noticed my heart was drumming fast, my chest tightening further with every beat as I ran back into the nursery. Senseless with panic, I pressed on the window but it was securely locked. I kicked open the door to the bathroom, peered around it and even looked in the bath and shower cubicle. Then I raced downstairs to the front door. It was closed, with no sign of a forced entry, and I opened it and looked out into the street. Her pram was still there at the bottom of the stairs. 'Joni!' I called out, but the street was empty save for one old man, who slowly turned and gave me a puzzled look.

My mind ticked over desperately. My thoughts felt muddled by the painful, thick *thump, thump, thump,* of my heart in my chest. I felt frantic. Then it hit me. Who could be so evil as to take my baby?

I ran back into the bedroom where my phone was still on the bedside table. My hands shaking, my finger hovered over calling 999, but instead I called Lucy.

CHAPTER FORTY-THREE

Lucy

After the stress and anxiety of the past week, I decided to book myself in for a yoga class. I'd gone to the local studio religiously during my pregnancy, but since Albie was born, and what with taking adequate time to recover from the C-section, my practice had completely fallen away. There didn't seem to be a single hour in the day when I could fit it in, and in the last few days I had felt too afraid of bumping into Jason or Aisha on my short walk to the studio, to risk going there.

But knowing the results were expected to arrive imminently, I needed to do something to relax, and Oscar was around to look after Albie for a couple of hours. It gave me a perfect window.

I put on one of Oscar's caps in an attempt to disguise myself slightly. On the short walk, I thought of Aisha again. My heart lurched as I tried to imagine the pain she must be in; the betrayal she must be feeling, not only from Jason, but me too. We had become good friends in a short space of time and I missed her in my life. I had thought about contacting her, of course. But what could I have possibly said without making the situation worse? It would all have been so much easier if I hated her, but almost from the moment I met her, that had proved impossible.

I was just about to turn a corner into the studio, when my phone vibrated. I thought about ignoring it – if it was Oscar asking something about Albie, he'd just have to cope – I really didn't want to have to abort this mission. But when I saw who was calling, my stomach flipped and I stopped dead in my tracks.

'Where is she? What have you done with her?' Aisha's voice screamed down the line, the second I answered. She sounded terror-stricken. Possessed. I wondered if she'd got the wrong number at first, she made no sense.

'Aisha. It's Lucy,' I said, as calmly as possible. 'Are you—'

'I know who it fucking is!' she cut me off. 'What have you done with Joni?' She was yelling loudly, hysterically; it was impossible not to shout back, just to be heard.

'I don't know what you're talking about! Where is Joni? Are you okay?'

'Of course I'm not okay. Do I sound it? Where is she?'

'Listen, I'm not far away – I'll come round.'

'I'm calling the police!' was the last thing I heard her shriek.

CHAPTER FORTY-FOUR

Aisha

Seconds after hanging up on Lucy I heard the key turn in the lock. I took the stairs two at a time and as the door opened I almost collapsed at the sight of Jason standing there with Joni in the baby carrier. I hadn't even noticed it was missing from the coat rack on the wall.

'Thank God!' I screeched, distraught.

Jason seemed nonplussed, as though this should have been a perfectly normal sight for me.

My arms automatically stretched out to reach for my baby. Joni was awake and her head turned in the carrier as she heard my voice. 'Thank God, you're okay, my baby girl!' I tenderly caressed the top of her head, stroked her cheek, double-checked it was really her and she was safe. Of course it was her. Relief slowly began to wash through me. 'Oh darling, thank goodness you are okay.'

Then I turned my attention to Jason, who was now looking shocked by my reaction to seeing him. 'What the fuck were you thinking? Breaking in here and taking her like that?'

'You didn't see the note, then,' he said, his calmness only accentuating my hysteria. 'I got off work early. You were sound asleep, I rang on the doorbell but there was no answer, so I let myself in.' I had almost forgotten he still had door keys. 'I was early, so at first I assumed you were out and thought I'd wait for you here. When I came in, I heard Joni stirring in her cot, and saw you were fast asleep. So I left a note on the kitchen table and took her out for a walk. We've only been gone ten minutes, Aisha. I thought I was doing you a favour, letting you have some extra sleep.'

How dare he make me feel ridiculous with this rational explanation? Relief was now turning into anger. But it felt as though I wasn't really here – that I was watching some other hysterical woman who was close to losing the plot. This couldn't be me. This couldn't have happened to my life. Could it?

Just then Lucy appeared behind him at the door. She was last person I wanted to see.

'Is everything okay?' she asked, looking at me. She could clearly see that Joni was here, with Jason.

I gaped at her. Where to begin?

Joni began to struggle in the carrier and my heart lurched for her. 'Pass her to me,' I ordered, as Jason obediently unclipped the carrier and loosened the straps so I could lift Joni's wriggling body out. I pulled her free and held her tightly against my chest, breathing in the comforting scent of the top of her head. She gave a little hungry cry.

As I turned to take her upstairs, I looked at the two adults by the door. They looked forlorn, scared with shadows beneath their eyes and no spark. At least I now knew that neither of them were psychotic baby kidnappers on top of being adulterers. That was something. Fired up from the emotion of the last minutes, I took a deep breath and then it was as if an other-worldly power took hold. I decided that if anyone was going to 'own' this moment it was me. The moment had come and they both owed it to me to tell the truth.

'Come in, both of you,' I said. 'It's time to talk.'

Jason immediately went to the kitchen to make coffee and I set about heating up a bottle for Joni. I noticed small beads of sweat on his nose; he was nervous too. My hands suddenly felt clammy. For a second, seeing Jason standing there, back in our flat, as if things were normal, I felt conflicted. Part of me could have folded him into my arms and given him a big hug. Then my mind flashed to an image of him and Lucy in this very room and fury began to erupt.

Lucy stood in the doorway awkwardly. 'Would you rather I leave?' she asked timidly.

It was as though Jason had only just registered she was there. 'What were you doing, Lucy?' he asked, his voice unfriendly, accusatory.

'I was going to yoga, when Aisha called me,' she replied. 'I was going to help her find—'

'Not right now, I mean what were you doing in The Baby Group?' he interrupted, sternly.

She paused, taking time to draw breath and consider her

response. 'The same as you,' she replied. 'Learning how to have a baby.'

'What the fuck, Lucy?' Jason was fidgety now, shifting his weight from foot to foot. He put a hand to his head and ran it through his hair nervously. 'It's not a time for sarcasm. Seriously – why did you have to mess everything up?'

Lucy scoffed loudly in response. 'Are you joking?'

I took a second to gather my thoughts. I hadn't planned for this moment to happen like this, in our kitchen. It was still so raw; for all of us.

'Stop!' I yelled. I lifted my head a little to study Jason's face, to look into his wide, panic-stricken eyes. 'If anyone should be angry right now, it's me. Let's go into the living room and talk like adults, while I feed Joni.'

Jason and I sat on the sofa, Lucy took the armchair and with Joni feeding in my arms, I took a deep breath and began. 'Lucy, I need you to tell me everything,' I said calmly.

'Half of me wanted you to guess that Jason and I knew each other, to give you enough clues that you might realize something. And so many times I was on the verge of telling you. But then I panicked and backed off,' she said. 'I wanted it all to be out in the open, but I was terrified at the same time. I knew you would be devastated and I didn't know what to do.'

'But why did you spin me a story about Albie being an IVF baby?'

'Because it's true.' She paused briefly to look at the side of Jason's face, to see if he understood what she was saying. He was still scowling, but he was quiet; at least listening. Then she continued as if he was not in the room: 'It was a really complicated time for me. I've never been able to fall pregnant, except for that time twenty years ago, when I aborted a baby at university. I suppose you know that part of the story.' She paused and I nodded sagely as she continued. 'Jason only told me that night – the night last September – that he knew about the abortion I'd had all that time ago. It hurt so much. Anyway, I underwent planned IVF the day after Jason and I spent the night together,' she continued. 'Using an embryo fertilised by an anonymous sperm donor.' She glanced across at me. 'Oscar and I were split up at the time. And that's why I genuinely don't know who Albie's father is – the sperm donor, or Jason. Aisha, I want you to know that I had not seen Jason prior to that night, or after.' Lucy continued; though her eyes were red, she was doing a good job of holding things together: 'There was no affair. We were both drunk. I was in a bad place. You don't deserve this and I am so sorry. Whatever happens with the result, I won't be bothering you again.'

'What about Oscar?' I asked. 'Does he know?'

'We only got together properly during my second trimester,' she explained, 'and before then, he had made it clear he didn't want another child. He already has two from a previous relationship – he's been married before, as you know. But then he changed his mind. I told you all this, and it's true. And yes, I've told him everything about Jason now.' She began to cry, and they were not crocodile tears, I could see the pain in her eyes. 'I'm so sorry,' she said, holding her head in her hands.

Adrenalin had pulsed through me as I listened to Lucy's

explanation, but now I felt more in control, I almost pitied her, as well as felt relieved that her story matched Jason's account. Lucy and I had become what I thought of as good friends over the past few months and although I held Jason completely accountable for his actions, there were two people involved in this awful situation, so it didn't seem fair that she shouldn't have to ever look me in the eye and explain herself.

Lucy had put her coat on and was about to leave, when she picked up her phone and looked at it. Her expression changed. At first I thought Oscar must have been calling, wondering where she was.

She spoke in a calm, low voice: 'The results are here.'

CHAPTER FORTY-FIVE

Aisha

January 2022, the following year

After discovering the test result, Jason and I lived apart for over five months as we tried to come to terms with what had happened. He came to the flat every weekend, to spend time with Joni.

'Do you think we can ever be happy again?' he asked me one evening, in the living room, after we had poured out our hearts again.

'I don't know,' I sighed. I wanted to say that I hoped so, but something seismic had shifted and I needed longer to decide if I could trust him again.

Jason had gathered some more clothes into a suitcase and as he left to go back to his sister's for an as yet 'undefined amount of time', he looked at me, clearly building up to say something. I waited.

It was so quiet in the flat that we could hear some people

laughing in the street outside, their mood at odds with the atmosphere in here.

He spoke slowly. 'I hope we can find a way through this, more than anything in the world.' He looked like a broken man.

Gradually, once the tears began to dry and we were able to meet up without combing over the past because he had answered everything I could possibly think of, there was a semblance of normal weekends together – we would cook, go for walks, explore new parts of London – yet for the most part we were too afraid to talk about the future.

We had spent Christmas together although half of me found it fake – like we were pretending to be a happy family. Watching saccharine festive family movies together was a continual reminder that we were not perfect. Our marriage had been smashed, like a glass bauble. I found it hard, but I didn't really have anywhere else to go – flying to Dubai to Dad was a much less appealing option – and we both owed it to Joni to try to make her first Christmas as happy as possible. We talked a lot and Jason continually assured me that we could, and would, get back to a place of trust. That we weren't just putting tinsel over what had happened – he would dig deep and do the work to build that trust again, day-by-day, week-by-week, year-by-year, for as long as it took. I observed Jason become an amazing father – he was patient, fun, kind and full of love. Joni was so content when she was with him. She adored her daddy.

In January, we decided to spend a few weeks 'dating'; we began flirting again and the spark between us returned. It felt like the days when we first met. Finally, I saw flashes of our old life return, but it felt deeper, more truthful, actually more exciting.

Some evenings, instead of going out, we would have a glass of wine and a takeaway together. We would talk about watching a film, but never got as far as finishing one because the conversation would turn to Joni and then back to us, our separation, our plans and each of us would air the latest thing on our mind.

As the weeks passed, I believed how remorseful Jason felt. He seemed fully committed to getting back together for the long-term future, and I knew I couldn't really imagine a life without him. On 28th January, the day Jason brought his suitcase back full, to stay, I knew with all my heart that it was what I wanted and what Joni needed too. I had found a way to let go of the past and embrace the new shape of our future. And I had learnt that love was messy, imperfect, painful at times, but true love always found a way to win through.

CHAPTER FORTY-SIX

Aisha

May

As summer approached, I had an irrepressible urge to holiday in a gîte in France. We had visited our gîte in the Loire Valley every year when I was a school child and my memories of those summers were idyllic. Messing around in boats on the river, exploring woods and running through fields, going to the *boulangerie*, BBQing, attempting to play tennis, and, in later years, beating my parents at tennis as I became an accomplished player.

But the highlight had always been the anticipation – the thought that the night before the holiday I'd be put to bed in my day clothes and then transferred, complete with *My Little Pony* pillow and duvet, in what felt like the middle of the night, into the back of the Audi to drive down to Portsmouth and board the ferry to Calais.

I could remember the oily smell of the lower deck, which

was generally where I'd have been when I was roused by my mother and led upstairs into the lounge for a cooked breakfast. It had always happened at the beginning of every August, and it had never lost its allure. I was devastated when Dad decided to sell the gîte soon after Mum passed away.

Now that I had a baby – a little family of my own – I wanted to recreate that feeling for Joni. I knew she'd be too young to remember it this year, she was still only little, but it would mean so much to me.

'Let's see it as a dry run – a recce for future holidays,' I had said to Jason.

Jason and I decided to go in mid-May, to coincide with Joni's first birthday. She was still at the stage of sleeping every time we turned on the car engine so we were optimistic it would be a fairly easy drive to and from the ferry. Before confirming the booking, Jason googled the weather in the Loire, which looked changeable, and asked if I was sure I wouldn't rather fly to Greece and stay in the nicest spa resort we could afford for guaranteed hot weather at this time of year.

'I really want to do this; it has to be France,' I replied, and he could tell by the intense look in my eyes that this wasn't the time to argue. Anything to do with Mum, especially my early childhood memories of happy times spent with her, felt even more sacred now. Having a baby girl had made me feel closer to her – like she was by my side, albeit invisibly. I felt her presence, gently encouraging me to keep going through the difficult times. I knew she would have been rooting for Jason and I to work things out, I just felt it. I hoped that taking Joni to the Loire would somehow make my baby girl feel close to her late grandmother too.

Since Jason had moved back in, life in London lost its thrill for me, and I needed to satiate my urge to break free and run wild in the French countryside. I also couldn't wait to stuff my face with brie, camembert and baguette, washed down with fantastically cheap red wine, because I'd missed that taste combination so much during pregnancy.

What I hadn't properly considered was that the weather in northern France in May could be a lot worse than even the long-term forecast had suggested. It rained for seven days solid. Literally from the moment we disembarked the ferry in pouring rain, it must have come down near constantly. I became obsessed with a variety of weather apps, moving from one to the next when I didn't like the look of the rain or dark cloud emoji it was showing, and feeling elated when I found one that indicated a hint of sunshine from behind a dark cloud.

'Look – a patch of blue on the horizon!' Jason would exclaim optimistically from time to time, only for it to dissipate into more heavy grey sky when our car reached it. We almost doubled our expected petrol costs for the holiday because we had to drive – along with every other holiday-maker in the area – to the nearest rainproof venues like a heated swimming pool or an ancient aquarium. There was only one moment, on Joni's first birthday, when we managed to lay out a rug on a vaguely dry patch of grass on a bank of the Loire, so that Joni could stretch out while we snacked on yet more baguette and cheese and toasted her with some delicious Bordeaux. Jason and I exchanged a look which said, 'This is what could have been!'

But conversely, despite the weather, Jason and I got on better than ever during that week away. He became his old, cheeky self – taking the mickey whenever I tried to order something in French, constantly asking what was happening in the book I was reading and insisting on competitive games of backgammon while Joni slept. I had forgotten how much backgammon we used to play in Hong Kong and was thrilled Jason had brought our old travel set along. I hadn't seen it in at least three years and it brought back such happy memories.

The old Jason brought the old me back to life. I felt less alone than I had done in the early months because we were properly sharing childcare duties. I found myself drawing again, and not only for work – though I did bring along the brief for a new children's picture book I'd been commissioned to do – but also for my own enjoyment. Sketching the scenery and copying images from photographs stored on my phone of Joni as a tiny baby; photographs I hadn't been able to revisit since that awful time because it had been too painful. It made any joy on our faces seem such a lie. On one particularly rainy afternoon, I spent an hour sketching Joni asleep in Jason's arms, noticing every last detail on his face, recognizing how he had aged over the years – more creases around the eyes, his skin slightly looser, nose a little wider and a few grey hairs. I swelled with love for them both. We had become an 'us' again, away from the stifling, hectic pace of London life.

On that holiday, Jason and I started having sex again too. I mean really passionate, great sex that felt more intense and meaningful than ever, with our baby snoozing away contentedly in her cot just a few feet away. Wanting to be with him again physically was one of the hardest parts for me. And despite the fact I felt slightly shy about how my body looked post-baby, Jason devoured me naked, commenting on how beautiful I looked, how he was lucky to have a wife who was so sexy and gorgeous and how he loved the taste of me. But most of all, he stared into my eyes and told me how much he loved me, over and over again. There was no expressing his love through my belly as he used to do when I was pregnant, or soppy, drunk declarations like in the early days of fatherhood; this was the real thing.

One evening, when we were sitting by the fire in the gîte reading books – it was so cold we'd felt the need to light an open fire each evening – I went and got something from my bag.

It was a tiny handwritten card I had received; it had been posted through the front door by Lucy, the day after the test results arrived. I'd been carrying it around, like some kind of talisman, almost as though having it in my possession was helping me to process things, upsetting as it was.

I thought about its contents – I knew it so well. But I'd gone past feeling angry with Lucy; I had almost been able to forgive her. Her desire to be a mother had been so strong she was blindsided. She had been willing to risk everything, including the man who truly loved her. I opened the card for a moment to read the words again. Just three short sentences:

'He was only ever yours. I'm so sorry. I'll miss you. Lucy x'

Without comment, I passed Jason the note. He looked

at me curiously before opening it. He read it in silence and then he stood up and unceremoniously tossed it into the fire.

We watched as the flames cackled and licked around the paper, then engulfed it. Within seconds it had turned into red-hot embers and finally to white ashes. It was gone. She was gone.

Jason went back to his armchair and I joined him, settling myself onto his lap. He let me sink into him, pulling me into a big bear hug with both arms. I sighed appreciatively and gently turned my face to his. I stopped, close enough to feel his warm breath on my lips.

'I love you,' he said.

'I love you too,' I replied.

It was the first time I'd told him that in months and I meant it.

We kissed passionately.

The three of us returned to London without any hint of a tan, but with our marriage buoyed and a new sense that we had won each other back, and that we could be a functioning family again, without Jason or I losing sight of one another in the process. While on holiday we made plans to leave London and move further out, to Sussex or Surrey, where we could probably afford a house rather than a flat, with a garden big enough for Joni to run around in. For the first time in a long while, I allowed myself to feel we had a long-term future.

CHAPTER FORTY-SEVEN

Lucy

The moment the DNA results had arrived, we had all taken a sharp intake of breath. Jason had immediately pulled out his phone to check the email at the same time, Aisha reading it next to him. And there it was, in black and white.

There was only one top line, so it had taken just seconds for us to discover the outcome. Then I had fled home to find Oscar...

'How was yoga?' he called out from the living room, where he and Albie, who was swaddled in his arms, were watching the rugby together.

'I didn't make it. Will explain in a minute – but right now there's something you need to look at.'

I sank down into the sofa next to him, grabbed his hand and laced his fingers with mine, squeezing them. We opened and read the email together.

Albie coughed in Oscar's arms, making him sit up straight,

giving me a reprieve from speaking as I took in the result again.

'You okay?' Oscar said softly.

I turned my face to his and swallowed. 'I'm fine,' I managed.

'No secrets, remember?' he said looking right at me, reading me.

'I guess it just feels weird,' I bowed my head. 'I can't help wishing his daddy was you.' I paused. 'You did ask for the truth.'

Oscar put his hand on my chin and lifted my face upwards, so I had no choice but to look into his eyes as he spoke. He slid his hand slowly around my shoulders and pulled me close.

'I'm so sorry for hurting you with this,' I said remorsefully. 'Albie and I are so lucky to have you.' I stopped and looked into his eyes. 'Kiss me, if it's going to be all right,' I whispered.

And he did.

My fortieth birthday came and went in October, without me really wanting to mark it at all. Oscar cooked me dinner at home and it was all very low-key. Once we had got through Christmas, the decorations had been packed away and the dust had settled on everything that had happened, Oscar and I had decided to move away from Clapham. We really needed a fresh start. Besides, we had always imagined the rented house was a stop-gap. In truth, it had been a trial for our relationship, and somehow, despite it all, we had managed to come out stronger.

We craved a house with a decent-sized garden for Albie, in close proximity to good schools and a station for Oscar's commute, but not too far from Pippa who lived with Evie and Ollie in Sheen.

We had viewed three houses in Kingston upon Thames, and had opted for the middle one. With Oscar's salary, plus the money from my flat, which I had sold to my tenant, we had been able to upscale to a five-bed with an ample garden. I had loved the house immediately – it was a new build, but in a traditional style. A proper family home. It had plenty of storage space, which appealed to my love of order and neatness, and there was a brand-new kitchen, with a white marble-topped island, which made my heart sing. I had got back into cooking over the last few months and was starting to foster dreams of starting a home-baking company and writing a cook book, once Albie started at nursery and I had some more time on my hands. I knew a great PR and marketing company who could take it on for me.

And now it was early summer. Albie was a lively boy, energetic and inquisitive, and was already walking and chatting nonsense by the time he turned one. He seemed to need constant entertaining so I embraced taking him to various classes and activities, being in the fortunate position of not having to rush back to work just yet, despite having been on maternity leave for just over a year.

We had just returned home from a local Gymboree session when the message appeared on my phone. It was the first message on the Baby Group thread in a long while and seeing that baby bottle icon again stopped me in my tracks. My stomach flipped.

Susie: Hello everyone, long time! Hope you and the little ones are all doing well? Hasn't time flown?! We're having a naming ceremony for Charlie, on Saturday 30th September on Clapham Common, 3 p.m., under the big oak tree by the Windmill pub. I know it's a little way off, but since most of you have moved away now, we thought we'd get the date booked in. Lin, Charlie and I would absolutely love to see you there. We can call it a reunion of sorts! No presents, just bring a dish – for old times' sake ;-). Pray for good weather.

Maggie is not invited!! Mooooo! Ha ha.
RSVP.
Love Susie xx

Then moments later, my phone lit up again.

Will: It's so great to hear from you. Count us in! xx

Helen: Aaaah, our babies are all ONE now! Hope everyone's well. Maddie is keeping us busy! We would love to join you. Ian and I are back to together btw :-) See you on the 30th. Hx

I looked at my online calendar – Oscar and I had no plans on 30th September, the weekend before my forty-first birthday. I hadn't yet thought about what I might do for it. I hadn't been in the mood to celebrate my fortieth last year, so Oscar had loosely mentioned that maybe we would make up for it this year. Perhaps we would end up going away, but for now, the date looked free.

CHAPTER FORTY-EIGHT

Aisha

Friday, 30th September

As we neared the gathering, my heart started to pound. The spot they had chosen for the ceremony was only a stone's throw from the bandstand on the Common, the place Jason chose to deliver the news, so the thought of coming back here had initially made a chill run up my spine. But I had wanted to come; to not let a bad memory beat me. I – *we* – had moved on.

Now we were here, though, I started having doubts.

'Do you think this is a good idea, Jason?' I asked, a lump in my throat. I was pretty sure Lucy and Oscar wouldn't turn up, but it wasn't unthinkable. Granted almost a year had gone past since it all came out, but I still felt queasy at the thought of coming face-to-face with them, especially with Lucy.

Although still some distance from us, the group was easy to spot: there was bunting hung on the lower branches, and a trestle table covered in a white cloth had been set up to one side. There were glasses and ice buckets on it, plus a large cake.

When we arrived, there was no sign of Lucy and Oscar. Susie and Lin greeted us with warm hugs like the old friends I supposed we now were. It was really lovely catching up with the others and seeing their not-so-little 'babies' again. We immediately began swapping stories about our children's first words, going back to work and how we were all adapting to a new lifestyle as parents.

But in a quiet moment later on, Susie pulled me to one side and examined my face carefully.

'Is everything okay?' she asked.

I had withdrawn from the WhatsApp group after that dreadful time, yet something made me unable to leave it completely, and I took an interest from afar in the occasional conversation about nursery places, first steps, first haircuts and moans about missing pelvic floors; they made for amusing anecdotes from time to time.

Of course Lucy stayed mute on the group too, although I noticed she hadn't exited it either. I had only told Susie what happened, when she had private messaged me, sensing something might be up because of my lack of communication. Of course she was floored when she heard.

'Bloody hell. You never can tell about people,' she had said, adding a shocked emoji.

Thankfully she didn't probe me today, when I simply beamed and said, honestly: 'Yes, we are great.' I even resisted asking her if Lucy was coming, because I didn't want to appear insecure.

'Joni is absolutely gorgeous,' Susie smiled.

'Gorgeous and full of attitude,' I replied.

'Isn't every sixteen-month old?' she looked across at Charlie who was sat down using a stick to dig a hole next to the tree, covering his smart little chinos in mud. 'Oh Charlie, really?' she shouted over. 'Is it too much to stay smart for just one day?'

'Don't worry, Joni will be joining him shortly,' I chuckled. 'Anyway, I brought you this, for Charlie's bedroom.' I handed her a brown A5 hard-backed envelope.

'Ooh, is it what I hope it is?' she asked, her eyes shining excitedly. 'Is it an Aisha original?' She'd always had such a warm and enthusiastic personality.

Carefully she teased the envelope open and pulled out the artwork inside. It was a pencil sketch of her holding a baby Charlie. I'd found the photo on my phone, I had taken it on one of our trips to the French café on the edge of the common, not far from where we were standing today. I had caught such a sweet moment as Susie, although so tired, sat gazing at her tiny boy with such utter love and pride, as he stared back up at her, his tiny hand in the air.

'Oh it's beautiful!' she exclaimed, throwing her arms around me, 'I love it. You're so clever, we'll treasure this forever.'

'I'm so pleased! The frame will be arriving in a few days, in the post. I didn't quite get my act...' My voice trailed off and my heart twisted as I recognized the couple striding towards us.

CHAPTER FORTY-NINE

Lucy

When the Naming Day came around, considering everything that had happened, I felt oddly calm. I was ready to draw a line under the past; to achieve closure. Oscar reached for my hand and I took it as we walked purposefully towards the tree on the common.

It felt funny being back on our old turf and, although Kingston wasn't so far away, this was the first time we'd come back to Clapham since the move. It was all so familiar, yet distant at the same time.

As we got closer, I slowed my pace. I felt my heart rate quicken and palms moisten. I was reminded of how I'd spotted Jason and Aisha near this very spot on the common on that terrible day. I felt nervous. We were running late, and it meant that everyone was already gathered. I felt like we were 'making an entrance'. I had let Susie know that we were hoping to drop by, but wouldn't stay long, we would just make a flying visit – I didn't want to commit to staying for the whole day in case we decided against it or the atmosphere was awkward. There was still time to change our mind.

I peered across and thought I could see Lin stood talking to an older man in a beige suit: probably the celebrant, as he then seemed to try to gather everyone together. There was a group of children of various ages and sizes yelling and chasing each other around the tree. One of them was probably Charlie, although I would be unlikely to spot him in a line-up; he was just a baby the last time I saw him. Then I noticed a fair-haired couple, with a little blonde girl toddling alongside them in a pretty dress and T-bar shoes – the mother looked pregnant. It was Helen, Ian and Maddie.

Back at the tree a crowd was gathering; Will and Christian plus their son Leo were easy to spot by their height and good looks. Leo was so tall, easily a head and shoulders on Albie. He was a stunning child with wild, curly hair. I strained to focus on some of the other faces.

Were Aisha and Jason there already? Where were they?

Without being conscious of it, my pace had slowed to little more than a crawl. Suddenly, Albie, who had been holding my hand and chattering non-stop about trains, stopped dead in his tracks.

'Mama – look – 'copter!' he squealed, pointing to the sky above us.

'Yes, darling, you're right, a helicopter!' I enthused, scooping him up.

I was glad to have a moment to stop, to collect myself.

I stole a moment to look across at the tree again, squinting as I tried to confirm the identity of more of the people gathering there. A few were hugging each other, and there were pats on the back and air kisses as they stood in groups of two or three to chat, the children playing around them. Many of them we didn't know.

Then I spotted Aisha, it was definitely her. She was standing with Susie, and Jason was nearby, swinging Joni between his legs. They looked really happy.

Did we *really* want to go through with this?

Oscar seemed to read my mind. He touched my arm. 'Oh no – the salad! We've left it in the car,' he said. 'I'll dash back and—'

'No point,' I interjected. 'I left it in the fridge. It felt too much, I'd feel embarrassed. The salad was a stupid idea, it reminds me too much of...' My voice trailed off into nothingness. We both knew what I meant – the fact I'd been so keen to make an impression at The Baby Group. My mind went back to that first morning and the effort I had put into preparing that squash and pine nut salad; into all of those over-the-top salads for the group. It seemed ridiculous now.

'Okay, deep breath time,' he said, taking my hand firmly. 'We can do this. We're a great team.'

Oscar squeezed my fingers and the three of us strode towards the group, our wide steps belying the butterflies in my stomach. Albie ran ahead, not thinking of anything other than the fact he'd spotted a big pile of brightly coloured bunting to play with.

'Just a brief hello, we'll stay for the ceremony and then go,' Oscar said.

As we approached the group, Susie spotted us and came over.

'Lucy, you came! It's really lovely to see you,' she exclaimed warmly. She had a red sun dress on.

'This colour looks great on you,' I told her.

My mind wandered back to that first Baby Group when I was hiding the biggest secret. The weight of it just as heavy as the nearly full-term baby inside me.

Helen came over to join us and I congratulated her on her obvious bump.

'It's very different, this pregnancy, not half as relaxing as the first time around,' she said. 'If only we were able to appreciate that at the time.'

I smiled in response. I had felt anything but relaxed during my pregnancy with Albie.

Sensing she may have unwittingly hit a nerve, she continued, 'So have you got your publishing deal for a cookbook yet?'

'Not yet,' I said. 'Even cooking has taken a back seat recently. These toddlers, they keep us too busy!'

I looked around to see where Oscar had got to with Albie and noticed Aisha, standing with Ian, Jason and Joni nearby. She paused and we locked eyes briefly. In that penetrating moment, her gaze upon my face, I wondered if she had received the note I posted through her door the day after the results came. Her face softened and the corners of her mouth turned up. I smiled back. In any other life I felt sure we could have been great friends.

Jason looked my way too, his green eyes shining as brightly as hers. They made such a strikingly handsome couple. He raised his hand to me in brief acknowledgement. It wasn't an overly enthusiastic gesture, but it was friendly. An olive branch for sure. In that moment, he acknowledged everything that had been between us and the child we once conceived. The baby I lost over twenty years ago, but only mentally laid to rest recently.

It struck me how we were two people who had shared so much, but also so little. I realized that for all those years, I thought I was so in love with him, but really it was just the idea of being in love with him that I was so obsessed with. Jason was my first taste of love – but he was only a tiny sample of the love that was to come.

For so long I had ached to know whether I meant something to him – even if it was just the smallest amount, knowing this would have given me some comfort, closure. But I didn't need to know now.

I cautiously smiled back, but was glad when Oscar returned to my side. I instinctively reached for his hand.

Oscar and I stayed for the ceremony and then Albie, becoming irritable because he needed his nap, gave us a reason to make a quick and quiet exit.

'Nice enough bunch, but I'm not sure I particularly want to stay friends,' he said.

'Know what you mean,' I added.

'Anyway, Lucy Raven, you didn't think I'd forgotten it's your birthday, next weekend, did you? I figured we probably wouldn't last long this afternoon, if we made it at all, so I took the liberty of making some plans on your behalf. To get the celebrations started.'

'You? Make plans?' I looked aghast, as he dropped this bombshell.

'We're going for a drink at our old local, the one we used to sneak kisses in, when we were dating. And we know we won't bump into anyone we don't want to because *they're* all here.' He threw a cursory glance over his shoulder. 'We're meeting the babysitter at the pub – my Evie is going to take Albie home, so I can escort you to dinner. And then, next weekend, well let's just say you'll need to pack a bag because I'm whisking you away for a night. See, I do have *some* secretarial skills, you know,' he smiled, even more broadly.

The little dimple that sometimes appeared on his cheek came out to play. He looked cute, in a black T-shirt and turned up jeans. I craned my neck and he lowered his lips towards mine.

'Do you love me?' he asked, just before our lips met.

'I love you,' I told him. 'I love you so much.'

And it was true. I loved Oscar more than I'd ever loved anyone.

'And Albie of course,' I added, beaming.

Albie chose that moment to fight me for his attention.

'Carry, Daddy! Carry!' he called, appearing between us and lifting his arms up to Oscar, demanding to be scooped up. Oscar reached down and whisked the little boy high into the air.

Although we had decided that marriage wasn't for us, not right now anyway, Oscar had been amazing, considering all we had been through.

Although I didn't know who Albie's biological dad was, and I might never know, unless Albie wanted to find his anonymous donor one day, Oscar really was Albie's father, in every other sense.

Oscar had taught me that love was rarely perfect – and that nobody was perfect; that was, until you fell in love with them. He had won my heart completely and, now that I believed he was here to stay, I had given myself permission to be happy.

'Shoulder ride you want, young man?' he asked Albie.

He was met with a beaming smile and enthusiastic shriek: 'Yeah Daddy! Yeah!'

A dimple appeared on Albie's cheek as he smiled. It struck me that he and Oscar had plenty of similarities.

'Here goes then.' And he carefully lifted the child behind his head.

'Look, Albie high!' the boy cried, as he sat upright, taller than us both on Oscar's shoulders, his small hands gripping the top of his head. 'Albie high, Mama!'

'You're the king of the castle!' I declared, his laughter so infectious.

Oscar began running back towards our car with the little boy bouncing on his shoulders, screaming with delight and excited giggles.

I watched them as they became silhouetted by the sun. I couldn't wipe the smile from my face, my love for them was so huge.

CHAPTER FIFTY

Aisha

When Lucy and I had caught each other's eye, I had felt wistful for a moment, reflecting on the camaraderie our Baby Group had shared. It had been such a bonding experience; we had invested a lot in our relationships, but for such a short amount of time. It was quite odd really – we had been living in a pregnancy and baby bubble; a parallel world of milk-drunk babies and sleep deprivation.

But although Lucy and I had become fast friends, I had always felt she was keeping something back, as though she'd been in possession of a box of secrets she hadn't decided whether to let me look into. Occasionally snippets had escaped, only for her to have slammed the box shut and locked it up again. How right I had been.

After the ceremony, Susie caught me daydreaming.

'You okay?' she asked. She intimated towards Lucy and Oscar, who had already turned their backs to us and were walking away with Albie. 'I really didn't think they would come.'

'It's fine,' I replied. 'I made peace with it all a while ago. And they weren't all bad, those Baby Group days. I have some fond – if slightly foggy – memories.' I smiled.

'Me too. Thank you for being such a great friend to me. I remember so vividly that afternoon you rescued me from Boots during that horrific colic phase he had.' She shuddered. 'So much for my plans to be an "Earth Mother" – they went out of the window in week one!'

'Ah, the colic era. It was, I recall, the time of the poo-mageddons for me!' I giggled. 'There was one day when I had to change Joni's whole outfit five times. I mean what was *in* my breast milk? And God, do you remember when I accidentally fake-tanned her cheek and almost got arrested by the health visitor?'

Susie clutched her belly as she laughed. 'Why people do it twice, I don't know,' she chuckled.

She must have noticed my cheeks colour slightly when she made that comment because she stopped and gave me a curious look.

I fiddled with a button on my dress. She clocked me.

'Aisha, are you trying to tell me something?'

'I'm not meant to say anything… It's still early,' I whispered. Susie's eyes widened. 'But yes, there is another one on the way… due mid-February. Utter madness, I know. Don't tell anyone!'

'You crazy woman!' she teased, before putting an arm around my waist and whispering into my ear: 'I'm thrilled for you, for all three of you, I really am. You're an amazing mother. A complete natural.'

I looked across at Jason, who was engaged in a competition with Ian to see who could swing their daughter highest. He was holding Joni under her arms, whooshing her upwards, like she was as light as a blade of grass as she shrieked with delight. I thought how lucky I was. He had been a changed man since we got the result – that he was not Albie's father. There was a joy and a lightness about him that I hadn't witnessed in a long time.

Now we had moved out of London and had a much better work/life balance, there was actually time to communicate properly in the evenings, and we tried to keep the weekends clear for family time. I mean, there were *still* software updates, you can't have it all, but at least they didn't occur almost every week like they once used to.

Looking back, I always had a feeling that I didn't have full ownership of Jason; that a bit of him had belonged to someone else. But I didn't think that any more.

At that moment Jason's gaze went from Joni's face to mine. He stopped tickling her and our eyes locked. I moved my hands across my stomach instinctively and thought about the second little bean growing in there. He smiled into my eyes and said everything he needed to say in one look.

ACKNOWLEDGEMENTS

Just Between Friends has been an epic three-year passion project with a number of twists and turns in the writing process which, ultimately, have led it to become a very different novel to my previous two, and one I feel really proud of. It wouldn't have come this far without the valued contributions from the talented, supportive team at HQ Stories: Lisa Milton and my editors Charlotte Mursell and Cicely Aspinall, thank you so much for your continued encouragement to keep pushing and pushing for the best possible plot. Yes it does feel like I have given birth a couple of times over, but the end prize is so worth it!

Also thanks to Jenny Savill for always championing me; Dr. Stuart Lavery for speaking to me about the IVF process; JmStorm for the perfect quote; so many of my friends for your anecdotes – we did have a lot of laughs looking back fondly on those days of baby groups, coping with a new-born and the madness of sleep deprivation.

Thank you to Callum, Heath and Rex, my three leading men, who gave me so much support to write this novel, even when it meant nights away from home burning the midnight oil. I am so deeply grateful for your encouragement and nurturing of my love of writing and I am inspired to see budding writers in you. Plus, as ever, I am so thankful to my parents, to whom this novel is dedicated.

And finally, I would like to thank Amy, Barbara, Corinne, Fede, Jemima, Natalie, Nicola, and Tanya – the eight wonderful women in my NCT Group. I have such happy memories of 2014, our first summer as mothers, but I want to assure you there were no huge secrets kept between us, and the characters of Aisha, Lucy and all of my Baby Group members, are not based on you or your other halves! But the 'poo-mageddon' episode, some of the baby group classes (Moo-ing), colic dramas and the copious amounts of coffee consumed in various Clapham cafes before pounding the common with our prams, might sound a little familiar and are remembered with great affection. Thank you for sharing such a special time with me; your support and friendship in the final stages of pregnancy and early months of motherhood and beyond, means so much and will never be forgotten. Especially now there's a book documenting some of it. I hope this novel makes you smile.

ONE PLACE. MANY STORIES

Bold, innovative and
empowering publishing.

FOLLOW US ON:

@HQStories